KISSING THE CEO

LAYLA HAGEN

Copyright

Chapter 1

Cade

"I have great news," I announced, looking around the table. My brothers and I were all gathered at my grandparents' home. I paid particular attention to my grandmother and grandfather, looking forward to seeing their expressions once I made my announcement. I knew it would mean a lot to them. Ever since our father left, my brothers and I were very close to our grandparents. "The Boston Coffee Expert will participate in The Fair-Trade Choice competition."

"That's the best news I've heard in a while." Grandfather looked at me with pride in his eyes.

Grandmother smiled. "Oh, you've done so well, Cade."

"In the first stage, all the competitors show off their blends in Harvard Square. I'll set up a booth. You're all invited. Once we're up and running, I'll probably only drop by the event a few times, but my team will be there to carry it through."

"We'll stop by," Grandfather said. "I have a good feeling that we'll win."

I was going to make sure of that. My grandfather founded the company fifty years ago. Then my father ran it for a decade and ruined everything my grandfather worked so hard to build. After my brother Jake discovered Dad's infidelity and his other family, he hightailed it out of town. Needless to say, he fucked up both the business and the family.

"Good. I look forward to coming and tasting everything," Jake said. He was the second oldest of us Whitley brothers. Since he'd only recently returned to Boston, we were all still getting used to seeing him at the family gatherings. "Maybe then I'll understand why you give me so much grief about coffee."

I'd always had an obsession with coffee. I was a connoisseur. Some people prided themselves on knowing wine. I knew coffee.

I turned to my eldest brother. "Colton, will you drop by too?"

He gave a noncommittal shrug. "I'll do my best."

I shook my head. "Man, you can't stay in your office all day."

He grinned. "I don't. Sometimes I go to the lab for a change of scenery."

"You know what I mean."

Colton was a workaholic. When he was working on a breakthrough invention, we struggled to pull him away from his building.

"When does the booth open?" Spencer asked.

"Next week."

"Got it. I'm going to be there."

Spencer was my twin. We weren't identical, so we looked nothing alike. My hair was a shade darker than his, and so were my eyes. When we were growing up, Grandmother said I was the one always stirring up trouble, and he was the one trying to fix things. As adults, we were both pretty good at causing trouble. The downside for me was I had to fix my own messes now.

"To The Boston Coffee Expert," Grandfather said, and we clinked our wineglasses. "I want to take the opportunity to thank all of you for everything you've done for Whitley Industries over these past years. Jake, you deserve a special thank-you. You truly went above and beyond."

"Will you look at that?" Gabe said. "The rest of us have been working hard for years, but the golden boy returns home and takes all the credit."

Our youngest brother was joking, but Grandfather still frowned. "We're grateful to all of you in equal measure. After your father left, those companies were up in the air, and you all stepped up to the plate without even having been asked."

It was my turn to frown. "It's our family legacy. I never felt anything but proud, continuing it."

My father had left a stain on our name, but I was honored to bring back its former glory. Of course, there were some wrongs we couldn't right. There was absolutely nothing we could've done for our mom. But with our combined efforts, we kept Whitley Industries from sinking. Colton was in charge of the biotech branch. Gabe ran the craft distillery. Spencer had taken over the publishing arm, and a few months ago, Jake bandaged the bleeding wound of Whitley Industries: Whitley Advertising. My older brother specialized in management consulting. He had a company in New York that turned around businesses for a living and had successfully done the same with Whitley Advertising. Now Jake had moved back to Boston to run it full-time.

THE ONLY POSITIVE THING ABOUT MY FATHER'S DOUBLE life was that we had three additional half brothers. I still couldn't believe he'd actually managed to have two families and neither of the women knew until the end. Ours was located here in Boston, and the other was in Maine. It was difficult to look back upon those years even though it was over a decade ago.

"I, for one, can't wait to taste all those new blends you told us about," Grandmother said. "You've been obsessed with our perfect roast since you were in high school. I've never seen a teenager so interested in coffee, except perhaps Meredith."

"Is there any reason you're bringing her up again?" I asked

suspiciously. Meredith Porter had tutored me in math in high school. We'd been good friends, but I hadn't seen her in years.

I noticed Gabe looked strangely at Grandmother, and Spencer also gave me a warning look. *Wait a second. What does that mean?* I cocked a brow at him before glancing back at Grandmother.

She'd mentioned Meredith when we celebrated Grandfather's birthday at Jake's property on Martha's Vineyard last week. It made me suspicious—two references in one week when we hadn't spoken about her in years?

"All this coffee talk just reminds me of you and her. It's such a pity you didn't keep in touch."

"People grow apart after high school. It's normal."

Grandmother smiled knowingly, making me even more suspicious. She'd taken up meddling lately and was far too serious about it. She'd conspired to bring Jake and his fiancée, Natalie, together, and the success had clearly gone to her head. But in the end, Natalie was the perfect match for my brother.

I decided to be up-front about it. "Are you planning something?"

She didn't reply, and the look on her face almost made me burst out laughing.

Jake shook his head. Next to him, Natalie was also fighting a smile.

"Jeannie, just because it worked out for Jake and me doesn't mean it will every time," Natalie said gently, practically voicing my thoughts. She could say things to our grandmother that none of us could.

"But I've turned ninety, dear, and still don't have any great-grandkids. Isn't that a sign to take matters into my own hands?"

Suddenly, Natalie had nothing to say—probably for fear of Grandmother badgering her.

"No, Grandmother, it's not." Spencer sounded uncharacteristically serious. "Things take time, and you can't butt in on something so personal."

I almost spit out my drink.

"Oh, well, I don't know, Spencer dear. Jake didn't mind," Grandmother said.

Jake chuckled, taking Natalie's hand and kissing it. The change in him was still shocking to see. He'd been distant for years, and not just physically, but Natalie came along and changed all that.

"No, I didn't mind... at least, I don't mind now, but I don't mean that as an encouragement, Grandmother." He squeezed Natalie's hand, kissing her cheek. He was clearly at peace, and I was happy for him. But I wasn't going down that path. At thirty-one, I knew I never intended to settle down. I liked to play the field—although I was never double-dipping my wick. I wasn't my father. But marriage wasn't for me.

"I'll take it as encouragement anyway. Who knows which of you is going to follow in Jake's footsteps?"

"I have a feeling you do," Spencer replied flatly, looking me squarely in the face.

Huh?

I cocked a brow at him again. *What is it with him today?*

I had no idea why Spencer was so up in arms. Yes, Grandmother was meddling sometimes, but she'd only mentioned Meredith twice.

Well, whatever was going on didn't matter because I had my hands full with the competition. To increase profits, my father had completely forsaken the fair-trade principle that was very dear to Grandfather. He'd kept production at a high standard, which included sourcing coffee from places where farmers and workers had acceptable working conditions. Father didn't care about any of that.

I'd worked very hard these last years to rebuild our reputation. This prize would mean a great deal to my family. I would do everything in my power to win and right some of the wrongs my father caused all those years ago.

Meredith

"Meredith, I think you'll enjoy your new office," my boss and CEO, Sonya, said.

"Oh yeah. Most definitely," I agreed, glancing around my quaint space in the Winthrop Building. Looking outside, I smiled, loving the view of the street below. I was on the fifth floor, and this room was such an improvement over the one I had before my promotion. There was so much light coming in, whereas the previous office only had a slim window with a view of a fire escape. "Thank you for this opportunity, Sonya."

I'd been with the company for six years, having started as a marketing trainee. Now I was an executive and would be responsible for the bottom line of the company. It was a lot of responsibility, but I relished the challenge.

"You'll do great. I'm sure of it." The confidence Sonya and others at the firm had shown in me was invaluable, and I was so lucky that I liked the people I worked with as much as I loved my job.

"Okay, I'll hit the ground running, then, and ensure everything is ready for the competition. I'm going to go over today to check our booth myself."

"I'm glad I went with my gut and didn't hire someone externally. I knew you'd go above and beyond."

"Of course. I want us to have the best shot at winning." Coffee was my lifelong passion. I started drinking it when I was only fourteen years old. My mother was fine with it once she realized I functioned much better after a cup in the morning. But only one cup; Mom teased that she didn't want it to stunt my growth. Over the years, my passion for the product evolved, and I'd become more of a connoisseur, especially as I started working in the industry.

I'd had various positions in our marketing department, and

now I'd reached my dream of becoming the vice president of marketing at thirty-one. I felt completely blessed with my career path. I was doing a job I loved in an industry I adored, and now I had a kick-ass office all to myself. That was probably the best part of being VP—I didn't have to share my space.

"I'll let you get started," Sonya said as if reading my thoughts.

"Thank you. I'm going to review the pressing to-dos this morning and then jump right on them."

"I like your energy, Meredith." Sonya winked before she left the room.

I went to the window, putting my hands on my hips as I looked down at Water Street one more time. *Oh yeah, I have a very good feeling about this.*

As I moved to sit at my desk, my phone beeped with a message from Mom.

Mom: Darling, at what time should we expect you?

I grinned. My parents insisted on taking me out to celebrate my new job. They were cute. Little did they know, *I* was going to spoil *them*. They couldn't afford to spend money on me right now.

Meredith: I think around six.

I was also going to surprise them with a basket full of the very best coffee flavors we had. I planned to buy some special treats for them, too, although I was certain Mom would lecture me about that.

Whenever I was near sweets, Mom pointed out that sugar wasn't good if I was trying to lose weight, which I wasn't. I'd been a bit heavier my whole life, and now at thirty-one, I was thoroughly embracing it. I was healthy. My waist had never been smaller than thirty-four inches. So what? I wasn't ashamed of my curves. I certainly didn't dress to cover them up or hide them. Currently, I was wearing a sweaterdress that molded to all my curves. I was proud of them. I'd learned from an early age that when you were different from the others, you either had to embrace it or be completely unhappy.

I was the first one in my class to get boobs and cellulite. I remembered a well-meaning teacher telling me, “Big girls don’t get very far in life. And they definitely don’t get the guy of their dreams.” I guess it was her way of motivating me to lose weight. I'd gotten used to my boobs pretty fast. As for the cellulite, that was still a bit of a sore point. Most of the time I accepted it, except when summer was right around the corner. Then I fell prey to the marketing techniques of beauty companies and bought a lot of the creams and massage machines they advertised. But now we were in pumpkin season, so I had six months before I'd be bombarded by ads targeted at making me feel uncomfortable.

Opening my bag, I took out my violet-scented candle and lit it, taking a deep breath before opening my computer.

Since I’d worked for my predecessor, Cammie, right until she left, I was up-to-date with everything. She’d been a great VP of marketing, but now she was pregnant and said she wanted to stay at home for a couple of years with her baby. I was honored that she and Sonya chose me for the job, as there had been a lot of candidates for this position.

Cammie told me she would be available for any questions I had in the beginning, but I was determined not to bother her too often. She should relax this last month of pregnancy, not stress out about any pending work.

I had a single folder on my desktop, and inside it were two files. One was titled "To-dos," and the other one was "Competition." I opened the one with to-dos first. I glanced over the list, sorting the tasks by priority. The most pressing was the booth at The Fair-Trade Choice competition. Cammie had wanted to stop by herself to make sure everything was ready, but in her own words, she could barely move around her home. I told her I’d take pictures and send them to her so she didn’t feel left out.

I wanted to check out the other booths, too, and see what our competitors were up to before meeting them at the black-tie event at the end of the week. The competition’s committee had published the list of all the participants over the weekend, but I hadn't had time to check. Deciding I'd better look at it now, I opened the browser, scrolling slowly as I read the names. My heart somersaulted when I reached The Boston Coffee Expert.

Oh my God, could it be?

I opened another browser, googling Cade Whitley. I clicked the first result. He was still the CEO of The Boston Coffee Expert.

I sank lower in my chair, my eyes glued to the screen. I hadn't seen Cade in years—ever since he abruptly changed high schools without telling me about it. As an eighteen-year-old with a secret crush on him, it had been heartbreaking. He'd turned into a fine man. The photo was probably retouched, but I remembered the dark brown hair and those vivid blue eyes, always sparkling with mischief as if he were up to no good. To be fair, he *had* been up to no good during school.

Would I see him? I couldn't imagine that the CEO would get directly involved in the competition. He'd probably have his marketing team manage it all for him. Sonya was hands-on, but we were a smaller company, whereas The Boston Coffee Expert was a giant. Despite working in the same industry for years, our paths had never crossed. And I was sure they wouldn't now either.

Back to work, Meredith. You've got lots to do. First, check the booth and make sure we kick ass. Then, spoil your family.

CHAPTER 2

CADE

"Boss, you don't have to go there. I'm handling it," my assistant, John, said to me on Monday morning.

"No problem, John. I want to be on top of everything." I'd arrived at our office on Boylston Street at eight o'clock. I wasn't leaving anything to chance when it came to the competition.

The booths in Harvard Square were opening at nine o'clock sharp. That gave me enough time to give my team a pep talk before heading over.

"Okay, understood. Want me to come with you?" he asked.

"No, I'll call with any instructions I have."

John looked like he was about to pee his pants. Good, he should. I wasn't going to accept anything less than perfection.

We both stepped into the big meeting room, looking around. My top management was sitting around the oval table. John took one of the two empty seats.

"Morning, team," I said, unbuttoning my suit jacket, taking it off, and draping it around the back of the chair at the head of the table. "I'm going to make this brief. These next few weeks will be crucial for us. As you know, winning the competition will go a long way in restoring the company's reputation. Now let's go through everything once to make sure everyone has their responsibilities covered. Mark, you can begin. The floor is yours." I took my seat as Mark stood.

Mark was the VP of marketing. He was in charge of coordinating everything. I sat up straight in my chair, my focus razor-sharp on his presentation. I didn't have anything to add, which was a good sign. He was as prepared as he could be.

"Good," I said at the end, and he looked relieved. I wasn't an asshole, but I didn't give praise too often. It had to be earned.

"You're still going to Harvard Square?" he double-checked.

I nodded. "Yes. We can regroup here in the afternoon. John will let you know when I'm back and send everyone a calendar invite. Now let's all get to work."

Although everyone smiled, I could see the apprehension on their faces as I got up from my chair. John was on my heels as I left the room.

"Why is everyone so tense?" I asked him.

"You're joking, right? You've been riding our asses for months about the competition."

"No, I'm just making sure everything is running smoothly."

He held up his hands. "I'm just saying. You're usually more easygoing, but with this event, you've become a little heavy-handed."

I swallowed hard. Noticing a cuff link had come undone, I fixed it.

"It's important" was all I said.

My dad had all but ruined the Whitley name while financially hurting our businesses. This was personal. Family meant everything to me and winning meant everything to my family. I'd been working on restoring the company's reputation since I took over. Winning would cement that reputation.

I Ubered to Harvard Square in Cambridge. Driving and having to find a parking spot was a waste of time. My brother Jake used a driver, and the idea had its merits, but in the age of Uber, I didn't see the need to have someone at my beck and call when I could just order a car with a few clicks.

When I stepped out of the vehicle, I took in my surroundings. Competitors were milling around the square, setting up the booths, but no visitors were allowed in yet. The day was cold, even for October. After the hellishly hot summer we'd had, everyone expected a mild fall and winter, but that was not the case. It didn't matter. Cold weather was great for business, as consumption of hot beverages went up considerably.

I headed straight to our booth. Monica and Darren, two people we'd picked from our sales team, were tending it.

They were junior interns who we hired last year, and I was certain they were the best people we could have here. They were energetic and passionate about our products. Some of our more senior members on the team were too formal and not as outgoing. They weren't people-people, but Monica and Darren were.

"Good morning, boss," Monica greeted me as I walked over.

"We didn't expect to see you here this early," Darren added.

I looked at our booth, glad our newest coffee blends were front and center. Each one of them had a handwritten note under it explaining its history.

There were several aspects to the competition. The first step was the taste, and the public decided the winners. They could come by all week and give points to every company. The sustainability part—the one that was more important to me—was awarded by a professional committee. They judged based on the coffee origins and how ethically it was sourced, as well as the sustainability of the packaging.

"We've prepped everything so we can walk people through every blend we have, and we're also going to give them shots of espresso to taste. For those who don't like that, we'll mix whatever drink they'd enjoy, of course," Monica said.

"Sounds great. I appreciate you two doing this. I know it goes way beyond the job description."

Darren shrugged. "I worked as a barista, so I know my way around a coffee machine and difficult customers."

"That's exactly the attitude I'm looking for," I replied honestly. As I said, praise had to be earned, and he'd more than done that.

Darren and Monica both had a bright future in the company. I had a knack for people, and I especially liked those who didn't mind going that extra step beyond what was required of them. They didn't mind getting their hands dirty, and that went a long way in my book.

"I'm going to take a look at the competition," I informed them.

"We already did," Monica said proudly. "Check out Sonya's Blends, especially."

"Really?" I racked my mind. "That's a very small player."

"Yes, but they did a fabulous job setting their booth up. I think they're kind of pushing the rules a bit. They took up more space than they're allowed, but it looks good."

"Thanks for the tip." *Interesting.* Usually everyone followed the rules in competition. The fact that this vendor wasn't made me curious. Plus, it gave me the upper hand if it was grounds for disqualification. Fair was fair, after all.

I took a quick walk around the perimeter. Most booths had a similar setup to The Boston Coffee Expert. Then again, this wasn't rocket science. You just had to make sure your top products were in the front. There was no point in displaying everything in your catalog because that would risk overwhelming the customer. It was a marketing best practice.

Unless you were Sonya's Blends.

I stopped in front of their booth, taking in everything with a critical eye. They'd displayed eight blends, and I could instantly see what Monica meant. Most of us only showcased four, which, in my opinion, gave the most visual impact. This looked like it was all over the place, making it hard for the customer to focus on the brand.

One of their guys came up to me. "Hey, I didn't know they were letting in customers already. Welcome!"

"They're not," I said, maybe a little coolly. So what? "I'm from The Boston Coffee Expert. You've spaced out these racks far more than you're allowed to according to committee rules."

"Our VP of marketing measured it." His demeanor abruptly changed. He was smiling before; now he looked dead serious.

Game on.

"Why are you displaying more than four blends, anyway?" Curiosity had gotten the best of me. *Is there a new marketing strategy our team isn't privy to?*

"Our new VP felt it was a better look. 'More is better' sort of thinking."

I snorted. "You've got a new hire now? My guess is they're just trying to prove their worth by coming up with an outlandish decision to stick out from the crowd."

"Are you talking from experience, Cade? I see you haven't changed. Still trying to boss everyone into doing what you want."

I turned around at the familiar voice and couldn't believe my eyes.

Meredith. I didn't realize she still lived in Boston.

"I wondered if I'd see you around here," she said, her smile tentative.

Wait, no, that was a smirk.

For a few seconds, I was too bewildered to reply. "You work for Sonya's Blends?"

"Yes, I'm the new VP you seem to know so much about."

I waved my hand. "I was talking in general."

"I doubt that."

"There's a reason best practices are called that."

She flashed me a sardonic smile, running a hand through her hair. It was light blonde, much lighter than in high school. It reached her waist, and I was kind of surprised by my reaction to her. Meredith looked great. "I don't really care about best practices. I make my own rules, Cade."

I seemed to have pissed her off. "That was different in high school." I took a step closer. Her eyes flashed. She set her mouth in a thin line and propped her hands on her hips like she was ready for a fight.

"I thought I might see you at the gala but not here," she said. "What are you doing down in the trenches?"

"I always double-check the important things. I don't mind getting my hands dirty."

She dropped her hands from her hips, rearranging the belt of her thick black coat. "That hasn't changed about you, at least."

"Since when do you work in the coffee industry?" I couldn't believe our paths had never crossed.

"Since I started working for Sonya."

"So she's letting someone brand-new be in charge of her booth?" There had to be more to it.

"What do you know? She trusts my skills, and since I caught the eye of the famous Cade Whitley, I must be doing something right."

She'd caught my eye all right, but not in the way she thought. It was taking all my self-restraint not to check her out. I liked what I saw so far.

"And you're completely off base," she continued. "I've worked for her for six years. She just recently promoted me to VP of marketing."

"Meredith, come on. We've known each other since high school. Clearly we've started on the wrong foot."

"You can say that again. So far, you've insulted my work experience and my marketing decisions."

"I'm a hard-ass. I admit it."

"Cade, I'm busy. We can continue this fascinating conversation another time." She undid her belt, taking off her coat. "The customers will come in soon, and I don't want you to scare them away. So by all means, go check out the rest of the competition."

She was kicking me to the curb. Granted, I did come on strong.

"Unless, of course, you want to apologize, and then we can call a truce." She raised an eyebrow, and that pouty bottom lip of hers called to me.

"I still stand by what I said about the number of blends. I'm right, and you know it."

She put her coat on a small stool behind the case displaying a variety of their coffee blends. Fuck me, she looked delicious. She wore a sweaterdress that fit her like a glove.

The guy I first spoke with handed her a cup of coffee, and she brought it under her nose, closing her eyes briefly before inhaling the aroma. I had a flashback to school. She used to do exactly that before taking her first sip. I didn't know anyone else who did the same. We were two of the few kids in high school who enjoyed a good cup of coffee.

"In that case, Cade, I'll see you around. I don't want you messing up my Zen when the customers come in."

Zen? What is she talking about?

"Have a great day, Meredith."

As the customers arrived, I made a quick trip around the perimeter. Monica was right. None of the booths stood out except Meredith's.

"So what did you think?" Monica asked when I came back to our booth.

"Yes, they certainly have an interesting setup. You both have my phone number. Send me updates throughout the day, okay?" It made no sense for me to stay here; I'd just be in their way, and I'd only intended to come here before they kicked things off anyway.

On the other hand, I hadn't planned to attend the gala, but now that I knew Meredith was going, I was rethinking that.

Chapter 3

Meredith

"Darling, you're so busy today. You didn't have to bother," Mom exclaimed on Friday. It was the second time this week I was stopping by with goodies. I loved to surprise my parents.

"But I like to spoil you."

"That's right. You do," Mom said with a shy smile, opening the front door wide. I went in with the small container of fruit, oranges, and grapefruits.

"Can you stay for a cup of coffee?" she asked as we stepped into the living room. Dad was watching the Red Sox with my sister, Everly. This was their last month in this house, as they were downsizing to a one-bedroom bungalow. I knew it hurt to sell our childhood home, but it couldn't be helped. They couldn't afford it anymore. My sister and I tried our best to keep this from happening, but it was the best solution.

"I don't have a lot of time before the gala. I need to get ready for tonight."

Mom beamed at me. "Look at you. You're so radiant and happy."

"I am," I said. I'd attended a few black-tie events over the years, so I was really looking forward to this. "It's going to be amazing."

"What will you be wearing?" Mom asked. Everly turned from the television to hear the details as well.

"Oh, I've got a nice red silk dress I keep for special occasions."

Mom pursed her lips. "Something black would look better. It's very flattering on any figure."

I sighed inwardly. Mom meant well, but she always hinted that I should wear *flattering* clothes. Whenever she bought me something, it was extremely loose, almost tent sized. I wasn't ashamed of my body and preferred more stylish clothes than the things my mother liked.

My sister, on the other hand, was thin and could wear anything she wanted. When I was younger, I'd always wanted to have a figure like hers, but I was more than happy with my size now. Fat-shaming didn't work on this girl.

"Red looks good on me, Mom," I said with a wink. "I want to make a splash."

"Mom, stop hassling Meredith. She looks great in anything she wears."

Did I mention how much I loved my sister? Everly was sitting next to Dad, her feet on the couch, one hand on her enormous belly. I smiled at her. I couldn't wait for my niece to be here.

"How are you holding up?" I asked her. Everly looked nothing like me. She was petite, brunette, and had Mom's slim figure. I loved her dearly and couldn't wait to hold her baby.

"Oh, I love my baby, but I want her out. I can't believe I still have a few months to go. I feel like I'm going to pop any moment."

"I didn't know you were here when I drove up," I said. "I bought you some goodies from the bakery. I've got them in my car." My sister had gestational diabetes. She'd been a bit depressed while reading about everything she wasn't allowed to eat, so I'd hunted down a bakery that made products especially for diabetics, and they were delicious.

"I'll come out with you before you leave so we can transfer them into my car."

"Want an orange? I can peel one for you now," I offered. "Vitamin C is good for you."

Something happened to my brain after my sister got pregnant. I suddenly got overprotective, pushing vitamins and stuff. I wondered where this second personality came from.

"Shh, girls," Dad said. My sister, Mom, and I groaned in unison. Mom always said that Dad's first and biggest love was the Red Sox, and I agreed with her. My parents were one of the happiest married couples I knew. They were two peas in a pod.

My sister had followed in her footsteps. Her husband, Derek, was a great guy.

"I'm going to help Mom put everything away in the kitchen," I said. Ever since I turned fourteen, I had taken it upon myself to organize the family pantry. Mom said it was my superpower, and she was right. I could organize even the tiniest of spaces.

"How's the competition?" Mom asked. "Do you know the other companies?"

"Yes, some of the big players are also participating. Guess who's one of the biggest? Remember Cade?"

I heard a movement on the couch. My sister's neck snapped back around as she turned to look at us.

"Cade, yes! You used to tutor him in math," Mom exclaimed but didn't seem too surprised.

"Yeah, I did. Good memory."

"How is he nowadays?" She glanced away, pushing a strand of hair behind her ear.

Is she avoiding my eyes?

"I haven't had the chance to talk to him too much. I just saw him at the booth on Monday."

In a matter of seconds, my sister joined Mom and me in the kitchen. I barely held back laughter. She liked to complain all day long about how difficult it was for her to move around, yet she practically teleported here.

"Cade, huh?" she said, giving me a knowing smile.

I glanced into the pantry and immediately took out a box with cleaning supplies. "Mom, we spoke about this. They go in the bathroom."

Mom nodded feverishly, taking the box from me. "Yeah, you're right. That's a much better place for them. I never need them in the pantry. I have no idea how they got there."

In a second, Mom was out of earshot. My sister stepped closer. "So, you've seen him in person?"

I nodded as I organized the oranges on the shelf.

"Spill it. How is the man? Did he turn out as gorgeous as we always thought he would?"

Guess who knew all about my crush on Cade? That's right, my sister. She'd always been my confidant. She'd even given me tips on how to capture his interest, but I failed miserably.

I turned to look at her with a huge smile after I finished stacking the oranges. "He seems to suffer from acute arrogance and has a particularly nasty case of know-it-all-itis."

My sister started laughing so hard that she had to grab the wall with her hand. "Jesus, woman, you can't do that to me."

I put a hand on her belly, watching her. "Are you in pain?"

"I'm not even sure. Laughing does strange things to my body these days."

"Okay, no more making you laugh, although I didn't mean that in a humorous way. The guy showed up at my booth, and the first thing he did was start criticizing everything I'd done."

Everly smiled. "That does sound like Cade. He thought very highly of himself even in high school."

"That he did," I said, "and it's only intensified with age."

"Do you still think he's hot?" She looked into my eyes, intent on my answer.

I cleared my throat, feeling my stomach somersault. It always did that when Everly caught me in a pinch. "Yes. I'm not blind, you know? I've got eyes, and I can admire a fine specimen of a man."

"Is he going to be there tonight?"

"I think so."

She wiggled her eyebrows. "Cool. I require photographic evidence."

"Of what?" I asked, bewildered.

"How hot he is."

I snorted. "Everly, I'm not going to snap pics of him."

"Ahh, you're so mean." She tapped my temple. "Fine. Then register every delicious detail there and call me to tell me all about it."

"You're even feistier since getting pregnant."

"Lots of changes going on in my brain. I can't remember what I had for breakfast, but I damn sure can remember every single detail about Cade in high school."

"Okay. You've distracted me enough. I have to go. It's going to take me a while to get ready."

She wiggled her eyebrows again. "Putting in extra effort for someone?"

"No," I said. "I always like to look my best."

"And you always do, sis. I'm so proud of you."

"Aww, thanks."

After goodbyes to Mom and Dad, we both went out to the car, and after transferring the goodies I got her to her trunk, I drove home.

I was already mentally putting together my outfit. I was sticking to my guns about the red dress and would pair it with tights, black pumps, and an elegant black coat. Even though it was only the end of October, it was windy enough for a thick coat.

I lived in a one-bedroom apartment in North End. The best part about it was that it was close to my workplace, only a fifteen-minute walk. Stepping into my living room, I threw my coat onto the gray couch. Then I stepped behind it, rearranging one of the three paintings hanging on the wall. It was always a bit lopsided and drove me nuts. Something was probably wrong with the hanger, but I never had time to check it. The wall was painted dark blue. It had thrown me off when I first visited the apartment—as did the dark green shade they'd painted the bedroom. The owner was adamant that I wasn't allowed to paint it white, so I did the best I could by covering it with paintings.

Afterward, I hurried to my bathroom, showering quickly. Then I put on the tights and the dress and secured the belt around my waist. I loved it. It was one of my favorite outfits. I always felt extra confident in it.

Moving into my bathroom, I took out my makeup kit. I applied plenty of mascara and a new lipstick I got the other week. I didn't like wearing too much makeup; it made me feel fake. I took special care of my hair, styling it with some of it up and some down. It looked sophisticated. Once I was done, I stepped back, glancing in the mirror I'd hung on the bathroom door, and nodded at myself.

Yes, I was ready for this evening.

As I gathered my things and walked back into the living room, I realized I still had a bit of time. I didn't want to be there too early, so, almost unwillingly, I headed to my bookshelf. Wedged between *Moby-Dick* and the *Harry Potter* series was my high school graduation yearbook. I had no clue why I wanted to look at it tonight. I hadn't done so in years.

I absentmindedly perused the pages. There was a blank space where Cade Whitley's photo should've been. He had transferred to a new school midway through our senior year. It had been a shock for everyone—most of all for me. One day, we were meeting early to do our math together, and the next day, he was gone. No text, no goodbye. He'd simply vanished. I never heard from him again.

Secretly, I'd feared for some time that he might transfer. His parents' divorce had made the news months earlier, and since then, Cade had become reckless. He'd always been a practical joker, but all of a sudden, his jokes weren't funny anymore. They were dangerous.

The school kept warning him to behave as his detentions kept mounting up. I was pretty sure he'd come close to expulsion. I'd feared his family would move him before that happened, so the fact that he left didn't surprise me.

The radio silence had.

Shaking my head, I closed the yearbook and put it back.

The sound of my phone beeping startled me. It was in the pocket of my coat on the couch. Taking it out, I only gave the screen a cursory glance before grinning.

Everly: You refused to send me pics of Cade, but I want to see one of you laughing.

I picked my phone up and went to the huge floor-to-ceiling mirror in the bathroom. I did a silly pose, kicking out my leg and throwing my head back like a diva.

I snapped a pic and sent it to my sister.

She replied right away.

Everly: Roar! You look absolutely stunning. I always love your style.

I smiled as I responded.

Meredith: Thanks, sis.

She was one of the few people around me who never tried to talk me into wearing loose clothes or styles that were supposed to complement a fuller figure. And I loved her even more for that. She simply accepted me as I was. A second message arrived.

Everly: By the way, I found some pictures of Cade online. And the man is a dictionary definition of hot as hell.

Meredith: Aren't you happily married, sister darling?

Everly: It was just an observation. In case you need an opinion.

Meredith: I don't. Now, have a relaxing evening. I've got to go.

I decided to go to the gala a little bit early after all, thinking I could run into traffic even though I wasn't too far away from the venue.

I put on my coat, ordering an Uber before I even left my apartment. One of the benefits of living in the city was that I never had to wait long for a car. By the time I reached the front door of the building, my app was informing me that my driver was one minute away. I took in a deep breath, smiling as I looked around. I *lived* for the months ending in "ber": September, October, November, December. The cozy factor was through the roof. I called it the hot-chocolate-and-pumpkin-spice-latte season. I loved that the entire city was full of color, primarily from the leaves on the trees and the Halloween decorations, which would be followed immediately by Christmas ones.

The party was being held in an elegant ballroom at the Boston Park Plaza Hotel. I wasn't the only one who'd arrived early. There was already a line of cabs and Ubers in front of the building, and elegantly dressed people were making their way to the front doors.

I buttoned up my coat as I got out of the car. It was windy here, so I walked inside with very quick steps. Thankfully, there were five people working the coatroom. I really would've liked to have kept my coat on for a few more seconds to warm up, but I gave it to the attendant, keeping only my silk scarf.

Once I was inside, I looked around appreciatively. I'd never been here. There were small round tables everywhere, and a huge chandelier hung at the center of the room. There were balconies on the upper level with white and gold ornaments. *Stunning.*

I'd been surprised when Sonya told me I was coming up here tonight by myself. As far as I could tell from looking around the room, most companies had sent two or more representatives. I wondered if I was going to see Cade here tonight. He could send his VP of marketing, after all, like Sonya had. A pang of disappointment settled in my stomach at the thought.

Wait, what was that? I didn't have anything to be disappointed about. I felt a little bit guilty about jumping the gun the other day.

I was a bit of a hothead, and when he'd suggested we start with a clean slate, I'd immediately shut him down.

Forget about it, Meredith. You probably won't see him for the rest of the competition.

I'd researched our competitors and recognized a few people in the room. Many here were VPs of marketing—a few were CEOs. I decided to find my seat and was happy to see my name on a center table. I was seated next to someone named Alex Delaware, and on my other side would be a woman named Alina Smith. The tables were small; most had four place settings where mine had only three. I didn't know either of these people. It should be fun chatting with someone else in the industry. No one was sitting down yet, so I simply made a mental note of where my table was and walked straight to the bar.

"A glass of Dom Perignon, please," I requested.

"Right away, ma'am," the bartender said, pouring me a glass.

I was watching the bubbles build as he filled my drink when a familiar voice said, "You've got great taste."

My entire body lit up, and I turned my head sideways to confirm my suspicion. Holy shit! I wasn't sure what kind of picture Everly had found of Cade, but if it was one with him wearing a tux, I could totally understand her reaction. The man looked like he was a superstar attending a movie premiere. I hadn't noticed that morning how tan he was and how his hair had sun-kissed blond streaks in between tufts of dark brown.

"Cade. I'm surprised again. I wasn't expecting you here tonight."

He winked at me. "That's why I came. I always do the unexpected. Helps me a great deal along the way."

I grabbed the glass the bartender put on the counter, wrapping my fingers around the stem. "Am I about to hear a lecture on some best practices again?" I challenged him. I still couldn't believe how arrogant he was on Monday about how we merchandised our booth. He was ready to call us out for the footprint we created—

how petty was that? It hadn't been against the rules to display more blends. I'd checked the guidelines twice afterward to make sure I was right.

"If you want to, I'm game. As you know, I have a wealth of information, and I'm an open book." Thankfully, he said that with a smirk.

"Has anyone ever told you that you're a bit of a know-it-all?"

He laughed, then said, "Several people tell me that multiple times a day."

"You sound almost proud of it." I *had* to tease him.

"I am," he said. "It's good seeing you, Meredith. Where are you sitting?"

"There." I pointed at my table. "No one's arrived, though, so that's why I'm milling around." As I glanced near the door, I mentioned, "I just noticed a few people here who I know from a coffee conference."

"Trying to escape talking with me already?"

"Don't flatter yourself." But actually, I was. Why was he making me feel nervous?

He looked at me knowingly. "I'll see you later, Meredith." Cade's eyes dropped from my face for a fraction of a second, and I felt a flash of heat coiling through my body. Was it my imagination, or did his appreciative gaze fall right to my hips? No, that couldn't be. I'd never been his type. But as he turned around and walked away, I had to admit to myself that he was still *my* type.

Putting on my work smile—the one pleasant enough to attract people but not wide enough to scare them away—I started making the rounds, approaching the two people I knew from the coffee conference. I looked over my shoulder a couple times because I had the uncanny feeling that I was being watched.

A loud bell sounded as a woman stepped up onto the platform that overlooked the room. "Everyone, if you could head to your seats, that would be wonderful. Our host is going to say a few words before dinner."

There was a shuffle in the room as everyone went to their table. I reached mine quickly, and to my astonishment, Cade was there.

"What are you doing here?" I asked.

"I sit here."

"No, you don't." I glanced down at the name on the card, seeing it no longer said Alex Delaware but Cade Whitley. The third chair and name-tag had been removed.

I bit the inside of my cheek, looking back up at him. "Your name was not there before."

"I know," he said, then whispered, "I switched the cards."

I swallowed hard, feeling suddenly very warm. I was too stunned to reply, but I quickly gathered my faculties.

"Cade," I said in a low voice. "The seats are assigned."

He gave me a cheeky grin, pulling my chair out and gesturing for me to sit down. "You know I don't like to play by the rules, Meredith. We have a lot to catch up on."

"We do? I disagree." *Oh my God. Is it getting hot in here or what?*

"I knew you would. That's why I needed this seat—to persuade you. And now I have all evening to do that."

Chapter 4

Cade

Was I an asshole for enjoying the way her mouth fell open? When I saw her tonight, I knew I couldn't let this evening pass without talking to her. She looked fucking amazing in that dress.

"You're used to getting whatever you want no matter what, aren't you, Cade?"

"Yes," I admitted.

"And you're not above cheating."

"Not for a good cause."

"Oh yeah. I remember that. What was your saying? 'Rules are never rules.' At most, you consider them guidelines, right? I hope you don't plan to cheat your way through the contest."

She pressed her lips together, crossing her arms over her chest. I'd managed to piss her off again. I truly felt like an asshole this time, because I enjoyed it. She looked hot when she was angry.

"No. Meredith, what do you take me for?" I teased, adding, "The title is important to me, but I want to win fair and square. Besides, you're the one who used more shelf space in your booth," I reminded her.

"You want to have another fight about that?" she asked as her eyes flashed.

"If you insist. I can give as good as I get, Meredith." I couldn't help myself. This woman brought out something in me.

"That's true."

SHE LOWERED HER ARMS, STILL LOOKING AT ME suspiciously, but she did sit down, and I sat next to her.

"Where are the people who were supposed to sit here?" she asked.

"I asked the waiter to move them. There was plenty of space around." I wanted to have all of Meredith's attention tonight. Now that I had both of them moved, she and I were alone at the table.

She dropped her head back, laughing. "You really are something. I was looking forward to getting to know my neighbors."

"Trust me, I'm much better company."

She half turned to me. Fucking hell, not looking down at her chest took considerable effort. I was taller, so I had a direct view of her cleavage.

"How can you be so sure of that?" she asked.

I pointed to the left. "Those were your neighbors. I had a long chat with them before. Dead boring, trust me."

She took a sip from her glass before putting it back down. "I'm not even sure how to reply to that."

"You have time to think about it while we listen to the keynote speaker. I'm certain you'll find a way to fight me on it."

"Oh yes, I will."

That sass was new, not at all like the Meredith from high school, and I fucking liked it. The studious, careful girl I knew was now a confident, hot woman.

We both looked at the stage as Harley Denver, the president of the committee, stepped up.

"Thank you all for coming here tonight. I'm happy we have such a great turnout. When I first suggested to meet this evening, my colleagues said, 'No one wants to fraternize with the competition.' I disagree. Yes, I know you're all competitors, but I also think there's something to be said about working together and forging bonds. This, after all, is how the industry has made massive improvements over the last decades. In the past years, you've all made remarkable progress in fair-trade sourcing and sustainability, as well as sensitizing the customers to these issues. The leaders in this market have varied over time, and even though there will only be one winner in this competition, I want you to know we're celebrating all of you."

The Boston Coffee Expert had been the front-runner of the pack decades ago when my grandfather was leading it, before my father went ahead and ruined everything. But I was going to make things right. I was determined. I knew everyone was going to bring their best game, but I also knew our strengths. We had a great shot.

I was familiar with most of the companies attending. At the neighboring table was Alfred Danvers from Boston Masters. He was a fucker. If we didn't win, I sure as hell hoped he wouldn't. I butted heads with him a couple years ago when he tried to stop my company from getting shelf-space in one of the biggest retail chains. Alfred Danvers was the leading coffee brand at that time—but my company surpassed him as number one only a year later. He was still pissed about it.

"Wow. That was a nice talk," Meredith mumbled under her breath.

"Disagree with her?"

She shrugged. "I think the point of a competition is to win it. Knowing you participated and did your best isn't really the point, right? Otherwise, there wouldn't be a winner."

"You and I are more alike than I thought," I said.

Despite my best intentions, I didn't get to talk to Meredith alone for long. I hadn't bothered to look at the agenda for tonight.

I'd assumed, since they spent good money asking us all to be here, that they'd actually give us an opportunity to socialize and enjoy the evening. The complete opposite was true. Every member of the committee seemed determined to give a speech, and each was more boring than the previous one. They also informed us of the steps of the competition. After the tasting week was over, they'd announce which of us would advance to the next level. The committee didn't want to waste time with any applicants who didn't meet the taste criteria.

The waiters served the food in the brief pauses between speeches. "It's a waste of this ballroom, if you ask me," I told Meredith amid bites of grilled salmon.

"Will you look at that? Something we can agree on," Meredith said. She'd watched the stage intently, but I saw her eyes glaze over a few times. "They're putting a dent in your plan, aren't they?" A smile was inching across her face.

I couldn't get over how gorgeous she was. Had she always been this pretty? I'd never paid attention to her in high school. Our friendship had been born out of *my* necessity. I'd been too busy being cool to pay attention in class, so when I asked her for help one day, I had no idea she'd ever agreed to tutor me. I was the proverbial jock who only got serious about life after my family imploded.

"Fuck yes, they are," I admitted. "I didn't come here tonight to listen to them."

She swallowed hard, fidgeting, and said, "Why did you come?"

"Told you. To catch up with you. By the looks of it, these old farts are determined to talk our ears off until the end."

She parted her lips, dipping the tip of her tongue between them.

My cock twitched at her action. *Fucking hell.* I moved closer, leaning toward her shoulder. "Let's bury the hatchet, at least for tonight."

"I was thinking about that too," she said, drumming her fingers on the stem of her empty glass. She hadn't asked the waiter for a refill. "But I'm reconsidering it."

“Based on what?" I teased.

"Your behavior."

"Is that so?" I straightened back up in my chair.

“Yeah. I felt guilty about roasting your ass the other day at the booth, but you deserved it."

"Do I get any credit if I admit that I did?"

She jerked her head back, clearly surprised. "Yes. Yes, you do."

"Good. We're inching closer to burying that hatchet and getting out of here."

Meredith sighed. "Yeah, but it'll have to be after the last speech. God, why do they all need to go on and on?"

"My thoughts exactly."

After the last speech, which coincided with the cheesecake dessert, the organizers announced that the evening was over. As far as events were concerned, this one was atrocious. You didn't just dismiss your guests after you'd bored them to tears the whole evening. But Meredith and I had been ready to go for the last hour anyway.

"Why did they even mention fraternizing with the enemy? We didn't have time to do any of that," Meredith said as we all crowded toward the entrance.

“Give me your coat number and I’ll get them both,” I offered.

Meredith didn’t hesitate. She reached into her purse, handing me a metal plate with a 27 on it.

“Thanks a lot. I’ll wait for you here.” She stepped into the corner between the two doors, shivering. I immediately took off my suit jacket, draping it around her shoulders.

“Cade—”

She sounded belligerent, and I wasn’t having it.

“You need it!”

“Yes, I do. Thanks.”

I liked how it looked on her.

Five minutes later, I returned with both our coats. After she gave me back the jacket, I held her coat, and she immediately put it on. I had a perfect view of her cleavage as she slipped her arms into the sleeves. Black lace hugged her breasts. I cleared my throat, looking away, but I knew the image of her nipple pushing against lace had been branded on my mind.

Her hair smelled amazing up close. Like spices, or something along those lines. I had no idea except that it was addictive.

As she stepped away, buttoning up her coat, I slid on mine. It was apparent that the committee organizers hadn't thought this through, as we all came out at the same time, and it was getting really crowded.

"How are we supposed to find an Uber?" Meredith said, tapping her phone and refreshing the app every few seconds. Everyone else appeared to be doing the same, making it difficult to call a car. Putting the phone in her pocket, she looked around. "I'm going to walk a few blocks. I'm sure that once I'm at considerable distance, it'll be easier to a find a car."

"Great idea. I'll walk with you."

"No, you won't. You don't even know what direction I'm heading."

"It doesn't matter." My tone was determined. "I won't let you roam the streets alone at this hour."

She gave me a soft laugh. "I'm a grown-up, and I'm quite used to roaming the streets alone. This is Boston."

"Yes, exactly."

She narrowed her eyes. "Cade, I do this often."

"Not tonight—not with me. I'm going with you." Was she insane? Why would she want to go alone? It was true that we were in a relatively well-lit neighborhood, but still.

"I swear to God, you're stubborn," she said.

"And so are you. I'm not budging on this. I'll follow you whichever way you go."

She clasped her hands together. She'd already put on gloves.

Was she that cold? I wanted to reach out and take her hands in mine, warm them up. I could call Jake's driver, but I wasn't sure if Meredith would be cool with it, or if he'd be available. For now, all I wanted was some alone time with this beautiful woman.

"You're not really making a case for burying that hatchet right now," she said, but we walked away from the group and down Columbus Avenue.

"I wonder if there's some big event we don't know about in the city. The traffic is insane. Is there a hockey game or something?"

"Not that I know of. And I'd know if there was any baseball happening. My dad can't stop talking about it."

"He's still a Red Sox fan?" I asked.

"Yes. How do you remember that?"

"First time I came over to your house, he was watching a game. Questioned me about my favorite team. He made it clear that any answer except the Red Sox wasn't acceptable."

Meredith grinned. "Yeah, that sounds like my dad. He's still a fan."

"How are your parents?" I asked.

Her eyes clouded for a bit. "They're okay."

I was sure that wasn't the whole story, but she didn't add anything else, and I didn't press. I knew all about people asking questions you didn't want to answer.

"How are your brothers?" she continued when we turned onto Stuart Street.

"All good." It was my standard answer. "Jake returned to Boston a short while ago."

"He'd moved? I didn't know he left."

"Yeah, to New York for a couple years. Grandmother is happy about having everyone home."

"How old is Jeannie now? Is she still as feisty as I remember her?" Meredith asked.

"She's ninety and has only gotten better with age," I explained, glancing around. I liked to be aware of my surroundings.

"Is she still acting?"

"No, she retired years ago. She keeps busy. Maybe too much so. We're trying to convince her and Grandfather to get more help around the house. It's an ongoing battle."

"My parents are retired too. I drop by to check on them a couple times a week and bring them goodies."

"Very thoughtful."

I liked that she wanted to make them happy because that meant family was important to her. I remembered Meredith's family surprisingly well. Her parents had an easygoing relationship that had seemed alien to me as a teenager. Even before my parents' marriage collapsed, they were always stiff with each other. I thought that was normal until I went to Meredith's house.

"So what's Jeannie doing to keep busy these days?" she asked.

"Throwing parties and nagging us about grandkids."

"Oh my God, I can't believe it. She sounds like my parents."

"She even meddled to bring Jake and his fiancée together." I'd never shared that with anyone. In general, I had a strict rule about not bringing up my family. It invited personal questions I had no intention of answering. Everyone usually brought up the scandal one way or another, but talking to Meredith was different.

She ran her hand through her hair, pulling her coat tighter.

"Are you cold?" I asked her. "I can give you my coat too."

"No, it's just cozier if I pull it together tighter. You were saying about Jeannie meddling?" She sounded incredulous.

"We're all having a collective reaction that's very similar to yours."

It felt good talking about something other than business. Meredith was genuinely interested in knowing how everyone was, and that was comforting.

"Do you think we've walked far enough?" she asked.

"Let's check." I took out my phone, bringing up the app showing us cars. "I think it's good. We can share one," I said. "I'll drop you off first and then head home."

"What are you afraid of? That I won't be able to find my own way from the Uber to my building?"

"Meredith," I said in a warning tone, and she sucked in a breath. I locked my eyes on hers as she shifted her weight from one leg to the other, shaking her head. Her thick, shiny hair fell on her face, and she pushed it away behind her ear. An image popped into my mind of her under me, hair messed up while I was thrusting inside her.

Whoa, not going there.

I wasn't going to even fantasize about that. She wasn't going to end up in my bed.

Out. Of. The. Question.

"You bossed me into walking with me, which did make sense, but sharing a car doesn't. So, I'm ordering my own." She took out her phone, clicking on the app. "It's coming in two minutes."

I'd done the same. "Mine in three." At least that gave me some peace of mind; I could see her get in the car.

"Things didn't really go your way this evening, huh?" she teased.

"And you're enjoying it."

"Immensely."

It was true. We didn't catch up nearly as much as I'd intended.

Her car arrived less than two minutes later.

"Tonight was fun. Admit it," I said as I opened the door for her.

The corners of her mouth twitched. "I think I can admit that without the risk of it going to your head."

"Excellent. That's all I wanted to know."

She cocked an eyebrow as she lowered herself into the car. I breathed in another whiff of her shampoo—or maybe it was perfume—making me only want more.

"I find that hard to believe," she replied.

"That's because you don't know me very well anymore, Meredith. It doesn't mean I'm giving up."

She bit her lower lip. I barely kept my composure. I wanted to bend down and capture her mouth.

“Meaning?”

"Ma'am, we really should get going," the driver said.

"Just a second," she told him before focusing on me.

I winked. “No, he’s right. We wouldn’t want to waste his time, would we?”

I closed the door, enjoying the look on her face far too much.

Yeah, I was definitely an ass, but I liked surprising her. I’d come here tonight intent on burying the hatchet and catching up with an old friend. I hadn’t counted on being so attracted to her that I couldn’t think straight.

Chapter 5

Meredith

Oh God. This evening hadn't gone at all how I thought it would. The way he'd slipped into the seat next to me at the dinner still boggled my mind. How could anyone be so daring? He acted as if the world was his to spin whichever way he wanted. Though his overprotectiveness when he insisted to walk with me was sexy as hell.

As I was about to slip my phone into my purse, I noticed Everly texted me.

Everly: Hey, call me when you're home. I'm up with heartburn again.

I made a split-second decision. Her house was on the way to my apartment. I could stop by for ten or twenty minutes.

I cleared my throat. "I'd like to change my address."

The driver looked at me in the rearview mirror, clearly displeased. I wasn't his favorite person tonight after having made him wait while saying goodbye to Cade, that was for sure.

"Ma'am," he said lazily, "you can't change the address. You already put it in the app."

"Please? I need to drop by somewhere first."

He huffed again, clearly annoyed. "Fine. Where do you want to go?"

I gave him my sister's address. At the same time, I texted Everly.

Meredith: I'll do one better. I'll stop by.

Everly: Oh, sister time. Good. Derek is sleeping.

It was only nine o'clock in the evening, but Derek worked in construction, so he always woke up early. I arrived at my sister's house fifteen minutes later. She was sprawled on her couch, watching *The Vampire Diaries* again. It was one of her guilty pleasures.

"Season three, I see."

"Yeah, it's my favorite."

It was mine as well. She was eating one of the muffins I'd bought her today. I sat at the foot of the couch and started massaging her feet.

"I'm also looking at cheap moving companies for our parents," she told me.

"No way. I told you I'm handling that."

"But I can help. I feel so useless all the time."

"Don't even think about it. I'm handling everything with Mom and Dad. You need to relax and take care of my niece."

Our parents had had a few rough years. After losing their business, they couldn't make their payments on the house, which was why they had to sell it. A large portion of the money they made from the sale went into settling the debts from their business. I was helping them with the rent for the new house until they could get back on their feet.

"But you've got a lot on your plate with the new job."

"I'm warning you, Everly, or I'm taking all these goodies back."

The last thing I wanted was for my sister to worry about anything. She'd had some absolutely shitty years with fertility treatments, and now she was finally looking forward to some peace and quiet, enjoying the time with her baby. I hadn't been able to do anything for her these past few years, but I could help my parents.

Even though Everly was the older sister, I was used to handling everything, and I didn't mind in the least. I had this covered.

"Huh? You can't," she said.

"These things are really good," I said, munching on a muffin. It went way beyond not using sugar. They also didn't use wheat flour. I had no idea what the ingredients were, but it was delicious.

"How were things with Cade tonight?"

"Outlandish. I feel like I'm different around him."

She giggled. "Yeah, it was like that in school too."

"I know, right? I was trying to be a completely different person for him, and yet he never saw me as more than his dork friend when we were young. But now it's different. I'm constantly teasing and challenging him. Fighting, even."

My sister yawned. Her eyes were sleepy.

"Why did you let me come over if you're that tired?" I asked her.

"I'm always tired. I fall asleep everywhere these days. Just stay with me and watch this episode."

I sighed. "I never can say no to *The Vampire Diaries*."

"And you can tell me more about Cade."

"I still have to wrap my mind around this evening, to be honest. Besides, he's a competitor, so I've got to be careful."

My sister gestured as if she were zipping her lips. "Okay, I promise not to say anything more until you give me the green light."

"That's unlike you."

"I know, but I've decided to have mercy on you tonight."

We cuddled on the couch like we did as kids. She fell asleep before the episode even ended. I tiptoed around her, covering her up with a blanket that had a pumpkin pattern on it. My sister loved the fall season as much as I did.

I requested an Uber and arrived in front of my building fifteen minutes later. The tips of my ears were ice-cold from the moment I stepped out of the car until I entered the front door. The cold was a big minus of the cozy months.

I put my palms over my ears, warming them up after I pressed the button for the elevator. I wasn't in the mood for stairs, even though this was the slowest elevator in the world. It always took forever to arrive, but tonight took the cake.

When the doors dinged, my phone vibrated in my purse. I rummaged in my bag but only found it when I was in the elevator. Of course, I lost my signal as the doors closed. Taking it out, I glanced at the screen. My stomach somersaulted. I had a missed call from a number I didn't have saved.

Oh God. What if something happened to my parents? Or sister?

Don't panic, Meredith. You have all their numbers.

But what if it's a paramedic or something?

The second I stepped inside my apartment, I intended to call back, but my phone vibrated. The same number was calling.

I pressed the green button to answer, drawing in a sharp breath as I brought the phone to my ear.

"Hello?" I was sure I sounded panicked.

"Good evening, Meredith."

It was Cade. Relief raced through my body. I couldn't believe I'd gotten myself so worked up. But how did he get my number?

"Cade. It's you. So this was your master plan? Bribe your way into getting my phone number?"

"Of course. I actually thought I'd only find your email, but the organizers had your phone number too. You still haven't told me what you've been up to all these years."

"Why would you even want to know?"

"I just do."

I had no idea what to say to that.

"Cade?"

"Yeah."

"We're competitors."

"I know that. There's no clause saying we can't fraternize. Hell, they held an event for that."

"You've checked the clauses? I thought you didn't care about rules."

"I don't want to mess this up for either of us."

I respected him for that.

"I just got home. Let me take off my coat."

"Only now? Did the car break down or something?"

That alpha tone was coming through again. My pulse sped up, and my mouth went dry. I loved this about him.

"No, I stopped by my sister's house," I replied, awkwardly holding the phone between my ear and my shoulder as I took off my coat, hanging it up before taking off my shoes. I tiptoed into the living room. My heart had rate accelerated just from hearing his voice on the phone.

"How is Everly?" he asked.

"She's pregnant and excited for the baby."

"Congratulations."

"She also has gestational diabetes, so I had to find a special bakery to make sugar-free sweets." I had no idea why I told him that. It was Everly's private health matter, after all.

"You always went above and beyond for your sister. I remember that."

"Of course. She's my sister. I always look after her. You were close to your brothers too. Is that still true?"

"Yeah. Especially with Spencer."

I grinned for no reason. "The terrible duo. Jeannie always said you weren't just responsible for her gray hair but also for that of every one of your teachers, and that your mother's was probably going to turn white before she hit fifty. How is your mom?"

I walked straight into the bedroom, sitting on the edge of my mattress.

There was a long pause, and then his voice sounded completely different when he answered. "She passed away."

"Oh my God. I'm so sorry." I stood straighter, suddenly feeling like I had a huge weight pressing on my heart. "Recently? God, she was so young."

"No. She got sick right around when I changed schools."

His words felt like a shock to me. "Why didn't you say anything?"

"I was too busy breaking into the school lab. My family was too busy keeping me out of juvie. I don't know. I guess I just didn't want anyone to know."

"I'm so sorry." I felt like utter shit. I always prided myself in saying that I'd been his friend, yet I hadn't known his mother was sick.

"It happened a long time ago, Meredith."

"Losing a parent, is always hard."

The abrupt change of schools made more sense now. Suddenly I wanted to know what he'd been doing these past few years too.

I yawned and quickly covered it with my palm. "Sorry," I said, smiling sheepishly even though he couldn't see me. "I had a long day."

"Then I won't keep you any longer."

"Oh." I was disappointed. "Giving up so soon?" I hoped my voice sounded teasing and not needy. I was all over the place tonight, and I wasn't used to it. I liked to think I was in control of things in all areas of my life: my work, my personal life, my parents' financial situation—just everything. But where Cade was concerned, the opposite was true. The man rattled me.

"No. But catching up on all the years in between is going to take a long time. Unless you want to make this a sleepless night?"

The thought was exciting. I considered it for a brief second before shaking myself out of it. *Meredith, you're already losing your mind.*

I lay down on the bed without slipping under the covers, simply putting my duvet over me.

"Nope. Still sounds like giving up to me," I teased.

"Not at all. I have your number now, remember? I can use it any time I want."

"I bet you will." *Time to end this call before I combust.* "Good night, Cade."

"Good night."

Chapter 6

Cade

"Oh, you two are making me so happy," Grandmother exclaimed the next Saturday.

We were all gathered at my grandparents' house again, except for Colton. Jake and his fiancée, Natalie, had just informed us that they'd decided on a wedding date next summer, and Grandmother was over the moon.

"I do wish it was sooner than next summer, though," she continued.

"There's no pleasing you, is there, Grandmother?" Jake asked.

"I might croak before then. Neither I nor your grandfather are getting any younger."

There was a collective groan around the table.

"That's a low blow," Spencer said. "You can't use the age card on us every time you want something."

"Yes, I can," Grandmother said, winking. "Besides, that means you won't give me any great-grandkids any time soon."

"That's a private matter," Jake said.

"You've been in New York for too long," I informed him. "Grandmother doesn't understand the meaning of the word *private*."

"Oh, and the rest of you do?" Grandmother retaliated.

"She has a point," Grandfather said, backing her up as always. It was nice, though. I was grateful that we had an example in our lives of what a healthy relationship looked like.

"Okay, everyone. Dig in," Grandmother said.

I looked appreciatively at the table. It bugged me that she was still spending so much time in the kitchen when we got together. She definitely didn't have to cook so many meals, but she was determined to please everyone. Whenever I confronted her about it, she said they would have leftovers for the whole week after, which made sense, I supposed. But still, I didn't like the idea of her being on her feet for so many hours. She could more than afford a private chef, but Grandmother had never wanted any of that.

“By the way, for Thanksgiving, I'd love for all of you to come here to celebrate. I want to be surrounded by all my grandchildren." Jake cleared his throat. "Oh, yes. Jake, I already invited your half brothers. I don't want to hear anything about it.”

“You won’t from me. Have you told Colton yet?” I asked.

“No, but he’ll come around,” Grandmother replied.

Colton and Jake were the most distant from our half brothers, although Jake had interacted more with them ever since Natalie started working for Maddox. Colton was another story.

"So, Cade, tell us about the contest. And how is Meredith? I heard she’s participating too," Grandmother said.

I stared at her. "The jig's up. You name-dropped her last time, and I thought it was a coincidence, but clearly you know something. What is it?"

Jake was looking in fascination at Grandmother. Natalie was chuckling, and Gabe looked stunned. Spencer shook his head when Natalie glanced at him, and when he frowned, I realized he knew something.

"Whatever's going on, I want to know," I said firmly, pointing at him. “I invoke twin privilege.”

Spencer held up his hands. "I don't even know that much. But when we were at Martha's Vineyard, it was obvious that Grandmother was planning something from the way she mentioned Meredith."

"I think planning is too strong a word," Grandmother said in an innocent tone of voice. "Several things just fell into place the way I wanted them to at the right time."

"And what are those things?" Jake asked.

She cleared her throat. “Her mom and I met two months ago when I joined a new book club. It was lovely catching up with her. Imagine my surprise when she told me Meredith was in the coffee industry too. Now, let’s all focus on this delicious meal I've prepared. We don't want it to get cold."

We were all silent as we ate. Clearly I wasn't the only one blindsided by our grandmother's craftiness. I also admired it.

After we finished eating, we each took as many plates as we could and carried them to the kitchen.

"You’re not mad at your old gran, are you?" she asked as I put the plates in the dishwasher.

"I'm just surprised that you openly admitted it. I know you schemed when it came to Jake, but you were more subtle about it." I winked at her. I couldn’t be mad at my grandmother.

"Ah, yes, but that was different. I knew your brother would fight me if I admitted to him that I was matchmaking him and Natalie."

My eyes bulged. "Matchmaking? That's what you're trying to do here?"

"Yes." Her grin was huge, and she put her hands on her hips. "I always thought you and Meredith could’ve had something going on in high school."

"Grandmother, that was years ago."

"My instincts never lie."

She looked so excited that I chose not to contradict her. Did I like Meredith? Hell yes. Was I attracted to her? Fuck yes. But that didn't mean Grandmother was right. I was a flirt through and through, even though I'd been having a dry spell for almost a month. I owned up to my reputation. That wouldn't earn me any points with Meredith, I was sure of it. As opposed to my father, I didn't hide that I didn't want to get serious about a woman. I told my dates that up front—and usually pursued women who only wanted something casual.

"And there. Seed planted," Grandmother said triumphantly. "My job here is done."

I shook my head, laughing as she walked away from the kitchen.

Spencer came in. "Should I be worried? Grandmother was a bit too cheerful, like she already got her way."

"Yeah, that's what she thinks," I informed my twin. "For some reason, she got it in her head that Meredith and I should be a thing. She even used the word *matchmaking*."

Spencer winced, rinsing the plates before I loaded them. "She's really determined about it lately, isn't she?"

I shrugged. "It's important to her. I get it. Just won't happen when it comes to me."

"I wonder why she's so fixated on you. I mean, she could've chosen Colton to focus on."

"Hardly," I said, starting the dishwasher. "The dude won't come out of his lab."

"Yeah, what are we doing about that?" Spencer asked.

I groaned. "I don't know. I'll think of something."

Our brother was approaching burnout. While I didn't appreciate my grandmother's meddling, I did agree with Spencer that we needed to look after each other and interfere whenever we thought one of us needed it.

We hadn't been quick enough when it came to Grandfather. Last year, when Whitley Advertising was approaching bankruptcy, he insisted it was fine for him to go back to work. Deep down, I knew that wasn't right. The man was ninety, and he'd had a heart attack many years ago, and the doctor had told him he needed to rest. But he was stubborn and ended up getting sick again. At least it hadn't been another heart attack, thank fuck. But after we brought him home, I swore I would always follow my instincts. And Colton needed saving from himself.

"You two, I see that look on your faces. What are you planning?" Grandmother asked, coming back to the kitchen.

"Ways to get Colton out of his lab."

"Oh, good. I hope you come up with something. I've run out of ideas."

"Out of curiosity," Spencer asked, "does this matchmaking plan of yours extend to our half brothers as well?"

She grinned. "Of course. They just don't know it. Not that it's a secret, dear. You're welcome to share it with them. I don't have any specific plans for them as of yet."

"Just for me," I said sarcastically.

"Just for you." There was no trace of irony in her voice.

I wasn't going to tell her how I felt about it. I mean, the woman was ninety. If this brought her joy and peace of mind, then so be it.

I WAS THE FIRST TO LEAVE OUR GRANDPARENTS' HOUSE. I was heading to Colton's office and called him on the way. Ambushing him wouldn't help; knowing him, he'd just push me away.

"Let's go for a round of boxing," I said instead of hello. He liked to do that in his free time. It was the best way to blow off steam. I joined him in the ring sometimes, though he was better at sparring than me.

"I don't have time for that."

Someone's in a mood.

"It's Saturday afternoon, and you say you always concentrate better after boxing."

He sighed. "Fuck it. You're right. Okay."

I arrived at his headquarters fifteen minutes later. He was already in front of the building in his BMW.

His boxing ring was one block away from the company. We parked our cars in the underground garage. I took my workout bag from the trunk before joining my brother.

"I knew I could always lure you out for a good old brawl," I said.

"You're right. It relaxes me."

"Are you ever planning on taking it slower?"

"As soon as we get a breakthrough. It's eluding us. I mean, it's *right there*."

“You’ve got to start taking it easier or you’ll have a nervous breakdown. You've been talking about that ‘breakthrough’ for at least a year. Anyway, it’ll happen when it does."

He scoffed. “Pot, kettle. You’ve been terrorizing your team ever since you started preparing for that contest thing.”

I blinked. "Who told you that?"

"I called you a couple days ago. You didn't pick up. Then I called your office. Your assistant sounded like he was about to shit his pants."

"How did you get them to tell you what was going on?"

"I didn’t do anything. He just spilled his guts. No idea why."

“Me neither." It wasn't like Colton was a people person or someone who invited you to open up and tell him all your worries. I had to review my management style. If my assistant had volunteered this information to Colton, it meant he was stressed out of his mind, and that wasn't how I did things. I respected my employees and certainly didn’t want them working under duress.

We went inside, and Darren, the owner of the gym, welcomed us. He was behind the reception desk, although he was a trainer too. He ran the place efficiently with only three others on the staff. My brother had brought him a lot of business over the years.

"I've got gloves for you two," he said, handing them to us after we changed. I never bothered buying gloves. Colton did, and he kept all his equipment here.

"Okay, give me your best shot," I told him as we stepped into the ring.

The place was full, which was normal for a Saturday afternoon. There were four rings, and each was occupied.

Colton and I had a rule about not bruising each other; we wanted to let off steam, not look like banged-up idiots.

"What's got you up in arms?" Colton asked as he landed the first punch.

"Nothing." I punched back, and he blocked me right away. He was better than me at this, but he also had more practice. It didn't matter. I didn't come here to win.

"You're the one who suggested boxing."

Punch. Punch back. Punch. Block. Punch.

"That's because I knew it was the only thing that would get you out of the office."

We went back and forth, back and forth. I wasn't in fighting shape. Colton was. I went to the gym religiously, but my workout didn't include dodging my brother's fists. My reflexes weren't as quick.

"All right, I think that's enough," Colton said forty minutes later. We were both drenched in sweat, and I was panting like a dog. "Fuck, this was good." He took off his gloves and put them on the bench next to the ring. I did the same.

"I agree. Feels surprisingly good."

He grinned. "That was a win. And you're still insisting that nothing's wrong? Did Grandmother get on your nerves?"

"No. You know she admitted to matchmaking Jake and Natalie?"

Colton jerked his head back. " I don't like that word."

"Neither do I, especially since she informed me that she's hoping to do the same with Meredith and me."

"Oh, yeah. Spencer told me that."

"Dude, I thought you didn't have time to go out with any of us, but you have time for all the gossip in the family? You know more stuff than I do."

"What can I say? People just tell me stuff. I never ask them for it." He paused, then said, "I don't remember Meredith."

"You weren't in high school anymore."

"But I know Mom liked her."

That caught me off guard. "Mom talked to you about Meredith?"

"Yeah. After you failed some test in math. She said it was a good thing Meredith agreed to tutor you and also that she liked her."

I had no idea why that impacted me. I had so few good memories of that period. Whenever I thought back on that time, I only remembered Dad's betrayal and my shitty reaction to it. I should've been there for Mom. We all should've. Instead, we gave her headaches on top of everything else she had to deal with.

As we went to the showers, I racked my brain, trying to remember when Mom and Meredith had interacted. For the life of me, I couldn't remember. I had to ask Meredith.

Colton and I showered and changed quickly. We were out of the place ten minutes later.

"We made great time, and I still have hours of work ahead of me."

I groaned. "Dude, come on. I thought this would motivate you to take today off. Let's get a drink or bite to eat."

"No can do."

"Do you have an Off button?" I asked in exasperation. "The world won't stop if you take a break."

Colton swallowed hard. His eyes turned cold. "No, but some people might unnecessarily lose their lives."

"What are you talking about?" I asked. My brother was losing it.

"This is medicine, Cade, not coffee."

"I know. Don't be a jackass about it," I snapped back.

"Ever stop to wonder what would've happened if there had been a good medicine for Mom?"

His words were like a punch to my gut. I always knew Mom's illness made him get into biotech, but I never realized it was what still drove him to this day. I chose my words carefully.

"I did. I still do. Sometimes. Not all the time, Colton. It's not healthy."

"That's not what I meant. I feel a responsibility for getting a good product on the market every time."

"That's admirable. But if you work yourself into the ground, you won't be able to help anyone at all."

"See, now you almost sound like Grandmother."

"Well, I *have* been attending her lunches more often than you. By the way, she invited Maddox, Leo, and Nick for Thanksgiving too."

Colton set his jaw, glancing away. "Fine."

This wasn't news. Grandmother insisted we all get together a few times a year, but Colton always needed a warning. In the past, so had Jake, but he'd changed his attitude toward our half brothers as of late. As of Natalie.

"Colton, it's not their fault—"

"I know. I have no time for a lecture again. See you when I see you," he added as we both went to our respective cars.

Our grandmother was right about Colton. Almost unwillingly, I wondered if she was right about Meredith and me too. This intervention of hers was working. It was reverse psychology at its best, and I knew it. We often used it for our coffee ads, and now my grandmother was using it against me.

People weren't meant for each other. I was sure of that. The concept didn't exist. Grandmother was wrong on that one. But attraction was a real thing. I felt it every time I was around Meredith.

I'd teased her enough about catching up on old times. Now I just wanted to hear her voice, to be around her.

Once I got to my brownstone in Back Bay, I poured myself a glass of whiskey, sitting in the huge armchair I had in front of the fireplace. On instinct, I called her.

"Hi, Cade." She sounded uncharacteristically shy.

"Meredith! Are you alone?"

"Yeah. I'm driving to my parents' house. You?"

"I went boxing with Colton."

"Oh wow. Talk about the unexpected. I thought you'd be a tennis guy or something like that."

"I am. I play with my half brothers on weekends."

"Your half brothers? They live here?" She sounded surprised. Then I realized that happened after I changed schools, so she wouldn't have known.

"They moved here after college. We grew closer over the years."

"That's cool. So now you have seven brothers, huh? I thought four was a lot."

That made me laugh. "Yeah."

"When I was little, I always envied your family."

"Why?" I couldn't fathom it. Her parents were warm people who cared for each other.

"Well, I only have my sister, and I love her, don't get me wrong, but I always hoped for more. I want to have at least three kids myself."

"Three!" Not only did that seem like a huge number to me, but it also drove home how different Meredith and I were. There were no children in my future. No plans for a family.

"You're acting as if I told you I want to commit a federal crime. Let me guess—you're an eternal bachelor."

I sipped from my glass, choosing my words carefully. "I don't believe in family."

“Cade!" Her tone was exasperated but also soft.

"I had one, and then it imploded. I kind of expect everyone to lead a double life now. I lay all my cards on the table when I’m dating. I'm easy—or, if you believe my family, a flirt.”

“You certainly have the looks for that."

"That's high praise from you. So, tell me everything you've done these past few years, Meredith."

“I went to UCLA for college. Tried to major in astronomy before deciding to pursue something more serious. Something I could actually get a job with after I graduated.”

“Astronomy?”

“Yeah, I’ve always been fascinated with the universe. But the job prospects weren’t interesting, so now I’m just an amateur astronomer. Anyway, then I spent a couple years in San Francisco before moving back here."

"How come? Most people I know who moved to California didn’t come back."

“I missed being closer to my family. My parents had a bit of a rough time."

"Why?" I sat up straight, frowning.

"The business went from okay to bad. And then to worse. They never told me that. If I had known, I wouldn’t have accepted money from them to pay my tuition. Anyway, now I'm helping them as much as I can."

"I'm sorry to hear about their business. I quite liked their store."

I’d been to it a couple times. They sold outdoor equipment, kind of like a Cabela’s.

"I know. So did I, but times change. People order their stuff online, and I can't even blame them. I order everything online too. Anyway, back to boxing. I still can’t believe it. How is Colton?”

"He's running a biotech company."

"Wait, wasn’t he into soccer?"

"Yes, he was. Until Mom passed away."

"Wow. It impacted him so much."

"More than I knew." The whiskey was loosening my tongue. Or was it Meredith's voice? It was so easy to talk to her about things I usually didn't even think about. "I don't think I ever realized that it's what still drives him until today when he mentioned it."

"Oh my God."

"He also mentioned something else. That Mom liked you. I don't even remember you interacting with her."

"What are you talking about? She was there every time I came to your house, always coming to your room with snacks and things. I think she wanted to make sure we were actually studying, not doing anything else. Just like my dad did."

Interesting that our parents would think we might be up to funny business. At the time, I liked Meredith, but only as a friend. "I don't remember any of that."

"Well, I do. Then one afternoon, you literally forgot I was coming to your house. You were too busy being part of the cool group. Your mom was baking a cake, and I helped her."

I cleared my throat. Remembering those adolescent years made me realize how much I didn't like who I was back then. "I was an ass in high school."

"You were just a teenage guy. Don't be so hard on yourself. It was a long time ago. Your turn."

I disagreed. I should've been a better person. But hindsight was twenty-twenty, as they say.

"Did you go away for college?" she asked.

"Yeah, I was in DC. Hated it. I even went on an exchange semester in London."

"Wow. That's amazing."

"It was all right. There was no doubt in my mind that I wanted to come back and take over the coffee branch of Whitley Industries after I graduated."

"Do you work with your dad?"

I stiffened. "No. He fucked off to Sydney years ago. Never heard from him again. It's like we don't even exist."

"I'm sorry about that." The sincerity in her voice did something to me. I liked it. Liked that she cared.

"Don't be. I'm not. If I don't see him again, I won't be sorry. We don't miss him around here. He left most of the companies in Whitley Industries in shambles. The Boston Coffee Expert was still in relatively good shape, just with a shit reputation. I want to restore it. I know it would mean a great deal to my grandparents. That's why I entered the competition."

"That's a valid reason," she said. "How are your grandparents?"

"They're doing great. Grandfather had a health scare, but now he's feeling good. Grandmother is meddling in our lives more than usual. By the way, apparently she and your mother are in the same book club, and, well, you can see where this is going."

"Oh my God. That's why Mom didn't seem surprised when I mentioned you. That's sneaky. She didn't tell me that."

"Yeah." I flexed my right hand. "I need to put some ice on my knuckles."

"Are you bruised?"

"If I say yes, will you come over and take care of me?"

She sucked in her breath. "Cade."

I groaned. "I'd say it's the whiskey talking, but that's not entirely true. Ever since we met again, I've been obsessed with you."

"Oh! That's... I'm not even... I'll... Okay, I'll stop before I embarrass myself." She drew a deep breath before adding, "I don't know what to say. I'm at my parents' house now."

"Have fun. Tell them I said hello."

"No, I'm not going to do that. Mom would know we've been talking, and who knows what idea would pop into her head?"

"If she's hanging out with my grandmother behind our backs, she's probably got too many ideas already."

"True."

We said our goodbyes a few seconds later, but instead of letting this drop, I followed my instinct and messaged her.

Cade: You can still come over and take care of me.

Meredith: My mom wants to watch a movie. She's made popcorn and pie. I don't think you can top that.

Cade: I'm patient, Meredith. I can bide my time.

CHAPTER 7

MEREDITH

I had an addiction, and my addiction had a name: texting Cade Whitley. I had no idea how it even started, but ever since our phone call last week, my heart somersaulted every time my phone vibrated. Five times out of ten, I was disappointed because it wasn't from him. The other five times, my knees weakened, and then butterflies churned in my stomach. I felt like that nerdy girl again, waiting for the popular guy to text her.

That evening when I went to my parents' house, I texted back more in jest than anything else. I liked riling him up.

But lately, he was the one riling *me* up.

"Oh, this is a great day," I said as I picked up my Starbucks: a pumpkin spice latte. Tonight after work, I was attending the second event of the competition. I was heading straight there from the office, so I was wearing a dress that could be considered office attire and a cocktail dress as well.

Once inside, I went directly to my desk. I turned on my computer and glanced at my phone. I noticed a message.

Cade: I can't wait to see you tonight. You looked deliciously gorgeous last time.

Oh Lord. That was exactly what I meant. I was already riled up.

I rolled my shoulders, ready to tackle the day, and tried to shake off the tingles in my body from Cade's message.

A few seconds later, Sonya came into my office. "Morning, Meredith."

"Good morning." Sonya had been super supportive. She was overall the best boss ever. I pinched myself every day that I'd landed this job.

"Excited about tonight?" she asked.

I nodded eagerly. "Oh yeah. I have a good feeling about it." We were having yet another "gala," as they called it, this evening, when the committee would announce who was moving on to the next stage of the competition. I was confident we had nothing to worry about. I'd asked our team to send me a report twice a day, informing me of how many customers we had and how many flavors they tasted. I didn't know anyone else's scores, but my gut feeling told me we were a sure thing.

"I'm coming tonight too," Sonya said.

"That's great! I've been thinking of ways to convince you to join me. I think it'll look good to the judges to have the CEO there."

"Are there other CEOs who attend?" she asked.

"I've noticed a couple." I'd really only noticed Cade, but Sonya didn't need to know that.

"Okay, I'll meet you here at six o'clock, and then we'll ride together?"

"Yes, sounds great." There was another reason I was grateful that she was coming. Sonya would be a great chaperone and keep me out of trouble.

Not a chaperone, a voice in my mind said. There was absolutely no need for that. I wasn't interested in Cade like that. Did my body go up in flames every time I was around him? Yes, it most certainly did. But I knew better than to act on that chemistry.

Why, then, was I on pins and needles the whole day? It wasn't because I feared we wouldn't make it to the next stage of the competition.

As the afternoon went by, I became downright restless. At five, I threw in the towel. I wasn't going to do anything productive today, so instead, I looked up Cade online. He didn't have much going on. Not much was posted on his social media profile—that the public could see, anyway. I had to friend or follow him if I wanted to see his timeline, and I wanted to do neither. I could imagine his smug smile if he saw me following him.

He had both high schools listed on his profile, though. I searched around for the status, but it didn't say if he was in a relationship or not. He'd referred to himself as a flirt, so probably not, but still.

Oh damn it, Meredith. It doesn't matter.

But I wanted to know. How silly was that?

"Meredith, you went to the same high school as Cade Whitley?" Sonya's voice startled me so badly that I nearly fell off my chair. I hadn't heard her come in, and now she was standing beside me, looking over my shoulder.

"Yes, we were classmates," I said. There was no reason for me to lie.

My heart started beating faster.

Calm down, Meredith. You're not doing anything wrong.

"Well, well," Sonya said with an uncharacteristic smile. "Now, that's some very interesting news."

Was it good or bad news? I couldn't tell from her expression.

"I came to tell you that I need to do some errands before we go, so I'll meet you there," she continued.

I pressed my lips together. She was going to leave me hanging like that?

"Sure. I'll meet you there, Sonya."

"We'll talk more about it later."

It was on the tip of my tongue to ask if it was a problem that I knew Cade, but I couldn't see why it would be. I wasn't required to disclose everyone I knew, even if that someone was a competitor. But despite my confident pep talk when Sonya left, I wasn't just on pins and needles anymore. I was a basket case.

Forty-five minutes later, I hurried to the bathroom, checking my appearance in the mirror. I was conscious of the fact that I was unnecessarily refreshing my makeup. My mood lifted as I left the building.

The restaurant was downtown. The second I entered, I was on alert. I wasn't on the lookout for Sonya but for Cade. My heart was hammering in my rib cage.

Would he be even more shameless than usual? Would I? I wasn't sure.

"Meredith!" I heard his voice behind me. My entire body lit up before I even turned around. I could smell his aftershave. There were a gazillion men around me, but somehow I knew it was *his* fragrance. I turned slowly, just as I gave my coat to the attendant.

"Cade!" I drew in a sharp breath, watching him take off his coat. I was fixating on his hands undoing every button with care and dexterity, and I had a flash of dirty images. I'd bet he was good with his hands in every way.

Jesus, Meredith, you definitely have a second personality when you're around him.

"You look amazing tonight," he said as he took off his coat.

It was on the tip of my tongue to return the compliment, but I simply couldn't. I needed to tell him that Sonya knew we knew each other. I had no clue if that was relevant, but knowing his impulsive nature, I figured it was better if he was prepared. I had no idea what Sonya had in mind.

"We need to talk," I said.

He gave me a wicked grin. "I'm all ears. What are you going to challenge me about tonight? Work events seem to be our favorite places for sparring."

I sucked in a breath as we moved away from the coat room to make space for others. "I wasn't challenging you last time."

"Really? That's just the way you talk to everyone?" he questioned.

"No," I replied.

"Just me, then? I see."

"Oh my God, you're insufferable. Will you just let me finish my thought?"

"No, I enjoy rattling you. Your blush is delicious." He wasn't making this easy.

I licked my lips, clearing my throat.

"Meredith, you're here!" Sonya exclaimed, coming up behind us. Cade's expression changed immediately. His smile was instantly polite, not wicked. His eyes expressed a pleasant interest. "And you must be Cade Whitley," she said.

If Cade was surprised that she knew who he was, he didn't let it show.

"Yes, I am. A pleasure to meet you. You must be Sonya."

"Yes." She smiled when he shook her hand. I had a flash of memory from years ago. Cade and I were studying at his home, and his mom came home with a friend. She introduced her to both of us.

Cade just greeted her, but then his mom pinned him with her stare, and he immediately shook the woman's hand.

"Meredith tells me you two know each other from way back when. High school, was it, Meredith?"

Out of the corner of my eye, I saw Cade's expression change once more. His smile faded, and there was a slight crease on his forehead.

Damn it. I really should've warned him earlier.

"That's right," I said.

"What a small world, huh? Let's go inside and see what they'll feed us tonight," Sonya said.

Really? This woman's driving me crazy.

The setup was different tonight. There were three long tables, and the seats were assigned once more. I couldn't help but wonder if Cade would've switched seats again if Sonya wasn't here. I peeked at him at the other end of the table and saw him look right back at me.

Holy shit, my entire body turned to goose bumps. Even from this distance, his gaze affected me. And by the way he was looking directly at me, I had my answer. He *definitely* would've switched seats. And look at that—I had sweaty palms and a dry mouth. My traitorous body was signaling that it would've liked that very much. I didn't even recognize myself when he was near.

Sonya and I sat next to each other. Her expression was too neutral for me to be able to tell if she was pleased or not. It was unnerving.

"Welcome back, everyone," Harley—the head of the competition—said, standing up at her table. "I know everyone is anxiously waiting to find out, and I wanted to reassure you that everyone we've invited here tonight is going forward to the next stage."

There was a round of applause. I let out a breath of relief. Even though I'd been certain of our success, you never really knew.

"Oh, that's clever of them," Sonya said. "Even though it would've been very awkward otherwise."

She had a point. I was too nervous to enjoy the food. I'd worked for Sonya for six years, and she wasn't a secretive or mysterious boss. On the contrary, she was always to the point, and we worked well together, but tonight she was holding back.

We'd been asked for feedback after the last event at the Plaza, and I was sure they'd gotten several complaints about everything ending so abruptly. Tonight, however, they left plenty of time to mingle after dessert. There were no speeches either; it was much more of a meet-and-greet atmosphere.

Sonya was way more sociable than usual. Later on in the evening, I noticed her conversing with the CEO of Boston Masters, Alfred Danvers, at the bar.

"Is this seat empty?" Cade startled me for the second time tonight.

“You’re asking for permission? That’s new.”

“Your boss is here. I’m *trying* to behave.”

The emphasis made me chuckle.

“She’s behaving oddly tonight. She’s been like this ever since she saw me look at your profile."

"You stalked me?"

Shoot. Why did I bring that up?

I cleared my throat. “I was curious.”

He leaned in closer. "You can ask me anything you want."

I held his gaze, determined not to balk even though I was melting from the sheer heat and masculinity rolling off him.

"Meredith, Cade. Good to see you two together,” Sonya said. I hadn’t noticed her return. *Damn, she’s been like a ninja today.*

She looked back and forth between the two of us with a smile. "You've been holding out on me. You didn't tell me you’re such good friends. This is even better than I hoped."

Better? For what?

"Since you have an in with Cade, I'll just lay all my cards on the table," Sonya continued. "I’m interested in selling Sonya's Blends. To be honest, the reason I entered this competition at all was in the hopes of catching the eye of a big fish."

I felt as if she'd thrown a bucket of ice-cold water at me.

She wants to sell? What the hell? When did she start planning this? I’d just gotten this promotion, and she hadn’t said one word.

My vision blurred for a few seconds. I drew a deep breath, but I couldn’t help the panicky feeling in my throat.

My job was not secure, and I'd had no clue of that until now.

If Sonya ended up selling, that was bad news. The buyer usually brought their own management team, too, and got rid of the old one.

"I see," Cade replied in a measured tone.

"We should set up a meeting to discuss this in more detail. Meredith, I’m sure you can arrange something for us,” Sonya said with a wink. "Now, I'm going to grab a glass of champagne and toast to your friendship."

I was too stunned to react at all. I watched her walk to the bar as if she hadn't just rocked my world.

"Meredith?" Cade asked. He sounded tentative for the first time.

I looked up at him. "What was up with that? Why didn't you tell her we just met again last week?"

"Why didn't you?"

"I was too shocked." Surely he could tell by the look on my face.

The slight grin was back. "And I was just playing along."

"What would you have done if she thought we were dating?"

His eyes flashed as he leaned in. "Kissed you right here in front of her to seal the deal."

I licked my lips. "I can't believe that's where your mind went."

"Yep. I was surprised by that myself."

Did I secretly want him to kiss me? My nipples perked up at the thought alone.

I sighed. "I need to talk to Sonya."

His brow furrowed. "She blindsided you with this information, didn't she?"

"Completely," I admitted. "I have no idea why she didn't even warn me before." I really didn't. I was a little hurt.

The corner of his mouth lifted. "Give her hell."

"She's my boss. That would be a career-limiting move."

"Didn't you say you don't play by the rules, Meredith?"

I didn't usually. But I wanted to keep my job, not antagonize my boss.

I honestly couldn't believe this was happening.

"I'll talk to my assistant," Cade said. "He'll contact you with meeting options."

"You're considering this?"

"Why not? We're always looking to grow our business."

I didn't know if it was a good thing or a bad thing that he was considering it.

"It was good seeing you tonight."

"You're leaving already?" I asked him.

"Do I detect a bit of regret?"

"You're not a terrible conversation partner," I teased. "When you're not mocking my work ethic."

He laughed, arranging his tie. "Colton texted me that he wants to go out for a drink. He's been locked in his lab for almost a year, so I can't pass up this opportunity. Knowing him, he'd probably just go back to work."

Oh, that warmed my heart. The Whitley brothers had always been close, and I was happy to see things hadn't changed.

"Go have fun with your brother." Probably for the best anyway. I needed to figure out what the heck was going on with Sonya and my job.

After he left, I scoured the room for my boss. She was at the bar, alone, watching me as I approached.

"The champagne is really good," she said. "Do you want a glass?"

I might not want to antagonize her, but I didn't want to tiptoe around her either. "No, thank you. I wanted to talk to you about the potential sale of the company."

"Oh yes, I thought you seemed a bit surprised."

I decided to be honest with her—after all, that was how we'd always worked in the past. "To be frank, Sonya, I was blindsided. You didn't mention any plans to sell when you promoted me."

Sonya shrugged. "Would you have taken the job?"

"No," I admitted. It would look bad on my résumé if I was promoted to a position of leadership only to lose it in a couple months. And she obviously knew that. So much for our stellar working relationship. Like Dad always said, business was business.

"See? That's why I didn't disclose it. I needed someone very good at marketing who could make sure we stayed in this competition for as long as possible. And I knew you were just that person."

"Do you have a timeline for the sale?"

"As soon as possible." Her quick response bothered me, and I was sure she could tell. "I want to retire, girl. I've worked hard for forty years. I'm tired. I want to take whatever money they're willing to give me and enjoy myself. I've had my eye on one of those around-the-world cruises for quite some time." My jaw was practically on the floor. She obviously noticed. "Meredith, I know this is a surprise. Just see me through this competition. Besides, you never know if the sale will work out or not."

"What if it doesn't?" I asked. "Do you have a contingency plan?"

She sighed, taking a sip of champagne. I was completely unnerved, waiting for her answer as I watched her swallow. I felt like she was searching for the right words and buying herself time before she responded. "I could try taking longer breaks, more vacations or long weekend getaways as long as I find someone trustworthy to lead the company while I'm gone." She looked at me speculatively. "You're a candidate."

"Me?" I was stunned now. Was this just Sonya buttering me up, or was she really considering me for this level of responsibility?

"Yes, you have what it takes to be CEO. I could become an advisor or something. It would require less of my time and give me an opportunity to enjoy life a bit more."

Nah, I knew what she was doing. She was baiting me so I wouldn't be tempted to search for another job. *Damn it. This is so frustrating.* All I wanted was a good salary so I could afford my rent and also help my parents with theirs. I didn't need this kind of insecurity.

"Look, Meredith, if the sale is successful, I can vouch for you so the buyer keeps you as head of marketing. You're a valuable person. I can't imagine that they wouldn't find a place for you in the company. Especially if the buyer ends up being Cade Whitley. I'm sure he wouldn't leave you without employment." She winked at me.

Oh. My. God. The boss who I thought I got along with so well, the boss who I thought confided in me wholeheartedly was giving me a line of *bullshit*.

"I don't take handouts," I replied instantly.

"And I admire you for that. Just stick with me through this competition."

I swallowed hard. "I will, of course, because I was promoted to do this job well and I don't do anything half-assed."

Chapter 8

Cade

"What do you mean, why?" My grandmother had called, wanting to stop by my office. "I don't need a reason to visit my grandson at his workplace."

The corners of my mouth twitched as I sat back in my chair, spinning it around. I had an impressive view of Boston from my office; in my opinion, it was the best in the entire city.

I couldn't remember the last time my grandmother stopped by without having a reason. She'd been here a few months ago, asking my advice about how to convince Jake to take over Whitley Advertising.

I wondered what she was up to now. I was going to find out soon enough. I always made time for my grandmother. She didn't leave the house much, so whenever she ventured out, I was all for it. This time, however, I sensed I might be walking into a trap.

"Look, I have a meeting that will start in ten minutes. It shouldn't take longer than two hours, and then we can go for lunch."

"Perfect," Grandmother exclaimed. "I'll come early and shop around a bit. I miss milling around Boylston Street. There's just something about that building that draws me. Back when your grandfather was still managing Whitley Industries, I was always looking for an excuse to visit him when he was there."

"I don't blame you. It's a great location. See you later, Grandmother. I need to prep for the meeting."

"See you later, Grandson. Say hi to Meredith for me."

Bingo! I sensed that had something to do with her visit. I'd let it slip that Meredith was coming by today. I wasn't even sure I wanted to know what was going on in my grandmother's mind.

After hanging up, I spun my chair back, looking at the presentation my assistant had printed. Meredith and Sonya's chief financial officer, Arthur, sent it yesterday evening. I'd reviewed it once, but I wanted to look it over again with fresh eyes. It was one of the best pitches I'd seen in a while. Then again, I didn't expect anything less of Meredith. She did everything to perfection.

Sonya had niche products. Their business primarily catered to connoisseurs. A few years ago, I would've dismissed even entertaining buying a company like this. Back then, I needed something that appealed to the masses. But the coffee market had changed since then, and now, acquiring a high-quality brand such as this had its benefits. Customers typically wanted to at least try a fancier, more sophisticated brands. From that perspective, Sonya's Blends would complement our product range.

Today was just an introductory meeting with Arthur. If we decided to move forward, I would include my own CFO in future conversations. Their initial asking price seemed too high, but my CFO would tell me with certainty if that was just a hunch, and if we should negotiate. I had one strict rule in business: I always paid for the value of the product. But I refused to overpay, no matter how much I wanted something.

A couple minutes later, John poked his head in. "They're here."

"Thanks."

"Are you going to the large conference room?"

"No. Bring them in here, please." My office was big enough,

with two chairs on the opposite side of my desk. The conference room was too large and formal for this type of meeting. It was only the three of us, and I preferred the more intimate setting of my office for a smaller group.

The door opened, and Meredith walked in. She wore a dark orange suit with a huge belt around her middle. I'd never seen anyone wear something like it in a business meeting, but Meredith rocked it. She didn't just look sexy—she looked downright delicious. It made me want to slowly peel off each layer, watching her every reaction while I explored her. Her blonde hair was bound in a ponytail, showing off her beautiful face.

"Meredith," I said, and she flashed me a smile before pressing her lips together, pointing at the man next to her. I hadn't even looked at him, too transfixed by her. She captivated me every time we were in the same room.

This had to stop. I had to keep it professional, at least while Arthur was cockblocking me.

"It's great to meet you, Arthur. Cade Whitley."

"Honored to meet you, too, Cade. I've read a lot about the company—even more so now." His smile was forced, and I surmised that he didn't agree with his boss about the sale. Then again, the existing management team rarely looked forward to a merger or an acquisition, mostly because they were concerned they could lose their jobs.

"We'll talk here in the office. Take a seat. Would either of you like anything to drink? Coffee, water? We already have water bottles here, but I can bring in a bottle of sparkling water if you'd prefer."

Arthur's eyes widened. "You're the first CEO I've met who actually asks that himself."

"I'll take it as a compliment."

Arthur looked away. I barely stifled a laugh, and so did Meredith.

Maybe Arthur preferred old-school owners who barked out commands and considered everyone their personal servants.

"We don't need anything, but thank you just the same. I can go with you through the presentation if you want," Meredith said.

"Sure. Let's get started. First of all, I'm surprised Sonya didn't come. I got the impression she wanted to be at the meeting."

Arthur straightened up, arranging his tie. Definitely an old-school type of guy. "Yes, she said we should probably talk numbers first. As chief financial officer of the company, Sonya thought it was best I handle this portion of the sale."

I tapped a finger on my chin, measuring him. "Even so, that's no way to start a negotiation, Arthur."

Meredith visibly winced. I didn't want this to be uncomfortable for her, but I was nobody's fool. And Sonya's absence made me think she wasn't serious about this.

"She needs to know that you're okay with the ballpark number, at least," Arthur added.

I was getting annoyed now. For a company that appeared eager to sell, this was an odd way to go about it.

"Let's start by reviewing the presentation," Meredith interjected.

"No, no. Let's set something clear right now, Arthur." I put both forearms on the desk. "I like the brand's unique selling proposition. I like the blends. The sales numbers are good, but my instinct tells me that your asking price is at least 20 percent too high."

Arthur opened his mouth. I fixed him with my stare. He closed it again. Good. I wasn't done. "Now, I don't make decisions based on my gut feeling. So if the interest is mutual and we want to move forward, I'd have my own CFO double-check everything and run a company valuation. I sincerely hope Sonya doesn't expect me to make a decision based on her asking price. If that's the case, you're welcome to leave right now." I pointed to the door.

Arthur turned white. He glanced at Meredith and then back at me. Clearly he hadn't expected this reaction. And that bothered me. He apparently thought I didn't know how to run a business. Why? Because I was nice, and I'd offered him water? Asshole.

"There's no need to be hasty," Meredith said, trying to level the tension building in the room.

Arthur nodded. "Sonya is open to future conversations, of course."

"Can we start?" Meredith interjected, her eyes now fiery. She was pissed off at her associate too. I suspected Sonya thought she might get away with a higher asking price because Meredith and I had a backstory. She was in for a surprise. I'd never willingly go into a bad deal, not even for Meredith, and she would never want that either.

She walked me through the first part of the presentation. Arthur took over once we reached the numbers.

He told a clever story for why their sales numbers weren't up where they should be, then added, "Besides, with your distribution network, you could easily double that in a year."

"No doubt I can strengthen this business in the first year, but that doesn't mean your asking price is correct." He wasn't going to weasel me, thinking he'd get the best of me. His tone deafness to the situation annoyed me. "I'll put my CFO in contact with you. He'll tell you what financial documents he needs to start the valuation."

"That sounds like a good start," Arthur concurred, looking somewhat relieved. The guy was not as savvy as he thought he was.

I checked my watch. We still had half an hour remaining. "Do you have any other questions? Otherwise, we can wrap up early."

"I think we're good," Arthur said just as Meredith nodded in agreement.

"I'm going to call Sonya real quick to ensure she doesn't have any other questions, and then we can go, Meredith," Arthur said. "I'll wait for you outside."

"Sure."

"I've got a couple more questions for Meredith," I said, noticing her cheeks instantly pinken. Had she always blushed like that? I didn't remember it happening in high school. Then again, I'd been a fucking fool back then. I hadn't noticed her in that way at all.

Arthur stood and shook my hand. The second he left the room, Meredith squirmed in her chair.

"What did you want to ask me?"

I walked around to her, sitting at the edge of my desk. She pushed her chair back, looking up at me.

"I want your honest opinion. If you were in my place, would you go ahead with this acquisition?"

"Oh, that's what you... Okay."

"You thought I was asking you to stay so I could make you blush?"

Meredith cleared her throat, putting her hands in her lap and picking invisible lint from her dark orange pants. She jutted her chin forward, eyes fixed on me. "It crossed my mind."

"Don't worry. I'll get to that too."

Her mouth formed an *O*. She put a hand to her ear as if she wanted to push a strand of hair behind it, but it was all pulled up.

"But no, I honestly want your professional opinion. You're very good at what you do, and you have a lot of experience. I value your thoughts."

"Thank you," she said, maybe even surprised by my compliment. "I think you could use Sonya's brands to attract those customers who think they're too good for the mass-market products. But I also think you have the in-house knowledge to develop those high-end products yourself. Granted, it would take longer to establish them, of course. Sonya already has a reputation among *amateur connoisseurs*." She'd coined the term in the presentation, and I couldn't agree with her more. She truly was a marketing genius.

"So it's all a matter of how fast you want to move into that market," she continued. "If I were you, I'd want to do it as quickly as possible. It's growing, and there are a lot of players trying to dominate that market. By using Sonya's branding, you'd already have a foot in the door and can build upon that."

"Thank you. I appreciate the honesty." I shifted a bit closer. She didn't make any move to back away. "And now, as to the blushing part..." I was so close to her now. I could barely keep myself from kissing her.

"Meredith!" My grandmother's voice rang out through the room as the door banged open.

I straightened up fast, grasping the edge of the desk.

Meredith spun around, eyes wide. "Jeannie, how lovely to see you again!"

"Oh, I can't believe it. I was certain it would take you two a bit longer to admit what's happening between you."

Meredith blinked, glancing at me, at a loss for words.

I recovered quickly. Then again, I had much more experience with my grandmother than Meredith did. I opened my mouth to tell her to dial down the meddling. Then I was struck by how astonishingly happy she looked. Grandmother's smile was wide. Her eyes were warm, maybe even misty. So, instead of telling her to mind her own business, I said, "What can I say, Grandmother? Your instinct was right." I put my arm around Meredith's shoulders.

She glanced up. "What are you doing?" she mouthed.

"Oh, lovely," Grandmother said. "Well, I don't want to disturb you two. I assumed you were available because your assistant told me your meeting was over. I'll just wait for you in the lobby."

"I'll be with you in a moment, and then we can go to lunch."

My ninety-year-old grandmother winked before closing the door.

"What was that all about?" Meredith asked.

"I told you she was thinking about matchmaking the two of us."

"Yes, but I don't understand why you went along with it just now."

I swallowed hard. "Honestly, I'm not sure how to answer that. I think I just saw her enthusiasm and didn't want to wipe that happiness away. No harm done. It'll just get her off my back for a while."

"Right. I'm going to leave before this gets even more out of hand."

I raised a brow. "How exactly could it get out of hand?"

"I don't know. That interaction with Jeannie is already more than my imagination can handle."

A whiff of her intoxicating perfume reached me. I tilted closer, needing more.

Meredith drew in a breath, darting out the tip of her tongue and licking her lower lip. This time, she did push her chair back, and she rose to her feet.

I walked her to the door, opening it for her.

"My CFO will be in touch," I told her, noticing that John was now watching me. *Wonder how Grandmother got past him. Probably used her sweet-talking or the age card.*

"And will you be?" She held her chin high.

"Do you want me to?"

"Does it matter?"

I frowned. "Of course. Meredith, I'd never do anything that would make you uncomfortable."

"No, I know you wouldn't. That's not what I meant." She shifted her weight from one leg to the other before stepping back from the door. On instinct, I closed it, wanting to be alone with her. I didn't want anyone to see or hear us.

"I don't want you to be uncomfortable," I repeated because I wanted that to be clear. "If this is bothering you, tell me."

She licked her lower lip. I glanced away, biting down a groan. I caught another whiff of her perfume. It was going to be my undoing.

“It doesn’t.”

I stepped closer to her without even thinking. She drew in a sharp breath. I lost it and kissed her, putting a hand on the back of her head. I fisted her ponytail with the other hand and pushed her against the door with my body against hers. Her taste was incredible. This kiss wasn't going to be enough, not even close. I wanted to devour her. I wanted to make her mine.

She moaned against my mouth. The sound reverberated through me, fueling my desire for her. This desperate need was foreign to me. All I wanted right now was to give free rein to my instincts. Her breasts were full and soft against my chest. It was all I could do not to peel off her clothes.

"Did Meredith already leave?" Arthur's voice resounded from the corridor.

I took a step back as Meredith winced, her hand now covering her mouth.

"No," my assistant's voice answered. "I didn't see her come out of the office. They're probably not done yet, but you can wait in the lobby."

"Sure," Arthur said.

Meredith still didn't lower her hand as we both listened intently until footsteps indicated they’d moved away.

"I've got to go," she muttered.

I needed her to stay, but I didn't want to cause her any discomfort. I opened the door for her again.

"I'll be in touch, then, Meredith."

She gave me a small smile before darting out the door, then glanced at me over her shoulder.

This woman would be my undoing.

Chapter 9

Cade

I took my grandmother to one of the best Italian restaurants in the city.

"I missed this place," she said, looking around. My grandmother usually spoke with fervor. She did everything that way, but today she was even more full of energy. "I can't believe you and Meredith already found your way to each other. It was all I wanted for the two of you, even when you were in high school."

I stopped cutting my pepperoni pizza. This was news to me.

Grandmother was eating cannelloni and had taken a bite when I responded, "All I remember from high school was you lecturing me about not getting expelled."

Her eyes dimmed as she swallowed and said, "Of course you'd remember that because it was the worst time of your life."

She was right. High school had been a blur of parties and living the good life, right until it all took a nosedive. First with Dad leaving and then Mom getting sick. Come to think of it, I couldn't remember anything from those years except how angry I was at the whole world.

"To be quite honest, I'm glad you and Meredith didn't have

anything going on back then," she said. "There was no way it would've lasted. You were on a self-destructive path."

"That's a bit dramatic," I said, continuing to cut my pizza.

Antonio, the owner, came back with a bottle of red wine. "Signora Whitley, some more Montepulciano for you?" He spoke with a fake Italian accent. He was Spanish.

She nudged her glass. "Yes, please. I've hidden all my bottles at home. I'll have to dine out more often."

"What do you mean, you've hidden the bottles?" I asked.

"The doctor insists your grandfather shouldn't drink, and I don't want to tempt him."

My grandparents' relationship never ceased to amaze me. They were the "poster grandparents" for a long and happy marriage. How had my father fucked it up so badly? Was it a conscious choice he made? Of course it was, but sometimes I wondered if there was something wrong deep in his DNA. Had he passed it on to us?

"I think I'll have some dessert too. The doctor said he should cut back on sugar, and that was my one saving grace. Whenever he got grumpy, I baked for him."

It dawned on me for the first time that Grandmother truly hadn't come here for a reason. She just needed to get out of the house and do all the things she couldn't do with Grandfather, fearing he'd fall ill again.

In a split second, I decided to change my plans for the evening.

"What time does Grandfather expect you home?"

"I told him I might stay out for a bit. A friend is visiting him, someone from the office who's also retired. They'll talk for hours."

"Would you accompany me to a play?"

Grandmother beamed widely. "Can we go to my old theater?"

"Of course. That was the plan."

"Are you sure? Don't you have anything lined up this evening?"

"No, I don't, and besides, I would cancel anything for a chance to spend some time with my grandmother." She'd been an actress for nearly sixty years before deciding she couldn't keep up with the pace of the stage anymore. In her honor, the theater kept two tickets reserved in the Whitley name for every show they booked.

"That would be lovely."

"I'll make all the arrangements," I said.

After lunch, I instructed my assistant to get me the tickets. My grandmother spent the rest of the day shopping, and we arrived at the theater at six o'clock. The John Druitt Nash Theater was a small venue downtown, but it had a very loyal clientele. I especially liked that they treated my grandmother like a queen.

"I haven't been here in two years," she said, looking around the lobby, probably trying to see what's new.

Fuck me, we're bad grandsons. I was going to have a chat with my brothers so one of us could take her out once a week, or at least offer to.

"Come on, let's go in. This musical is one of my favorites," she added.

Musicals were the bane of my existence, but there wasn't much I wouldn't do for my grandmother. Being here gave me a flashback to my teenage years. Had I truly been down a dark hole when I was a teen the way she'd described? I remembered the rage but nothing else.

Well, that wasn't true. I remembered Meredith as well. I spent the entire show thinking about her, trying to figure out a way to see her outside of the competition's events and meetings.

Before I even realized it, the show was over, and Grandmother and I were heading out of the theater to my BMW. It was ten o'clock in the evening when I dropped her off at home, and Grandfather was waiting up to make sure everything was okay.

Afterward, I started to drive back home but changed my mind and headed to my old high school. I couldn't say why. Maybe my grandmother had stirred something in my brain. When I arrived, I parked next to the main entrance. There were two lampposts at each side of the gate. Only one was working. The whole street was dark, and on instinct, I decided to call the one person who was my rock at the time—Meredith.

"Hey," she answered.

"Hey. Guess where I am."

"If you say you're outside my bedroom window, ready to throw stones, I'm going to be creeped out because you shouldn't know my address." She made me laugh, and it felt good. Those teen years were tough, and I'd missed out on a lot by being so angry at everything. I knew that now. But everyone went through something, right? We learned and moved on. That's what life was all about.

"I'm at the high school."

"Oh? What are you doing there?"

"I don't know."

"I haven't been there in a long time, even though I live just a few blocks away. How does it look?"

"Dark," I said. "But it's still the same layout. I can even see the backyard where we used to sneak a smoke."

"*You* smoked, not me. I just lectured you," she reminded me.

"True. I never could tempt you with that."

"Tempt me? I was sure you were going to give yourself lung cancer. Remember, I was the nerd."

I remembered it like yesterday. She was so concerned that I'd get sick. She was always like that. Meredith always cared.

"I need to see you," I said.

"Right now?" Her voice sounded strained.

"Yeah."

"Well, I *am* close to the high school. You could drop by. " She sounded nervous, but she didn't say no, and that was a good thing.

My phone buzzed with an incoming message; she'd sent her address to me. Did she need to see me just as badly? I flipped it to my phone's GPS and realized she was only five minutes away. I kept the phone on speaker as I drove.

"Okay, I'm almost there," I said when I turned onto her street.

"Really? Oh my God. Okay, um, I need to make myself decent."

"Don't trouble yourself on my account," I responded. I'd love to see a discombobulated Meredith; I was sure she'd look adorable.

"Cade!" She sounded half exasperated, half excited.

I parked right in front of her building. Getting out of the car, I noticed a few stones at the base of an oak tree that gave me an idea. I picked small ones, glancing up at the second floor. There were lights on in all the windows. I saw her silhouette at the second window and threw one stone. Nothing happened after the first one, so I threw two more until she opened the window.

"Cade!"

"You mentioned something about throwing stones."

"I'll let you in right away. Just call number 12," she said. Even that glimpse of her at the window was enough to cause a stirring in my jeans and a tug in my chest.

She disappeared from view, and I walked up the stairs to the front door, pressing the button next to "Apartment 12." She answered quickly.

"Second floor." She sounded breathless.

"I know."

The buzzer went off the next second, and I pushed the door open. A couple people were waiting for the elevator, so I took the stairs.

At the second floor, I immediately saw her door. It was slightly open.

"Meredith," I said, walking toward it with determined steps.

She opened it wider.

"Cade," she muttered. She was wearing a robe but was fully clothed underneath, at least from what I could tell. I barely kept my hands from reaching out and pulling her closer to me.

I stepped inside.

“So… the high school, huh?" she asked. "Were you in the area, and that’s what made you visit the school?"

"Not really. I went with Grandmother to a musical."

Her eyes bulged. "You hated musicals in high school."

"I still do."

"Not much you wouldn't do for your grandmother, huh?" Meredith looked pleased with me, and for some reason, that made my whole day.

"Damn straight."

"Including pretending that her matchmaking was successful."

I looked straight at her. "I don't regret it. And I'm not sorry about the kiss either."

Her chest was rising and falling rapidly. Suddenly, all I could think about was pulling off her robe.

"Neither am I," she murmured.

I closed the distance between us, stepping right into her personal space. She'd put a spell on me, and I was a goner.

"Tell me you want it to happen again," I said, putting a hand on her cheek. I wasn't brushing her lips, not yet.

"Cade. This is... It feels very sudden."

"It is, but I don't want to overthink any of this."

"Don't you? I thought flirting was your territory." Her tone was teasing, but I knew she was serious. I couldn't even tell how I knew.

Her chest was rising and falling even quicker now. I was a flirt. I wasn’t serious about women. So why was I after her? I knew she wanted an explanation. I didn't have one. I couldn't make sense of things at all.

The sound of a phone ringing broke the silence.

"Oops, that's my phone." She took it out of her pocket.

"Take it," I said.

She brought it to her ear. "Hey," she said, walking away from me. "Sure. Yeah. Oh, you're already... How many minutes do you need?" She looked up at me, panicked. "Yeah, of course you can. No problem."

The second she closed the phone, I moved next to her again. "Who was that?"

She narrowed her eyes. "I don't like that tone of voice."

"Meredith! You're seeing someone?"

"Why would you jump to that conclusion?" she asked defensively.

"Who else would come uninvited this late into the evening?"

"I don't know, someone like you?"

"I mean it." Fucking hell, I was jealous. I couldn't believe it.

"It's my sister. She's going to spend the night with me."

"Is she okay?"

"Yeah. Her husband is working out of town this weekend, and she doesn't like to be alone at night. So I'm pampering her a bit."

I groaned. She grinned. "Your plan is being thwarted again?"

"What are you doing tomorrow?" My voice sounded raspy. I cleared my throat.

"Tomorrow I'm leaving for a weekend trip with Everly."

I dropped my head back. "Jesus."

Meredith looked at the clock on the wall, then said, "You have to go now."

"You're kicking me out?"

"Cade, if she sees you here, she's going to ask questions, and I don't have answers."

"Meredith, I want to see you when you're back."

"I want to see you too. Now go, go, go."

Chuckling, I walked out the front door, straight to the elevator. Sunday couldn't come soon enough.

Chapter 10

Meredith

"This weekend is just what the doctor ordered," Everly exclaimed.

"I know. This place is amazing." We'd planned this girls' weekend away ages ago.

We were in the Stone House Manor in the White Mountains, and the scenery was gorgeous this time of the year. On the B&B's website, all the pictures had been taken in spring and summer because everything was green, but now the town was a million shades of red, brown, and yellow. In my opinion, it looked even better. Then again, this cozy-month-loving girl wasn't exactly objective.

As soon as we checked in and put our things away, we got ready to go to the indoor pool. They also had an outdoor one, but it was only open in the warmer months. I could already feel the Christmas spirit in the air now that we were midway through November.

When we stepped inside the pool area, the warmth engulfed us. My sister was already kicking off her shoes and dropping her cover-up on a chaise lounge.

"Let's get in," Everly said as my phone beeped.

I immediately checked it, wondering if it was my mom. It was from Cade.

Cade: How are you doing today, gorgeous? I can't stop imagining what would've happened last night if we weren't interrupted.

I was on fire in seconds. It had to be a record.

"You go. I'll come in just a second," I said to Everly. I hoped the pool wasn't too warm because I already needed a cold shower—or in this case, a cold pool.

I typed back as I sat on the lounge chair next to my sister's, sending him a picture of the fall colors through the enormous window.

Meredith: I'm on my getaway, remember?

He replied instantly.

Cade: I wish I were there with you.

I drew in a deep breath. *Oh God, he really means that?* I thought last night might have been... an impulsive moment. Following the other impulsive moment in his office.

Meredith: I don't think it's your style. It's small.

Cade: Meredith, you're my style. I don't care where we would be.

I swallowed hard, my thumbs hovering above the screen. My chest heaved up and down as my stomach somersaulted. *Cade, Cade, Cade.*

Cade: Are you sharing a room with your sister?

I stared at the screen. *That was an odd thing to ask.*

Meredith: No, I'm alone.

I'd wanted to share a room, but my sister said she snored so loudly since her belly expanded that I wouldn't be able to sleep a wink. We'd asked for adjacent rooms, but there weren't any available.

Cade: Okay, good.

Oh come on. He can't leave me hanging like this. Can he?

Meredith: Good what?

Cade: That means I can call you later and we can talk without anyone around.

Why was I swooning for him already? Was it perhaps because I was still feeling the lingering sensations of his kiss? I seriously needed a good swim not only to cool off, but also to burn off some sexual tension.

Meredith: I was thinking about watching a movie and eating a crap ton of junk food in the evening, but they don't have anything good here. Not even beef jerky or popcorn. Boo-hoo.

Cade: I can think of a better way to entertain you.

Meredith: Game on.

I was letting my inner siren come out to play. I hadn't done that in a while, but Cade simply demanded it.

I took off my cover-up and sandals, then lowered myself into the pool. Everly swam to me. There were three other guests in the water, but the pool was big, and there was plenty of room.

"You look like you were flirting, sitting there with your phone," she said with a smile.

"How could you tell that?"

"Am I right? I saw it."

"Yes, you are. I wasn't even sure I was flirting until you pointed it out."

She wiggled her eyebrows sexily. "Who was it?"

"I'm only telling you if you promise not to tell anyone."

"Who would I tell?"

"Mom?"

"Oh yeah, that's true." Everly then added, "Okay. I'll keep my mouth shut."

"It's Cade."

Her brows shot up her forehead. "Whitley? Mom will have a field day."

"Uh-uh-uh, now what did I say? Not to tell her."

"Well, that was before I knew this was about Cade. It's not fair," she pouted.

"You wanted to know. Now, come on—race me a couple laps."

"Why? You need to work off all that sexual energy?"

I winked at her. "You know it."

"You're playing a dangerous game, sister."

Everly always saw right through me, and I couldn't pretend to be anyone other than who I was with her.

She was right. Maybe this was a dangerous game I was playing. I'd had a crush on Cade for years in high school. I still remembered the sting of rejection. Although, it had never been an outright *rejection*. More like a lack of acknowledging me as a girl. I was just the nerdy, oversized friend. And that had hurt. But things were different now, and I never liked to dwell on the past. What good would it do? I was a different person now and so was Cade. He definitely knew how to flirt and kiss. And I wanted more of those things.

Everly and I stayed in the pool until our teeth started chattering. She said she felt so buoyant that she could almost forget she was pregnant.

Once I was in my room, I showered and dried my hair before wrapping the bathrobe tight around myself. For dinner, we were going to a nearby steak house, and I couldn't wait. I loved my steaks rare and was looking forward to a good one.

I was shocked when I noticed a package on my bed. It must have been there when I walked in, but I didn't notice it. I opened it and gasped. Ladies and gentlemen, I was the proud owner of three bags of beef jerky and two bags of microwave popcorn. There was a note too: ***Miss Meredith, compliments of Cade Whitley.***

Holy shit! The man had called the concierge and asked them to buy this for me.

I grinned instantly, snapping a picture and sending it to him. I glanced at the picture and deleted it. No, I wanted something to make a statement. I sat next to the bounty, stretching my arm up to take a selfie. Yeah, now he could see my silly grin. I snapped the picture and sent it to him before I could change my mind.

Meredith: Thank you for saving my evening. What would I have done without you? See, it's actually better that you're not here. This way, I can go ahead with my plan to treat myself to beef jerky and popcorn.

My phone vibrated a few seconds later.

Cade: Yeah. But if I were there, you could have beef jerky, popcorn, and me.

Oh yeah. The game was definitely on, and he was beating me at it.

Cade

"DUDE, ARE YOU THROWING THE GAME ON PURPOSE?" MY half brother Maddox asked. On Sunday afternoon, I met him along with my other two half brothers, Nick and Leo, for a tennis match. We played every week at one of the fitness clubs Nick owned in Jamaica Plain.

"No. I'm having trouble focusing," I admitted, which sounded strange even to my own ears. I lived for tennis. I started playing when I was in college, and now it was my favorite pastime sport.

"You sure? Because you're really bad. You must be doing this on purpose," Nick replied.

"Why don't we call it a game? I'm not in my best shape today. Don't want to ruin our reputation."

"Yeah, I agree," Maddox said.

"Not so fast," Leo replied. "We have a fair chance of beating you today, don't we?"

"It wouldn't be fair and square," I pointed out, "if I can't focus."

"That sounds like a Cade problem, not a tennis problem." Leo gave me a shit-eating grin.

Nick frowned. "Dude, is something wrong with Gran that we should know about?"

"No, that's not it at all." All these years later, I wasn't used to them calling her Gran. To us, she was Grandmother. My mother always insisted we call her that.

Nick looked at Leo. "You know, I wouldn't feel good about a victory today with this one having his head up his ass."

Leo waved his hand. "Fine. We'll continue next Sunday. Let's get something to drink."

The sports club was more of a hangout place for most members. I only used it to play tennis on Sundays with my half brothers. Sometimes it was still strange to hang out with them. After discovering my father's infidelity, I'd felt guilty for wanting to meet them. Colton and Jake had been far too furious even to entertain the thought. But even though I was pissed at my father, I still wanted to meet my three other brothers. None of this was their fault, after all.

It was months after Mom passed that my grandparents invited them to their house. It had been a very awkward day. They felt like strangers. Gabe immediately befriended them. Even today, they were closest to him.

We were better at navigating our relationship now. We rarely spoke of our childhood. Sometimes we mentioned Dad by accident. Nick was especially prone to bringing up that he took them fishing, and all those resentments came right back, slamming into me. He'd never done that with us. He was gone almost every weekend with "work" projects.

We tried to limit family talk to one subject: our grandparents. That way we didn't slip into dangerous territory. My brothers and half brothers were all focused on their well-being. As far as I knew, they weren't in contact with Dad.

As we sat down at the bar, the waiter brought us four menus.

"Coffee for me," I said.

"Yeah, for me too," Maddox said. Nick and Leo both went with a Coke. Everyone around us seemed to be drinking some sort of green juice, probably one of those health concoctions. I'd never understood the fad.

"Hey, look at that group," Leo said. "How about asking them if they want to play with us today?" He glanced at Maddox. "Since these two bozos are sitting out?"

Maddox turned to look at the ladies Leo was referencing. "I wouldn't mind if we went out with them instead of playing tennis."

Nick grinned. "You two, turn that down. Don't pick up women at the club. It's tacky, and that's not what Whitleys do."

"Why not?" Leo asked. "That's why most people come here."

"Running into them again here will be awkward," I pointed out. "It's just not a good look."

"Thank you," Nick said. "Finally, someone with a good head on his shoulders."

"Yeah," Leo remarked.

"True," Maddox agreed.

I had to laugh at how similar these guys were to my blood brothers. The apple doesn't fall far from the tree.

It was good that my brothers weren't here because they'd immediately pick up on why I was playing so shitty today. My family had a sixth sense when it came to that. I had to make an effort to stop them from guessing what was wrong with me, but I could relax around my half brothers, since they didn't know me as well.

My mind was on Meredith, plain and simple. She was getting back tonight.

While my half brothers continued discussing the pros and cons of hooking up with someone at the club, I texted Meredith.

Cade: What time do you get back today?

Meredith: Six o'clock.

Cade: When and where should I pick you up?

Meredith: Can I text you later? My parents moved into their new home. I promised I'll help them unpack or they'll never be done. We can go out after?

Cade: I'll drop by and help.

Meredith: Really? I'm sure you have better things to do on a Sunday evening.

Cade: Nah, I'd like to spend it with your parents. I haven't caught up with them in a while. And with you. Especially with you.

She didn't reply. I was 100 percent sure she was blushing.

"Dude, I thought you couldn't focus. But this is different. It's like you're in a trance," Nick said.

I looked up from the phone.

Leo narrowed his eyes. "I have an idea about what's going on."

"Don't try guessing. You're going to be wrong. Besides, my focus is back," I said.

Maddox clapped his hands. "Fantastic. Then let's go and beat the hell out of these two guys."

The competitive streak was strong in the Whitley family.

But unfortunately, Maddox and I lost spectacularly.

I was too busy imagining all the things I'd do to Meredith tonight after she and I left her parents' house.

"Dude," Maddox exclaimed. "What the hell was that? You said you were back in the game."

"Yeah, I was wrong, obviously," I said, patting his shoulder. "I'll make it up to you next week."

He was looking at me with a stunned expression. "Tell me the truth. Did you do it on purpose so those two bozos could win?"

"No, I'm just off my game today."

"I still have an idea," Leo said loudly.

"I don't want to hear it," Nick said. "I'm too busy basking in our glory."

"If I was a betting man," Leo went on as if he hadn't heard anything.

"You *are* a betting man," Maddox pointed out.

"True. I'd say Cade's got some woman troubles."

I jerked my head back. *Did I step into an alternate universe where my half brothers were onto me now?*

"Why would you think that?" I asked out of interest.

"Spencer thinks Gran's got her eyes on you with her whole matchmaking project," Leo explained.

"She does," I confirmed.

"Good. Keep her occupied for as long as possible," Leo said. "You never know when the woman will turn her sights on us."

"Knowing Grandmother, she already has plans for each of us," I said.

Leo and Nick both looked downright horrified by that prospect.

Maddox simply chuckled. "You know, I've never been happier that there are so many Whitleys to go through. It's going to be a while until my turn comes."

"We should ask Spencer to join us next weekend for a game," Maddox suggested as we headed out of the club.

"Already thinking about replacing me?" I chuckled.

He held his palms up. "Dude, I can forgive you this once. But if you're playing just as shitty next week, Spencer will definitely take your place."

"That's a fair deal."

Ten minutes later, I was in my car. I pulled up the address Meredith had texted me. This was insane. I was in a great mood just because I was going to spend the evening with her.

A few minutes later, Spencer called. Like Leo, I was a betting man, and I was certain he'd already heard about my spectacular loss. I answered right away.

"What's this I hear?" Spencer asked in a lazy voice. "You got your ass handed to you, and you took Maddox down with you."

"Guilty," I replied.

"Let me guess. You had Meredith on your mind."

I nearly bumped the car in front of me, barely pressing the brake on time. "This is a record, even for you," I said. "How would you even know about Meredith?"

"You think Grandmother keeps her successes to herself? The whole family is aware. Just so you know, she's already making plans about introducing Meredith to the family."

I stared at the phone. *Well done, Cade.* Why did I think it would appease Grandmother just to know her plan was working? Of course she'd want to ask Meredith to a family dinner.

I groaned. "I'll talk to Grandmother about that and ask her to hold off."

"Why?" Spencer asked.

I decided to fess up to my brother. "I told Grandmother she'd been successful just to get her to lay off of the whole matchmaking thing."

Spencer burst out laughing. "Dude, you're delusional. That will never work."

"I'm starting to realize that. Look at us talking about this. If anyone heard us talking about *matchmaking*, they'd think we're some weirdos, not grown men running their own companies."

"Relax. But wait! If you just said that for Grandmother's benefit, then why did you lose today? I mean, if Meredith really isn't on your mind?"

I didn't answer. *Shit.*

He laughed. "Your silence doesn't bode well, brother. I'm starting to get ideas."

"It's complicated," I replied.

"Damn. Grandmother's good."

"What's that supposed to mean?" I asked.

"Never mind. Anyway, do you foresee the need for me at next Sunday's tennis match or not?"

I considered this. "Yeah, there might be."

Then I remembered what I wanted to speak to my brothers about. "Since you called, I did want to talk about Grandmother. I think she's getting cabin fever. She's spending too much time indoors. She's trying to follow the same restrictions as Grandfather, and it's starting to get to her."

"That's why you went to the theater with her?"

"Yeah," I said.

"Okay. I'll rally the troops. We need to make more of an effort. Did you already talk to Maddox, Nick, and Leo?"

"No, I haven't."

"Why not?"

"I just didn't," I said. As much as my half brothers and I tried to focus our conversations on our grandparents, sometimes family talk spilled into darker topics, like our parents. Our father. Our tennis matches were a fun time, and I wanted to keep them that way.

"I'll ask Gabe to talk to them," Spencer said.

"Okay. Did you call to say something else, or did you just want to ride my ass?" I asked.

"No, nothing else. Just wait until Grandmother makes her next move."

"I'll talk to her before then," I said.

"Like that's ever worked."

I groaned as the call disconnected. He was 100 percent right.

I arrived at the address Meredith had given me a few minutes later. There was no moving truck in the driveway, which meant all the boxes were already unloaded. Meredith and a woman I recognized as her mother were in front of the house.

It was a good thing I'd told Spencer to join us at the club next Sunday. I had a feeling that spending more time with Meredith wasn't going to take my mind off her.

On the contrary.

Chapter 11

Cade

"Cade, you're here," her mother exclaimed when I got out of the car. "Let me take a look at you. It's been so long."

"Nice to see you again, Mrs. Porter." I gently shook her hand. Meredith watched with warm eyes. "And you, Meredith."

I looked directly at her and instantly realized this wasn't my best idea. Being with her around her parents was going to be torture. I needed to kiss and touch and devour her. What the hell had I been thinking?

Mr. Porter walked out of the house too. "Son, it's good to see you. I've been reading up on Whitley Industries. You've done well. Your brothers too."

"We're doing our best."

"Well, it's nice of you to come help us," Mrs. Porter said, now looking eagerly at Meredith. "I can't believe you convinced this young man to spend his Sunday evening helping us unpack and move things around."

"He offered," Meredith said in her trademark sexy voice.

I wanted to pin her against that wall and kiss her for the whole city to see.

Damn it. Rein it in, Cade. There's a time and place for that, and it's not here.

"Hm," Mrs. Porter said. "Come on inside the house. We already made some good headway."

"You've sold your old house?" I asked. I only vaguely remembered it, but I did know it was much bigger than this. This was a bungalow.

"Yes. We had to downsize," Mrs. Porter said, and I instantly realized she didn't want to talk about it. She turned to Meredith. "Our girl here was very kind and helped us find our footing."

"Of course, Mom. Now come on. Let's get to unpacking the rest of the things or we'll never be done."

As Mr. and Mrs. Porter went deeper inside the room, Mrs. Porter said, "We can work on the boxes in the living room. You two can work on the ones in the kitchen."

Yes! Fuck yes! I'd take some time alone with Meredith anywhere, even just in the next room.

"You look fantastic and well rested," I told Meredith as soon as we stepped into the kitchen.

She turned around, sucking in her breath. "No flirting while we're here."

"I wasn't flirting."

"Tell that to my lady bits."

I swallowed hard. "Well, fuck me, Meredith."

She covered her mouth with one hand. "I'm so sorry. I don't even know why I said that. You have a very strange effect on me."

I was relieved to know I wasn't the only one who was acting out of sorts lately.

"On one condition," I said. She bit her lower lip, running a hand through her hair. I looked at her mouth, and she licked her lips. I took a step closer and felt her suck in a breath as if she was bracing herself for me. "I want to kiss you."

"Cade," she murmured.

"I've been fantasizing about you the whole weekend, Meredith.

I barely talked myself out of getting in the car and just showing up at your hotel."

"Oh God, I wanted that so much. When I saw the package from you, I'd hoped you'd stop by too."

That was all I needed. I leaned in, kissing her the next moment. I'd been starved for this woman. She tasted like apples and mint, and I couldn't get enough of her. I first pulled her upper lip into my mouth, then the lower one before exploring her deeply, holding her close to me.

Her soft body melted against me, and she put her hands on my shoulders, sighing against my mouth. She was fierce, but one kiss was all it took for her to turn soft in my arms and open up for me.

She made a small sound in her throat, a moan. I couldn't stop at one kiss. I needed to find out what other sounds I could get out of her and all the ways in which I could bring her pleasure.

"Oh, I couldn't believe it when Jeannie told me."

Shit.

Meredith

THE SOUND OF MOM'S VOICE SLICED THROUGH THE AIR. I took a step back, and so did Cade. We both turned to face Mom, who was smiling from ear to ear. She put her hands together, clasping her fingers.

"You know, at the last book club meeting, she said you kids might be into something, and I honestly thought it was just wishful thinking on her part. I can't believe it's true. My baby girl and Cade."

I was so stunned, I didn't know what to say. *This is karma coming for you, Meredith.* I made fun of Cade for indulging Jeannie, but now I could see what he meant. Looking at Mom's expression, I didn't want to wipe away that smile. Besides, what exactly could I tell her? *"No, Cade and I aren't in a relationship. We're just shamelessly kissing in your kitchen."* That wouldn't go over well, and it wasn't a good look on either of us.

I was sure she saw the flush on my face.

"Mom," I said calmly. *Oh Lord, how to approach this?*

"No, no, you two carry on. I didn't want to disturb. I just wanted to say that the boxes in the corner belong in the living room."

"I'll move them right now," Cade said, looking every bit as uncomfortable as I felt.

Mom stared at him with a dreamy expression. "In high school, I really wanted to shake you a couple times for not noticing my baby girl."

Oh God. Ground, please swallow me. The last thing I needed was for him to know I had a crush on him.

"She was waiting for you to ask her to prom, and it didn't even cross your mind," she continued.

Yep, that's it. I need to get her out of here. My heart was beating out of my chest.

Cade hung his head. "Ma'am, I can't say I'm proud of a lot of things I did in high school, but I've matured a lot since then."

Mom laughed. "That you have, young man. Meredith, your dad and I will be in the living room, not listening to a thing."

"I'm so sorry about that," I said as soon as Mom was out of the room.

"About what? Your mom catching us and you not denying anything, just like I didn't with Grandmother? Or that I found out your secret?"

"Ummm... all of the above." I was hoping to distract him from the last part.

"Tell me about that crush. You've been holding out on me."

I swallowed hard. "It was nothing," I said, trying to wave it away. "Just a high school crush."

"Meredith." He stepped closer to me, putting his fingers under my chin and tilting my head up. "I was a blind moron. I didn't know any better, but now I do."

I bit my lip, holding my breath. I loved every word coming out of his mouth. And yet the part of me that had crushed on him all those years ago was alive and well. My poor heart had hurt for him once before. I couldn't put it in the same position.

His eyes were fixed on mine. I nodded. I wasn't even sure what I was agreeing to, but I was powerless to fight it—at least right now.

He seemed to know there was something on my mind, though. "Tell me what you're afraid of."

I shook my head. "Not now."

"Later, then." His voice was strong, like it wouldn't allow an argument. And though I liked to verbally spar with him, I couldn't deny that I also liked it when he unleashed that alpha voice on me. It definitely made my knees weak and set my panties on fire.

I nodded again and stepped back. "Okay."

"And I'm not going to come anywhere near you again while we're in your parents' house."

"Why not?" I asked, miffed.

"Because I can't seem to keep my hands or mouth off you. Being caught once by your mother is enough."

"Oh yeah, I agree," I said.

Wits, hello? Where did I lose you? Thank God Cade has some left.

"How rough of a time are your parents having?" he asked.

"Enough that they had to downsize. Selling the old house crushed them. They'd hoped to rent it out instead, but there were no takers. So my brother-in-law and I flipped that house and sold it. My sister also helped in the early months of her pregnancy. Most of my savings went into it, but it was worth it. They used most of the money they got for the house to pay the debts they still had from the store."

Cade looked straight at me as we opened one of the boxes that revealed plates and cutlery. "You're a great person, Meredith."

"They're my parents. Of course I'll help them," I replied. "Anyway, that's why I'm going to spend the better part of next week here, helping them unpack and put together the furniture. It's a good thing they have the bed, otherwise they couldn't even sleep here, and getting the kitchen situated is important too."

"No moving company?" he asked.

I shook my head. "It's just us. Maybe my sister's husband, but he's been working overtime."

"I'll help."

"No. No, come on," I protested, shocked. "You don't have to do that. There's a lot of work yet to do."

"Precisely."

I swallowed hard, totally speechless. "Thanks. But just so you know, if you change your mind, it's also okay."

"I don't make promises I can't keep, Meredith."

I jolted. "That's not what I meant. But this is exhausting work."

He stepped closer to me. "Which is exactly why I want to help."

He pressed his thumb to the corner of my mouth before drawing it over my lips. On instinct, I pushed my tongue out, licking his thumb.

"Fuck," he murmured, taking a step back.

"Oh, that's right. Now I understand why you said you're not coming near me. Shall we make it more official? Set a number of feet between us?"

He laughed. "That doesn't sound half bad."

It turned out we didn't have to, though, because my parents decided we should start assembling the dresser after all. They were excellent chaperones.

I couldn't believe Cade offered to help us put together the furniture. It was frustrating work, and he was the CEO of a big company; he certainly had better things to do with his time than doing this manual labor with me and my family.

Mom and I assembled the smaller pieces of the dresser while Dad and Cade did more of the muscle work. It gave me the opportunity to fully focus on Cade, as Mom and Dad were busy at their tasks and probably wouldn't notice. He was wearing a shirt underneath the sweater he'd taken off when he arrived at the house.

Who wore a dress shirt on weekends? Then again, when that's what you wore day in, day out, it probably became like a second skin.

I totally approved of his dress code. He looked mouthwatering, every single part of him—his tight ass, bulging biceps, that six-pack I thought I saw whenever he stretched and his shirt rode up.

It was late at night, almost midnight, by the time Mom practically shooed the two of us out of the house. The second we were outside on her porch, Cade came closer to me. Even though it was cold as all get-out, my body temperature skyrocketed the second he touched my lips with his fingers.

"Meredith..."

"I'm sorry this took so long tonight. Do you want to go to my place and order some takeout?" I asked. My parents had already ordered pizza for us all earlier, so I was certain neither of us was hungry, but I wanted an excuse to be with him.

"No." He said the word slowly and deliberately, as if he was trying to feel the weight of it on his tongue.

"No?" I was stricken. Had my parents already scared him away? Or had I?

"I realized one thing tonight, Meredith: I can't be close to you and not devour you."

"Yeah," I murmured. It felt great to be wanted so desperately by him.

"But then it got me thinking about some things your mother and my grandmother said, and I want to start this right."

I blinked. "What do you mean?"

"No rushing into things. No midnight quickie—not that it would be quick."

I laughed. "Right. So then, what great proposition do you have?"

"Tonight, I'm going to drive behind you to make sure you get home safe."

"Cade," I said. "Come on, I live, like, ten minutes away. Nothing's going to happen to me."

"I want to make sure you're safe. I'll drive behind you. I will definitely not get out of the car to walk you to your door, because I'd end up kissing you against it and taking you inside and having my way with you the whole night."

"But that sounds great."

"Taking it slow, remember?"

Stepping back, he took my hand and kissed it.

Is this real? Did this absolute god of a man just say all those romantic things to me?

His eyes shone in the dark. The intensity in them made me shiver. I knew he was right. If we went to my house, that was exactly what would happen. We would be all over each other, though, oddly, I didn't mind. But there was some part of me that was afraid to let myself go, and by tomorrow morning, my defenses were going to go right back up again. Cade did a great job tearing them down and getting beyond my insecurities. And that frightened me.

He walked me to my car, opening the door as I slipped in. He kept his promise and drove behind me, watching me until I entered my building. The second I was alone in my home, exhaustion slammed into me.

After showering, I went to bed, typing a quick message to Cade.

Meredith: I'm home. I just took a shower and forgot to text before.

He answered a couple minutes later while I tossed and turned in my bed.

Cade: I'm getting in my shower now.

I sat up a bit straighter, adrenaline coursing through me even though I was tired.

Meredith: A cold shower?

Cade: Hell yes.

Oh my God. He'd somehow found the self-restraint to only drive me to my door and not come inside. Cade Whitely was a total gentleman.

Meredith: Thank you for this evening.

Cade: My pleasure.

I shimmied on the mattress, settling down again and getting ready to fall asleep.

Meredith: All right then. Have fun in the shower.

Cade: Good night, beautiful.

I placed the phone on my nightstand, turning onto one side and smiling in the dark.

I was pining for my childhood crush all over again. But the difference? It wasn't unrequited this time.

Chapter 12

Meredith

The next morning, I practically jumped out of bed at six o'clock, even though I went to bed super late. Guess who was full of energy for no reason? Yep, this girl right here. I couldn't wait to start the day, even though all I had to look forward to was the same dreary routine at the office—and Cade's texts, of course.

I checked my phone before I brushed my teeth, after I brushed my teeth, before I combed my hair, and after I combed my hair, and yet I heard nothing from him.

Hmm, perhaps he isn't an early riser. Or, I thought to my horror, *maybe he changed his mind. Maybe last night he was caught in a whirl of—*

Oh, stop it, Meredith. Just accept it. This is happening.

Even though I had no clue what *this* was, I was still in a fantastic mood and checked my phone about twelve more times before I left my apartment.

It beeped for the first time when I was in the subway on the way to the office. It was a rainy morning, and I hadn't felt like walking. I didn't even know I had a signal, but I got an alert that said I had a message from Cade. I was so happy that I let out a very unladylike snort. Then I groaned because it turned out I didn't have a signal. I'd never gotten this notification before now: "Unable to display a message." Yeah, I had zero bars. Once I reached my station, I raced out onto the street.

In the lobby, I rested against the wall, nestled out of the way and read the message.

Cade: Good morning, Meredith. What time are we going to your parents' house tonight?

My heart was beating fast. I texted back so quickly that I nearly broke a nail, then waited until I pressed Send.

Don't seem too eager, Meredith. I drew in a deep breath and then exhaled through my nose. *Is ten seconds enough? Fifteen? Whatever.*

I pressed Send.

Meredith: We aren't. My parents forbid me to stop by to help tonight because we stayed so late there yesterday.

I held my breath, counting to... Yep, he replied four seconds later.

Cade: Then tell me when you finish work and I'll pick you up.

Meredith: For what?

Cade: You'll see.

Meredith: Cade!

Cade: Do you trust me, Meredith?

This time I didn't hesitate before replying.

Meredith: Yes.

Cade: Then text me when you're done with work.

Oh, this man. I didn't refuse because I knew he was even more stubborn than I was.

I headed to the elevators, smiling like a fool.

Cade: Wear something warm.

Damn. I could've used the warning before leaving home. At least my coat's thick. But where could he be taking me?

I considered the possibilities. It had to be somewhere outdoors, since he'd suggested I dress warm. The Christmas markets weren't open yet. There were plenty of autumn festivals, although I wasn't familiar with any of them. Maybe a walk in a botanical garden? I had no idea.

Just let the man surprise you, Meredith.

I stayed at the office until 6:55 p.m. before bolting out the door. I was alone in our office, as Sonya didn't believe in working late nights.

I went to my favorite Starbucks, debating whether I should move on from pumpkin spice lattes to eggnog lattes. No. I had to pace myself. I didn't want to start celebrating Christmas so early.

After buying my drink, I waited outside. A BMW pulled up in front of me. It was Cade. He opened his door to get out, but I yelled over the noise in the street, "No, don't bother. I'll just jump in the car."

I literally ran toward it, making sure not to slosh my latte anywhere. Even with a plastic lid, you could never be too careful. Getting in the car, I took a slurp before saying, "Hey."

What's wrong with my voice? Why is it so high-pitched?

“That drink smells weird,” he commented.

"It's a pumpkin spice latte," I said defensively.

"Explains the smell."

"Have you ever tasted one?"

"No."

"Want to try?"

"No."

"Then don't diss something you haven't tried. If I could just find *pastéis de nata* in this city, I'd be happy.”

“What's that?”

“Portuguese custard tarts. I had them when I went to a convention in Lisbon. They are delicious.” Cade had this weird look on his face. “Hey, don't look at me like that.”

“You like pumpkin drinks. I reserve judgment.”

“Hmm...”

“Excited about tonight?” he asked as the car lurched forward.

"Yes. I've tried to make a list of the possible places you might have in mind. I'm sure I have it wrong, so what is it?"

"I'll give you a hint. Boston University."

"I need a bit more."

"We're going up on the roof."

"We're taking a night tour of the university?" I guessed.

"No. It's a specific department." He hesitated, then said, "Astronomy."

"Oh, we're going stargazing?" My grin was huge.

"Yeah."

"I can't believe it." I frowned because I remembered one minor detail. "But today's Monday."

"I know."

I didn't want to rain on his parade—clearly he'd gone to some lengths to make this happen—but I knew for a fact that open nights for viewing were only on Wednesdays. I'd checked several times myself over the years.

"I don't think they're open today," I said.

"They are for us."

"What do you mean?"

"I booked us a private tour. A stargazing evening."

"That's possible?"

"For us, it is."

"Cade Whitley." I shimmied in the car seat, sipping from my latte. I was positively giddy when we turned onto Commonwealth Avenue, and even more so when we stopped at number 725.

The second he parked the car, I got out, taking in a deep breath. My pulse accelerated when he came up to me. God, he was so handsome. I couldn't believe he was taking me on the perfect date. This sexy man who insisted he was a flirt. Well, he might be, but clearly that didn't mean he couldn't pull together a fantastic date.

"You know your way around?" I asked.

"Yes. They explained on the phone what we needed to do, and

I jotted down the directions." He reached in his pocket and pulled out a piece of paper.

"Then lead the way."

I'd never been inside Boston University. It felt a bit eerie to walk through it at night, like we were doing something forbidden. It was utterly and completely empty except for a couple of night security guards. Cade had some credentials, so we just sailed on by and headed up to the fifth floor. The telescopes were above the astronomy department. There were a couple domes around us, and an older man was there waiting.

"Mr. Whitley?" he asked.

"Yes. I'm Cade. This is Meredith."

"I'm Professor Hastings. My colleague informed me that this is a private tour."

"Exactly," Cade replied.

"Allow me to take you to our telescopes. Follow me."

I looked around, mesmerized. This was so dreamy!

"I can't tell you how exciting it is to have a small, intimate group that I can share my knowledge with," Professor Hastings said

Cade didn't smile.

"Thank you so much," I said. I suspected this wasn't the romantic evening Cade had in mind. In fact, I was betting he'd imagined we'd be all alone up here. To be honest, so had I.

"Come here. Look through these telescopes. You can each take one. A perk of your private tour is that you don't have to wait your turn."

Once again, Cade said nothing. He was shooting daggers at the professor with his eyes, as if he wished Hastings would vanish into thin air.

I looked through the telescope and sighed. "The sky's beautiful."

"It is, isn't it? Now, let me tell you all about constellations."

For the next hour, he yapped nonstop. I had no idea how he even had time to breathe, but I loved every minute of it.

"Any more questions?" he asked once we stepped back from the telescopes.

Cade looked at me, so I offered the professor a polite smile. "No, I think that's everything."

"Really? I'm yours for the evening. Seriously. You can ask me anything."

"As Meredith said, I think we've heard a lot," Cade replied. "It was very informative. Thank you for your time."

"Okay," he said, clearly disappointed.

He walked with us through the university building, right out to the parking lot, where he got in a small Honda and drove away.

Cade groaned as we reached the car. I laughed. "The evening didn't go quite as you expected, huh?"

"When I booked a private tour, I expected us to be alone."

I narrowed my eyes. "What exactly did you expect we'd be doing at the astronomy building?"

"I wanted to have you all to myself, Meredith."

He moved to stand right in front of me. Instead of opening the door, he pinned me to the car and drew his thumb just under my jaw. "I want..."

"What?" I whispered, leaning forward.

"You." Then his lips were on mine.

Heat blasted inside me, gripping my body instantly. *Holy shit. How can he make me explode just by kissing me?* I lost all sense of time and space.

He explored my mouth shamelessly until I was shuddering.

"Meredith," he groaned.

"Let's go to your place," I whispered. "Or mine. It doesn't matter. I just want to be with you. I don’t care about taking it slow."

Chapter 13

Cade

We ended up at Meredith's. I threw my coat somewhere near the entrance, and I kissed her hard while walking her backward through the dark living room until we reached a door. I pushed her against it, kissing and kissing until she sighed against my mouth. I drank in every sound of pleasure, every reaction. She was going to be mine tonight, and I was going to make her come so damn hard. Her body was full of tension, and I couldn't wait to give her the release she craved. I couldn't take my mouth off her until I removed her coat, and then I took a step back.

"Where are the lights, Meredith? I want to watch you while I take your clothes off."

"There's a light switch." Her voice was low and shaky. With the light filtering through the window, I saw her pat the wall next to the door, flicking on the lights. Now I could see how red her mouth was from my kiss. I traced the contour of it with my thumb.

"I want you so damn much, Meredith."

"I want you too," she whispered back.

I grabbed the hem of her dress, pulling it up slowly and drawing my fingers along her thighs... until I felt her garters.

"Fuck me," I groaned, dropping my head back.

She flashed a wicked smile.

"You've had these on the whole day?"

She nodded.

I loved her curves, loved not just seeing them, for once, but feeling them under my fingers. I peeled off the dress easily, throwing it on the couch. She was an absolutely gorgeous woman. Her panties were connected to the bra by a series of crisscross spaghetti straps.

"This looks fucking sexy, but I need it out of the way. What's the fastest way to get it off, short of ripping it?"

She sucked in a breath. I was serious, and she knew it, because she didn't give me any sass.

"Here." She tugged on an end that was connected to the left cup of her bra, and the spaghetti strap started to come undone. I grabbed the end of it from her, and she gasped when our fingers touched. Once it was undone, I dropped it to the floor.

I went down on my knees, noticing there was a red line on her skin where the straps had dug in, and drew my fingers over it, then my mouth, starting from under her bra cups and moving in a straight line to her navel. Her muscles contracted beneath my touch.

"Cade," she murmured, rising on her toes, then lowering herself again. She could barely stand the contact, and I hadn't touched her pussy yet. I parted her legs wider, looking up at her gorgeous face while I rubbed my thumb up and down the fabric of her panties.

"Oh my God!"

I moved my thumb in decisive strokes until I felt the fabric get wet. Her thighs shook. She was ready for me.

"Cade, please, I need... Take them off."

"You need skin-on-skin contact?"

"Yes, please."

"What do you want exactly, Meredith? My fingers or my tongue?"

"I don't know. Both?"

"Greedy woman," I muttered, then pulled her panties down.

She lifted her feet as I peeled them off, stepping out of them. She was waxed clean. I started to slowly circle her clit with my fingers, all the time watching her. I wanted to taste her, too, but if I did that, I couldn't see her gorgeous face anymore. She squeezed her eyes shut and dropped her head back against the door.

Fuck, I need some release too. Lowering the zipper of my pants, I pushed them down enough to grip my cock, squeezing it good.

"Fuck," I muttered.

She opened her eyes, looking down at me and swallowing.

"You want me to do that?" she said.

"Later." I took my fingers away, then put my mouth right around her clit. She cried out loudly, and the sound spurred me on. I increased the pressure of my tongue, wanting to please her in every way possible. I didn't want to overwhelm her all at once, but I knew she could take more; I wanted to slowly increase the pressure, bringing her to the edge until she begged for me and my cock.

Tracing my free hand up her thigh, I moved to her ass, cupping her buttock, and then I slid it back to her inner thigh. I pushed two fingers inside as she gripped the doorway at her sides, parting her thighs even wider, crying my name.

“That's it.” She was clenching her muscles, and I pressed my tongue over her clit until she was completely done for.

I squeezed my erection hard, listening to her sounds, continuing my exploration of her until her muscles softened. Then and only then did I stand up. Her eyes were hooded, her smile sated.

"Cade! Now it's my turn."

"No, not yet. I'm not done making you come." I wanted to touch and explore every part of her gorgeous body.

Her eyes flashed. "Oh, by all means, then, go ahead. I don't want to ruin your plan. It sounds delicious."

“I haven't paid attention to these tonight. That's a shame.” The hook of her bra was between the cups. I immediately got rid of it. Her breasts were gorgeous, full, and round. I started with the right breast, drawing my mouth in an *S* shape all around, except the nipple. Both of them turned to pebbles. I knew she needed my touch there just as much as she needed it between her thighs.

"Cade... Oh God, how am I so on edge already?" Her breath was coming out in pants.

Smiling against her skin, I sealed my mouth over her nipple. She gasped, and then I felt her fingers curl around my cock. She squeezed once before moving her palm over the crown and twisting it on top. My vision blurred as I groaned against her skin.

I felt everything more intensely tonight. I took my mouth off her, straightening up and making eye contact. "Let's move to the bedroom, beautiful."

She nodded, biting her lower lip. Taking a step back, I grabbed her hand, leading her through the door to the huge bed. I liked that it was high enough. I had a lot in mind for tonight, and the angle looked perfect.

I got rid of all my clothes, but not before taking the condom out of my wallet and putting it on. I didn't want to lose my head and forget about it altogether. That had never happened, not once in my life, but instinctively I knew it was a real risk with Meredith. Everything was different with her. She made me forget myself in a way no one else had ever managed to. I was too wrapped up in her to think straight.

"How do you want me?" she asked.

My cock twitched. She was always so sassy and liked to be in charge, but here in the bedroom, she was willingly putting herself at my mercy.

“For now, turn around and stand in front of the bed.”

She did as I said, looking over her shoulder at me. I twisted her hair in one hand, kissing her shoulder. My cock pressed against her right ass cheek. With my free hand, I pushed it between her thighs, rubbing her pussy.

My eyes nearly rolled back in my head, and I wasn't even inside her. She gasped, liking the friction. I moved slowly back and forth, wanting to heighten the anticipation. Being here with this woman would be my ending. I could feel it in my bones. My entire body was on edge.

"Cade... Cade." She gasped and then bent at the waist, falling forward and putting her hands on the mattress. Her ass was up in the air.

I grabbed my cock at the base but didn't slide inside her. Instead, I circled her clit with the tip.

"Oh my God, how can this feel so good?" she asked. She buried her face in the mattress, and I slid inside her quickly because I knew this was going to push her over the edge completely. She'd barely come down from her last release but was already preparing for the next one. The way she called out my name and pulled at the sheets, I knew she was close. She was snug around my cock, making me close my eyes tight and breathe through my nose to regain my composure.

“Meredith, beautiful, you’re so amazing.”

She turned her head sideways, still pressing it against the mattress. I only saw one cheek, and it was beautifully flushed.

I pushed inside her to the hilt, stilling before leaning over her back until my mouth was on her shoulder.

"How are you feeling?" I murmured.

"This is perfect." She sounded surprised. Everything tonight was on an entirely different level. It filled me with immense satisfaction to know that this was the case for both of us.

I straightened up slowly, kissing her back as I went, and then pulled out. She gasped, looking back at me.

"Turn around," I commanded.

She parted her lips. "Now?"

"Yes, now. I want to see your face while I'm buried deep inside you." I took a step back, making space for her. Licking her lips, she turned around in a half-sitting position.

I took her legs, pulling her to the edge of the mattress until her pussy was level with my cock, and put both her feet on my chest. She wiggled her toes. Her nails were painted red. It suited her. I slid inside her slower this time, enjoying the way she clamped around every inch of my erection.

"Oh, Cade."

I dropped my head back, breathing in through my nose again. Energy gripped my body. This felt too intense already. *What is this woman doing to me?*

I slid in and out, feeling her tighten around my cock even more than I thought possible. I couldn't look away from her as she thrashed on the bed, pulling at the sheets, mirroring my desperation.

"That's it, babe. Come on."

"Cade, I don't think I can."

"Yes. I promise you can. You're going to come for me again."

I focused on her pleasure. It was the only way I could stave off my orgasm long enough to make her come. It felt out of this world, but I still wasn't going to give in to my climax before I felt her explode once again.

I pressed my hand on her belly and instantly felt a shift in her body. A groan tore out of her at the same time that I growled. We were connected on a primal level. I was done trying to rationalize this link between us. I just wanted to give in to it. It was beyond anything I'd ever felt, and it was glorious.

When I brushed my thumb over her clit again, her entire body shuddered. I felt her thighs shake as she wiggled her toes and then came hard the next second. Her cries were even louder than before.

She pulled me with her right away. One second I was looking at her beautiful face and hearing her sounds—the next I was lost in my own vortex. Nothing had ever felt like this. Instinctively, I knew nothing ever would.

I slowed my movements as we both came down from the cusp. She pushed herself back a bit farther on the bed, resting her heels at the edge of the mattress. I leaned forward, needing to support myself to give my thighs some relief. I pressed one hand on the bed, and with the other, I took off the condom. Looking up at her, I tried to check how she was doing, but I needed to regain my composure. My eyes weren't focused.

"Meredith," I asked, "are you sore?"

"Not at all."

She pushed herself up from the bed with a sigh. I straightened up to my feet and pushed her hair away over her shoulder, touching her face with the backs of my fingers.

"These muscles need some appreciation." She traced her fingers down my abdomen and then went directly to my thighs, then my ass, squeezing it. I started laughing. "They're in dire need of it," she said.

She grinned. I bent forward, kissing her.

"I was starting to get drowsy at the university, but now I feel like I could run a marathon. I wonder why." Her voice was playful.

"Come on, let's freshen up first."

We both made our way to the bathroom. Her apartment was cozy but very small. We had to take turns cleaning up.

She yawned, putting her hand to her mouth.

"Where did that come from?" I teased.

"It's just a fluke. I still have lots of energy." She batted her eyelashes.

I kissed her temple. The woman was adorable. She handed me a towel, and I put it around my lower body. As we stepped out of the bathroom, Meredith wasn't wearing anything. I was keeping my fingers crossed that she wanted to simply walk around naked. Then she grabbed a nightgown from her dresser, putting it on. It looked like a wet dream on her: white silk and lace.

"Why are you looking at me like that?" she asked, walking toward me with a shimmy in her hips.

"This looks great on you, but all I can think about is taking it off."

She grinned. "I love my lingerie. It makes me feel feminine and gorgeous."

"You *are* feminine and gorgeous."

Chapter 14

Cade

A smile played on her lips. I liked seeing her like this, completely sated and happy. I'd never seen this kind of smile on her before. "I'm so thirsty."

"Me too," I said.

"Come on, let's go into the living room. We need to hydrate."

"You first."

She looked at me over her shoulder. "Why?"

"I like the way you move your hips. You look stunning."

"Oh really? I love the effect my lingerie has on men."

My smile fell. Her words felt like a punch to the gut. *On men*.

Jesus, I wasn't the first one to see her wear these, obviously. Why was that a surprise?

It wasn't. What was surprising was my reaction to it. I couldn't bear the thought that someone else had seen her naked before me, that anyone had touched her.

"Meredith," I said. Something in my tone probably tipped her off. She turned and looked at me.

"What?" Her eyes searched my face.

I stepped so close to her that the front of my body was plastered against hers. I touched the side of her head, pressing my thumb at the base of her hairline. "Me, just me. I'm the only one who can see you like this from now on."

She parted her lips, surprise etched on her features. Was it because she didn't expect it or because she didn't want it?

"The only one who can make you come, who can make you feel everything you felt tonight."

"The only one," she agreed.

The knot unfurled in my chest. I hadn't been aware of it before then.

"Only you," she repeated, and I pulled her in for a kiss, needing to feel her close and to know she meant every word. I felt her smile against my mouth, and I pulled back, watching her. "I knew you were bossy, but I didn't think you'd be a possessive Neanderthal too."

"I don't know about Neanderthal—"

"Yes, you are," she interrupted.

"But you're right that I'm possessive. I won't share you."

She cleared her throat, looking up. "Neither will I. Word of warning: anyone gets close to you, I might claw her face."

"Fuck yes." Pride thumped in my chest.

She nodded, putting her hand on her throat. "Okay, I really need that water. My throat is aching a bit. Someone might have made me cry out too loud."

"There's no such thing as too loud. I loved hearing you."

I walked closer to her, bringing my mouth to her ear after she turned around. We walked in tandem to the kitchen with my arms around her middle. "To feel you, to see you."

"Wait. First, we drink water, and then you can go back to whatever it is you're doing. No clue what your endgame is, but I'm up for everything, and I like it."

Once at the kitchen island, I let go. I sliced two lemons while she filled two glasses with filtered water, and then I squeezed them into the glasses.

"Well, I have a squeezer, but why use it when I can make good use of your muscles and extremely talented fingers?"

I chuckled before we downed our glasses.

"This is good," I said. "Refreshing." I felt my body temperature cool down. I took her hand, lacing our fingers, and led us to the leather couch. Sitting down, I pointed to my lap. "Come on, sit here, pretty girl."

Grinning, she did as I said, although she planted her ass on the cushion next to me, placing her legs over my lap. Worked for me. I could see her better like this.

I ran my free hand up and down her calf, squeezing rhythmically.

"What are you doing?" she asked.

"Copping a feel."

"And I'm thoroughly enjoying it." She grinned, shimmying on the couch. "I can't believe you're here, in my place. It's like you're larger than life, you know? Though I have to say, you fit in much better without that suit."

"What's the suit got to do with it?"

"Well, your sexiness level is..." She waved her hand. "Never mind. It all makes sense in my head, but I can't explain it to you."

I was pleased that she was so relaxed around me, that she could say anything that was on her mind. She yawned, taking the last swig of water from her glass. "What do you know? I'm getting drowsy again."

"We were both full of adrenaline before. I'm feeling the tiredness too."

She pointed at my hand. "That's not stopping you from copping a feel, though, huh?"

"I could be hospitalized with the flu, and it still wouldn't stop me."

"I love your priorities." She wiggled her eyebrows, moving closer to the edge of the couch. "Want to lie down here with me? I'll make space for you."

"Very generous."

"No, it's just better. I can cop a feel and lie down too." She winked as I lay down next to her.

The second I was in a horizontal position, exhaustion slammed into me. I put my glass on the coffee table next to the couch, laughing when I felt her fingers on my torso.

"How did my fingers even get here? Never mind."

I put my head down on the armrest, intending to keep chatting for a while, but I went out like a light.

A PIERCING SOUND WOKE ME. I BLINKED MY EYES WIDE open and moved just in time to catch Meredith falling off the couch. Shit, we'd fallen asleep here. It was already morning. A blinding light was shining through the windows.

"Great reflexes," she mumbled.

Sassy even in the morning.

"It's a good thing I woke up," I said, pushing myself up on one elbow, looking at her face. Her eyes were a little swollen, and her lips too. She had dark smudges around her eyes.

"Oh my God," she exclaimed.

"What?" I asked as she sat up straight so fast that she nearly slid off again, then jumped to her feet.

"I forgot to remove my makeup last night." She smiled nervously, which was unlike her. "I'll be right back."

"Where are you going?" I asked, but she was gone before I even finished the question.

"Bathroom," she called from afar.

I pushed myself up to my feet too. My towel had slid off, obviously. I decided not to bother putting it back on. Walking into the kitchen, I glanced at the clock on the oven. It was seven in the morning already, but that wasn't a huge surprise. We'd gotten to bed late.

I found the coffee on the counter, loaded some in the filter, added water, and started the machine. While it was brewing, I looked around, taking in the place. On the side of the fridge were pictures of her family. I hadn't noticed them last night. One was of Meredith, her sister, and, I assumed, her brother-in-law. I took it off to get a closer look.

"My, my. What a sight."

I glanced up from the picture as she stood in front of me, still wearing the same camisole from last evening. She looked fresh-faced and even smelled of toothpaste.

I showed her the picture. "You look beautiful here."

"Thanks. Want to stop distracting me by dangling that gorgeous cock in my kitchen?"

My erection twitched. Hearing her say it was a damned turn-on. Next to the fridge, I noticed a black apron hanging on a hook, and that gave me an idea. Grabbing it, I put it over my head, tying it behind my back. It was all black, which was good. I didn't feel like a complete idiot wearing it.

"How about this?" I asked. "Make you breakfast? And I'm covered, so now the jewels won't distract you."

"Okay, I have to take a picture. Damn it, I can't." She smirked. "You know what? I will anyway, and obviously I'll be the only one who knows that you're completely commando." She grabbed her phone from the high table next to the entrance to the kitchen. I stood straight as she said, "No, don't move, not even one inch or everyone will know your ass is on display." She giggled, snapping a few pictures. "Okay, I've got it. I can't believe you're actually up for this."

"Why not?" I asked. "Come on, let's see what you've got in here. We both need sustenance."

"Yes, we do."

She didn't have a lot of food, but we made do with a platter of cheese, toast, and tomatoes. We ate while standing in the kitchen.

"What time do you have to be at the office?" I asked her.

"Nine at the latest. You?" she said between bites.

“I’m flexible. In the evening, I’ll come to your parents’ house.”

“We can handle everything on our own, really.”

“I promised I’d be there, Meredith. I’m not breaking my word.”

She smiled. “Thanks. I wonder when Mom meets Jeannie for the book club. They’ll surely have a lot to talk about.”

“No clue. I’m glad Grandmother’s getting out of the house for that. I like knowing she’s happy." I leaned against the edge of the counter, making more coffee as soon as we finished our light breakfast. "Sometimes I wonder if my brothers and I had made more of an effort with my mother, she would still be with us." Fuck me, I'd never voiced that thought. I never even realized I harbored it, and yet deep inside, I knew I'd always carried some guilt about those years.

"Why would you say that?"

"I don't know. I was so busy acting out that I wasn’t paying attention to her."

“Cade, you were a teenager. People usually act out at that age without any reasons, and you'd just found out your father had another family."

"I know, but I left all the heavy lifting to Colton and Jake. They didn't even tell us in the beginning that Mom was sick. She only told us later."

"It sucks how everything happened, but you shouldn't feel guilty." Her voice was soft. She came in front of me, putting both hands on my chest. My heartbeat calmed down in a matter of seconds. How did she intuitively know exactly what I needed? I clutched her wrist, rubbing my thumb over the pulse point.

"I don't know, maybe if we hadn't given her so much headache. If we'd bothered to take a look at her and suggest that she go to the doctor earlier. Maybe they could've helped her."

I usually hid this part of myself, mostly because people in business circles appreciated my cutthroat ability to make things happen. I didn’t want to appear vulnerable in negotiations. If people knew you had a soft spot, they used it. But Meredith was seeing both sides of me. That was rare. I typically didn't let them blend. I was breaking my rules for her.

"Cade, stop. That's not how illnesses work," she murmured.

"I know. I'm not sure what's gotten into me this morning. Anyway, back to Grandmother. There's a simple rule: when she's happy, we're all happy."

"Oh, so it's self-serving, huh?"

"Partly, yes."

She chuckled. "Why don't I believe you? You're actually a very thoughtful person. Who would've known?"

"I'm not sure that's a compliment," I said.

"Who says it is? I like keeping you on your toes."

A beeping sound filled the air.

"Not mine. Must be yours," she said.

"Yeah." I went to the entrance where I dropped my suit jacket yesterday and picked up my phone. "Speak of the devil. It's my grandmother," I said.

Meredith nodded, sipping her coffee.

I immediately answered. "Good morning, Grandmother."

"Darling, I didn't wake you up, did I?"

"No, all good. What's up?"

"Well, I called to tell you that I want us all to get together for dinner next week."

"Sure, Saturday?" That was our go-to day unless someone had plans.

"Yes, that works."

"Okay." I wasn't sure why she was calling to tell me that.

"More coffee?" Meredith asked.

"Who's that? Is it darling Meredith's voice?"

Meredith must have heard Grandmother because she pressed her lips together before mouthing, "Sorry."

"Yes."

"Oh good, the two of you are together. I was calling you because I'd love to have her here too."

Meredith heard her, clearly. She grimaced and then mouthed, "Sorry," again.

I waved my hand. It wasn't her fault. Grandmother was just meddling in our lives, as usual. I had a great deal of affection for both my grandparents, and I owed them everything I was today. If it hadn't been for them, I would've gone completely off the rails. But I didn't appreciate the way my grandmother liked to butt into my love life. I had no idea what had even gotten into her. She'd only started her matchmaking project—as she called it—last year.

"Grandmother, I'm sure Meredith is busy."

"Nonsense. I can totally change the day of the dinner to suit her."

"What are you talking about? You always say Saturday is the best day."

"Yes, but I don't want to inconvenience her. And I dearly want her to come. I'd invite her on Thursday for Thanksgiving, but I'm sure she already has plans with her family. And besides, I don't want to put pressure on you youngsters. Spencer lectured me on the fact that attending holiday events together is a sign of a big commitment."

"I'll ask her. Was that all?" I asked.

"Well, yes, actually."

I wondered if she knew I'd spent the night with Meredith before she called. I wouldn't put it past her. The woman had a scary amount of information.

"Take care, Grandmother. Say hi to Grandfather for me, and I'll talk to you later." After hanging up the phone, I looked straight at Meredith, then filled her in on the conversation.

"I can tell her no," I said.

A smile played on her lips. She put down her coffee cup, placing her hands back on my chest. "Can you? I'm not so sure."

"Look, I don't want you to feel pressured into anything. I was the one who got us into this by indulging my grandmother's idea that we're in a relationship."

"But we're not." That took me by surprise. True, one night of hot sex was not a relationship, but things had changed since Grandmother walked in on us. At least I thought they'd changed. Didn't Meredith?

Still, she was right. I'd made it clear to Meredith that I wanted her all for me. But one thing didn't imply the other.

Maybe it should.

"Come with me to the dinner," I said. "You'll have fun with me and my family. You know everyone." I needed her by my side. I couldn't explain that impulse, but when it came to Meredith, I was starting to learn to just take things as they came and act on them. "Grandmother will assume whatever she wants. And you and I know what we have."

"Which is what? Two adults enjoying each other's company, right?" she murmured.

"Enjoying it very, very much." I tilted closer.

She flashed a huge smile. "Okay. Then let's do this."

Chapter 15

Meredith

"Sonya, you're going to love this," I murmured on Tuesday morning, glancing at the printer. I was a little sleepy because *someone* kept me up late, but things at the office were crazy enough to give me an adrenaline boost.

The last quarter of the year always brought on more stress as everyone focused on filling sales quotas and making sure all our key performance indicators were on track. I was keeping an eye on our point-of-sale promos. I had to give kudos to my predecessor because she'd kept calm during these months. I felt like I was going to lose it every time someone emailed me that things weren't going according to plan. Sonya herself was also more operationally involved right now. She asked for updated sales reports twice a week. I went to her office as soon as the printer was done, as I couldn't wait for her to see the latest numbers. I knocked on her door; even though it was open, I didn't want to barge in.

"Meredith, come in," she said, massaging her temple. "What do you have for me?"

"The latest numbers. You'll like them." I put them on the desk in front of her.

She only threw them a cursory glance and then looked up at

me. I could tell she was happy. "This looks good. You're crushing it."

"Thanks. By the way, where are we with the sale? Did Arthur talk to Cade's CFO?"

Sonya shrugged, avoiding my eyes and looking back down at the report. "Don't stress over that. Cade's CFO reached out to us but we haven't moved forward in that direction. You just concern yourself with bringing more extraordinary numbers like this."

"Okay." My mood instantly lifted. *Does that mean she gave up on the idea of selling? Or maybe she's simply postponing everything until after the Christmas and New Year's rush are over.* That was more than fine by me.

"By the way, I know it's none of my business, but you and Cade are... more than friends?"

I blinked. My stomach lurched. "That's a personal question."

"It is. I'm not holding it against you or anything. I'm just curious. I saw you leaving Starbucks and getting in his car. You seemed more than friendly."

What the hell? Why wasn't I more cautious?

"We are more than friends, and that's all I'm going to say on that." Mostly because that was all I knew myself. Like Cade had said, we were enjoying our time together.

"Fair enough. Your private life is your own."

I couldn't get a good read on her. But I had enough on my plate without worrying about Sonya.

Still, when I sat at my desk, I shot Cade a message.

Meredith: Sonya saw us together yesterday.

He answered a few minutes later.

Cade: Is she giving you trouble?

Meredith: Not sure.

Cade: We'll deal with her if needed. I've got your back, Meredith. Can't let anyone roast that perfect ass.

I grinned, shaking my head as I got to work. I couldn't make up my mind what the best way was to describe Cade. After our evening together, I'd been firmly convinced that "sexy as hell" was his main attribute. But then the week rolled on, and the man revealed a completely different side of himself.

On Tuesday evening, he showed up at my parents' house, as promised. It turned out there wasn't that much to do because Derek took the day off work to help my parents assemble all the furniture. On Wednesday, I was already looking forward to the evening, even though we hadn't made any plans. To my intense disappointment, he sent me a message bearing bad news later in the afternoon.

Cade: I had to go out of town for an emergency at a packaging factory in Jacksonville.

Meredith: Fingers crossed you solve it fast!

Cade: Sorry about the short notice.

Meredith: Don't worry. I'm exhausted, so I wouldn't be much fun.

Cade: I disagree. What time do you finish work?

Meredith: 5:30. Why?

Cade: I'm sending someone to pick you up.

Meredith: Cade, really! That's not necessary.

Cade: Yes, it is. *If I were there, I'd take you, but I'm not. So Cal will look after you.*

Man, oh man! Why should I have disagreed with him? I didn't mind in the least. At five thirty, I practically ran out of the building.

A guy named Cal stood in front and introduced himself to me. "I'm Mr. Jake's driver, but Mr. Cade also uses my services from time to time. He told me to take you wherever you want."

I needed to do some shopping for Saturday. I wanted a present for Abe and Jeannie Whitley—I didn't want to show up empty-handed—and I was also looking for an outfit to wear, so I asked Cal to take me to Copley Square before texting Cade.

Meredith: When are you coming back?

Cade: Looks like I'll only make it back on Saturday.

There are more fires to put out than I anticipated. I even have a meeting on Saturday morning.

My heart plummeted. I couldn't even put into words the magnitude of the disappointment rolling through me. How could I even feel so down about this?

Meredith: You're spending Thanksgiving there?

Cade: Yes. Doesn't make sense to fly back and forth. One of our packaging lines is malfunctioning. I'm exploring several options so we can fulfill all the deliveries for the Christmas season.

Meredith: :-(Wish you could come back sooner.

Cade: Do you miss me?

Should I tone down my reaction? Maybe put a playful edge on it so I don't seem too needy?

But it felt so much easier to reply via text.

Meredith: Yes.

I sent it quickly, putting a hand on my chest, playing with the long pendant at my neck. It was a nervous habit of mine.

Cade: I miss you too. I planned on seeing you as soon as I got back. I wanted to surprise you at your home.

My heart jumped in my chest. I crossed and uncrossed my legs as a huge smile took over my face.

Okay, this is definitely slipping into romantic territory.

"We're here." Cal sat looking at me through the rearview mirror.

"Thanks so much. How much do I owe you?" I asked as I unhooked my seat belt.

"Nothing, of course. As I said, I work for Mr. Jake."

"Okay, well, thank you. Have a great evening, Cal."

"I'm not leaving. I'll park and wait for you."

"Oh! No, you don't have to. I'll just call an Uber once I'm done. I have no clue how long this is going to take."

"I have instructions to wait for you. In fact, I can give you my number, and if you have too many bags, I'll come and help you with them."

What is this life?

"Wow. Thank you." I got out of the car, hurrying down the bustling street, texting Cade.

Meredith: Okay, I've got to go. I'm off to buy something for your grandmother and a little something for me.

Cade: I demand pictures.

A shudder ran through me. My nipples turned hard, pushing against my bra. My panties felt hot against the skin between my legs.

Meredith: We'll see.

Cindy, one of the shop owners, welcomed me inside The Fashion Corner. I came here often. One of the things I loved most about the store was that it catered to all sizes and body shapes. They brought bigger sizes for most of their collections. I hated that most department stores only stocked up to size ten or twelve. They looked at me like I was an elephant every time I asked for a 14W.

More often than not, they gave me a cold smile and said I should probably try my luck at plus-size stores. I'd been through enough of those in my lifetime. They usually didn't have what I liked. Most of the collections found in plus-size stores looked like huge tents or blankets. They had no shape whatsoever. They were designed to hide. In my opinion, they simply magnified anyone's size.

Cindy smiled at me. "Meredith, it's so good to see you again. What are you looking for today?"

"I'm going to a family dinner on Saturday, and I'd like a cute outfit."

"Are your parents celebrating something? Did your sister give birth?" I was a regular, and they knew everything that went on with my family.

"No, it's not my family."

"You've got a boyfriend?"

I cleared my throat, but my smile betrayed me. "I'm seeing someone. I wouldn't call him my boyfriend."

"But you're meeting his family. I'm sensing you're getting your wires crossed."

I laughed nervously. "It's complicated, but we're having a good time together, and I'd like to wear something nice to the dinner. But not fancy. It's just a dinner at home." Remembering the Whitleys, I knew they didn't make a fuss, although a lot of time had passed, and Cade seemed to live in suits. I assumed his brothers did as well. Maybe they were more formal now. "On second thought, let me check."

I texted Cade quickly.

Meredith: What's the dress code? Do you guys wear a suit at dinner?

He replied right away.

Cade: I'll only exchange that information if you promise to send me pictures.

Heat pulsed between my thighs. He was a master at negotiations. I didn't want to give in, but I had to know.

Meredith: You've got a deal.

Cade: We wear casual clothes. Jeans, polo shirts, sweaters. That kind of thing.

I looked up. "Casual. I'm thinking a dress that looks Christmassy? But no, it's too early for that."

"Girl, it's already Thanksgiving. As soon as pumpkin season's over, Santa Claus is here."

I laughed. It was one of the reasons I loved her. She liked Christmas as much as I did.

"I'd love to see some sweaterdresses." They were my go-to in the cold weather season.

"You got it. Why don't you go to the changing room, and I'll bring you some outfits to choose from."

"Thank you."

I went inside a dressing room and took off my clothes, leaving on my tights. I tried a few poses, but I looked ridiculous like this. Nothing spelled unsexy more than wool tights, but it was the weather for them. I couldn't go out wearing sheer ones or I'd freeze my legs off. I made exceptions, like when I went on dates and wore sexy lingerie paired with sheer hose that reached to my upper thighs, but that was about it.

I could take them off and snap a few sexy pictures, but one, the light inside changing rooms was always, always awful. I looked like I had 3,000 percent more cellulite than I did in normal lighting. I never understood why they chose to put harsh light from above in changing rooms. It was depressing.

And two, I did need the tights for when I tried on the dresses so I could make sure you couldn't make out the elastic waistband. Sometimes the sweaterdresses were so thin that you could see it.

Cindy gave me five to choose from.

"You're so bad. Now I want all of them," I said. They were all rather similar, cut tight over the waist, where I was smallest, and then coming down in an A-line that molded to my body.

"I'd planned to message you one of these days to tell you we got sweaterdresses because I know how much you love them."

I tried them all on, snapping pictures of them, but I didn't send them to Cade right away. I might have agreed to send him pictures, but I was going to do it on my terms—namely sending them all at once, after I was out of the changing room. Otherwise, I suspected he might try to convince me to send him naked pictures too.

"They're all very tempting, but I'm going to stick with only two of them: the pink and the black ones," I said loudly while I changed into my own clothes.

"Great choices. I can text you when the others go on sale. Fingers crossed that we'll still have your size."

"Thanks, Cindy. I really appreciate it."

I came out, handing her the dresses I planned to buy. I appreciated that they never tried to be pushy.

My phone vibrated.

Cade: Meredith, pictures.

My body tensed. I could almost hear him say it in that rough bedroom voice he used when we were alone. I'd waited long enough, and I was out of the changing room, so I sent them.

He answered seconds later.

Cade: You look great in all of them, babe. Now, take them off, and send me a picture of your beautiful body.

Again, I imagined him *saying* the words, and his bedroom voice was so effective that I even contemplated finding an excuse to go back into the changing room and actually send him a naked pic.

Resist the temptation, Meredith. Resist the temptation. You're in public.

"Are you okay? You seem a bit flushed. Is the heat too much? Or did you get warm trying on all the clothes?" Cindy asked as she folded the dresses.

"Just a little warm," I said. *Because a shameless man sent me a shameless text.*

I replied right away.

Meredith: I'm out of the changing room already.

I sent him a wink too. *Let him do whatever he wanted with that.*

As I took out my card to swipe, I noticed a new collection of beanies and scarves.

"Oh my God, Mom and sis would love these," I said, grabbing the two white matching beanies. They both always complained that their heads froze in winter but insisted that most beanies were unflattering. These were great. "I'll buy two of those too."

The price was decent. One of the reasons I loved having a good-paying job was because I could spoil my family, and they deserved it 100 percent.

I left the store a couple minutes later, trying to decide what to buy for Abe and Jeannie. I strolled down the street, but nothing in the window displays inspired me.

Cindy was right. The stores were already putting out Christmas collections. I could definitely buy them something Christmas related.

That was how I found my way into my second-favorite store in the area. It was a pop-up set up during November and December only. They sold handmade glass globes that were downright exquisite. I sighed as I looked over the display. This place made my heart happy and was full to the brim with customers. It was two floors and had a cute spiral staircase running upstairs. Most of the time, this place was leased by a company selling bath and body products. I preferred the Christmas shop because the smell of the other one was overpowering whenever I passed through the rest of the year.

My eye caught on a gorgeous globe with an angel painted on it. It was huge, with its wings wide open. The halo above its head was particularly beautiful—a light yellow gold. It stole my heart.

I didn't even have to check with Cade. I was sure Jeannie and Abe would appreciate it. It was the type of gift anyone could like. Even if you didn't have a tree, you could still use it as a decoration piece in the house. On instinct, I bought it without giving myself time to reconsider.

Five minutes later, I walked out, super proud that I hadn't bought any trinkets for myself.

Cal texted me his location, and I quickly walked there. I'd bought gifts for Jeannie and Abe, Mom, and my sister. Everything was right in the world.

I stopped and bought an alcohol-free punch for Cal on the way back to the car. I knocked at the window, not wanting to startle him.

He immediately rolled it down. "Miss, do you need my help?"

"No, no. Just open the trunk. Here, this is for you." I handed him the punch.

"Oh, thank you. That's very kind of you."

"I thought you might need something warm. Actually, don't

even open the trunk. I just have these two bags, and they're not big."

"As you wish, ma'am."

As I slipped inside, he asked, "Where are we going?"

"Home."

I gave him my address, then leaned back in my seat. I checked my phone as Cal drove. I had a message from Cade.

Cade: Still waiting for that naked picture. When are you getting home?

I burst out laughing. Cal looked at me in the rearview mirror. I smiled sheepishly. "I'm good. I'm good." My voice sounded a bit rough. I'd blame it on Cade.

Meredith: You're going to have to do a lot more to get a naked pic from me.

Let's see what he'll do with that.

I felt hot from the tips of my toes to the apex between my thighs when his reply came only a few moments later.

Cade: Oh, I will. I'm going to romance you a bit more before asking you to take off your clothes :-)

I couldn't believe he'd actually typed that. I pressed the phone to my chest, smiling from ear to ear, fighting yet another unlady-like snort.

Goodness, the things this man did to me.

I really liked them.

Chapter 16

Meredith

Cade kept his word and didn't ask me for more naked pics. Not that I had the opportunity to send any. I spent Thursday at my parents' house. We all gathered to prepare Thanksgiving dinner. It was a lot of work for Mom and Everly, and I liked to help.

Mom proudly informed us that the whole dinner was prepped using recipes that were safe for diabetics. She'd then pulled me to one side, telling me that I'd benefit from the low-carb recipes book as well.

There was no stopping Mom and her incessant campaign that I lose weight. I knew she meant well, but it made me weary of holiday dinners. Still, the evening turned out amazing. We'd ended it by giving my sister and Derek unsolicited advice on baby names.

Friday was just as grueling as the first days of the week. Cade had wanted to send Cal to chauffeur me, but I told him it really wasn't necessary. I wanted to walk home, and I even took a detour to stretch my legs a bit. They'd grown stiff at the office, and I loved Boston at this time of the year.

So many people complained that Christmas had become a commercial holiday, and that was true, but that meant the city was full of lights a long time before Christmas. I had time to bask in it. The gorgeous streets were lit up in various colors, and I loved all of them. As much as I liked to match outfits and make sure everything went together impeccably, when it came to Christmas, the more color, the better.

Cade: Tell me when you're home.

I licked my lips. *Is he still trying to get nude pics?* He was wearing me down, which was probably his plan all along.

Meredith: In about ten minutes.

I arrived only eight minutes later, taking off my coat and boots once I stepped inside. *God, it was cold today.*

I barely made it to the kitchen when my doorbell rang. I exhaled sharply, turning around. *Oh my God, Cade's here.* I was sure of it. That was why he asked me when I would be home. He didn't have some perverted plan to get sexy pics after all. He was here in person.

I ran to the door, opening it wide without even thinking.

It wasn't Cade. Instead, a young woman carrying flowers and a box stood in the doorway.

"Hi," I said.

"Miss Meredith, yes?"

I nodded. "Yes."

"I have this delivery for you." She handed them to me with shaky hands.

"Have you been waiting for me this whole time?" I asked, feeling like shit for making her wait.

"Yes. My understanding was that you'd be home half an hour ago."

Oh crap. Me and my Christmas strolls. "I'm truly sorry. Do you want tea, or coffee, or something stronger? I have alcohol."

"Um, no, thank you."

Even her voice was shaking. I tipped her, taking the flowers and the treats, and put them in the foyer. "Are you sure? I feel so guilty."

"Don't worry. It's just part of the job. But you're very nice. Have a great evening. Enjoy your flowers."

"I will. Thank you."

I closed the door, turning around. Just like that, joy replaced the guilt. Well, didn't really replace it, because I was still thinking about the poor girl freezing her ass off outside my door, but it totally overpowered it.

Flowers! Cade Whitley sent me flowers.

I looked at the box, opening it immediately.

Holy shit. He found my Portuguese pastéis de nata. How is this possible? I breathed in the smell. My stomach rumbled.

I took my phone, snapping a picture and sending it to Cade.

Meredith: Thank you. I'm speechless.

He immediately called me. I sighed, putting in earbuds and setting the phone on the entrance console before answering. "I'd planned to bring them myself tonight, but just because I'm stuck here doesn't mean you don't get to enjoy them."

"You really wanted to come to my door with flowers and my favorite goodies in the world?"

"Yes."

God, this felt a lot like we were in a relationship. Why would he go to all this trouble otherwise? I narrowed my eyes, looking in the mirror in my foyer. I had an idea why.

"Are you still on your quest to get a naked picture of me?"

He laughed into the phone, but it sounded tired. "Maybe. Though I started looking for the sweets before I got the idea."

"Oh yeah, you say that to save face. Thank you so much. How was your day?" I asked in a softer voice. I put the box with the sweets on the console and arranged the flowers in a vase, placing them on the coffee table in the living room. Then I put two sweets on a plate and walked to the couch. Sitting down, I curled my legs next to me.

"Exhausting. Can't wait to be back in Boston and see you."

" I can't wait either," I admitted. "Tell me where you got the treats."

"Nah, I'm keeping that secret firmly up my sleeve."

"Cade!"

"I mean it. I've got to go now. I still have a call with overseas partners."

"Good luck. I can't wait to see you tomorrow."

We had an unspoken rule: we never asked for too many work details. It was easier to keep things completely separate.

As soon as the call disconnected, I savored my sweet treats. And despite my very best intentions of keeping the rest for my morning coffee tomorrow—I ended up eating all of them.

The next afternoon, I arrived at Jeannie and Abe's house at six o'clock on the dot. Cade was coming directly from the airport and offered to send Cal to pick me up. I declined once again. I appreciated being chauffeured around, but that wasn't who I was, and I felt a bit guilty to have someone who worked for Jake fuss over me.

I arrived at the same time as Cade, who stepped out of a cab.

"I was sure you'd come with Cal," I said as I walked up to him.

"No, he works for Jake."

"So you only make him work overtime for me?"

"Everything for my lady."

I was waiting for him to add a wink, but no, the man completely meant every word. Guess who was going to get all the naked pics he wanted later? Yep, I'd decided he deserved the reward.

"Is that a dress shirt? You said casual." He also wore a suit jacket and Oxford shoes. I had my UGG boots on and my thick winter jacket.

"I had a meeting this morning. Besides, jeans are casual."

“Is the packaging line functional again?”

“No. But we found a subcontractor willing to take us on. We’ll have a delay of two weeks, but we should be able to deliver most of the merchandise to stores.”

“I’m glad.”

“What’s that?" he asked, pointing to my bag.

"Isn't it obvious?" The word *Christmas* was written in classic gold lettering on the bag. "I brought a gift. I remember your grandmother liked to decorate the house when we were kids."

"She still does. I'm going to have to convince her to call a decoration company. Last year, she gave us a scare. She almost fell from the ladder she'd used to put garland over a bookshelf."

"I can totally help her.” I bit my lip. *Oh man, Christmas is a month away. Why am I inviting myself to his grandmother's home?*

"You truly love Christmas, don't you?"

"Heck yes," I said.

I realized he’d avoided answering my question in a very elegant way. My stomach lurched. *Don't be silly, Meredith. Who knows what might happen by then?*

We both went to the front door. I hadn’t been here too often —mostly we’d studied at my home, or the one where Cade grew up. But this place looked like I remembered it. The gorgeous porch and green siding were intact, and the gray slate roof looked idyllic.

"You think your brothers are here already?" I asked.

"A couple of them are. I saw their cars along the street."

We rang the doorbell, and the door opened almost immediately, as if someone was waiting behind it. Jeannie Whitley had changed tremendously since Cade and I were in high school. I had been too embarrassed in Cade’s office to pay too much attention to her, but now I saw her up close. Her hair was now completely white. It used to be pitch-black, though I always thought she colored it. The lines on her cheeks and neck were deeper than they were twelve years ago.

She was a beautiful woman at ninety, regardless.

"I'm so glad to see you again, Jeannie," I said.

"And you, too, Meredith." Her eyes were a bit glassy.

I looked at Cade and back at her, then stepped inside, hugging her. I hoped I wasn't overstepping, but I was a very huggy person. Jeannie returned it wholeheartedly.

Stepping back, I noticed Abe was behind her. I didn't have too many memories of him from when I was a kid. "Welcome, Meredith," he greeted me.

"Thank you so much for asking me to dinner. I'm honored, and I brought you a little keepsake for Christmas. You can put it on your tree or anywhere in the house, really."

Jeannie helped lift the bag for me, opening the box. "My God! This is beautiful. Is it from that pop-up store near Copley Square?"

"Yes!" I answered, stunned she was aware of the shop.

"You know, it's one of my favorite places. I do need to drop by this year and see what they've added from last year."

"Are you sure, darling? Don't you have quite enough?" Abe asked, sounding much like my dad.

"There are never enough Christmas decorations," she answered briskly.

Oh, I loved Jeannie Whitley, a woman after my own heart.

"Anyone happy to see me?" Cade asked from behind me.

Jeannie sighed. "Of course we are, darling boy. How was your trip?" She kissed his cheek.

"Grueling. But today's all about Meredith."

"Exactly. Besides, I don't like business talk at the table either. All it does is make people antsy."

"We don't really talk business anyway," I explained.

"Oh, true, since you're competitors." For some reason that seemed to highly amuse Jeannie. She squinted her eyes.

I peeked at Cade and saw he was looking at his grandmother with a strange expression. I couldn't decipher it.

"Shall we go inside?" I asked.

"Of course!" He put a hand on the small of my back, guiding me through the house.

"By the way, I didn't bring my brothers up-to-date about us," he whispered in my ear.

A strange pressure formed in my chest as I glanced up at him. What exactly did that mean? He hadn't told them that we weren't pretending? Did he want to keep us a secret? Was he ashamed?

Way to ruin this day, Meredith. Give the man some credit. He had a horrendous week.

But still, a small weight settled in my chest, and I couldn't seem to wish it away.

I nodded. "We'll improvise."

Chapter 17

Cade

Gabe, Spencer, and Colton were already here. Only Jake and Natalie were missing.

"Meredith," Spencer exclaimed. "Good to see you."

My brother winked at me. I knew exactly what he was thinking: *"You've got balls, brother, bringing her here."*

He didn't know the half of it.

"Oh, Gabe. I remember you, too. Great to see you after all this time." Meredith smiled at him.

Gabe was looking at us with a shit-eating grin.

"Glad you do." My smartass brother was checking my girl out in a way that was beginning to annoy me.

"We haven't met, but I've heard a lot about you through the grapevine," Colton said as he and Meredith shook hands.

He seemed amused. I took that as a win. In the past few years, nothing seemed to affect my oldest brother. He'd had a one-track mind in his lab, working on what he called his "breakthrough discovery." He'd explained it to me once, but biology had never been my forte, so I'd only half listened. I was good with numbers and sales, but I knew jack shit about developing medicine.

"Spencer, are you still covering up for this guy?" Meredith asked, pointing her thumb at me.

"Always."

"Hey now. None of that. I take care of myself these days," I teased.

Spencer clapped his hands once and then nodded. "Dude, your shit is becoming more complex. I'm learning from you these days, bro."

Meredith laughed. It was bizarre how at ease my brothers were around her. We weren't used to any of us showing up at family events with a woman on our arm. The first one who did that was Jake, and we ruthlessly mocked him. Then again, this was different. My brothers thought Meredith and I were keeping up a ruse for grandmother's sake.

Meredith focused on Gabe again. "And you're still getting away with everything because you're the youngest?"

Gabe laughed. My girl was giving it to them like a pro. "Oh, my older brothers usually stirred up so much shit themselves that all the focus was on them. Not my fault I got away with my shenanigans. And yet that continues to be true."

Everyone laughed at that, and a few of us contradicted and challenged him with verbal jabs.

"And the eternally brooding Colton," Meredith said with a smile. God, she was beautiful.

Colton jerked his head back. "Wait, that's a thing?" He looked around the group. "You all call me that?"

Meredith pressed her lips together, looking at me out of the corner of her eye. "Was that supposed to be a secret? I thought it was common knowledge."

"It is," I said, walking up to her and putting an arm around her shoulders.

Spencer narrowed his eyes, zeroing in on my hand. My grandparents weren't in the room, so there was no reason to pretend.

Cat's out of the bag.

I'd be up for an interrogation later. Fine, I'd let them take a shot at me. I was fucking exhausted, as the last two days had been a marathon of meetings and reviewing documentation, trying to troubleshoot all the problems.

I acted on instinct, grabbing Meredith's hand. I needed contact with her. I'd missed her. Did I even tell her that? I had no clue.

My grandparents joined us at that second, followed by Jake and Natalie. I hadn't even heard them come in.

"Meredith," Jake exclaimed. "Good to see you again." He shook her hand before introducing her to Natalie. "This is my fiancée, Natalie."

"It's nice to meet you, Natalie," Meredith said.

Natalie glanced at Meredith's outfit. "I love your scarf. Where did you get it?"

Meredith smiled. "I have this favorite cute little shop that always buys the most amazing collections. I'll give you the address."

"Oh, thank you, Meredith. Straight to the point. I like that."

Meredith smiled as they exchanged more info about the store.

"That's my girl," I said, noticing Grandmother looking pleased with herself.

"What's that?" I asked, pointing at the cake she was carrying to the table.

"It's coffee cake. I was in the mood for it. I know it's a bit early for a Christmas treat, but someone in this room is definitely already feeling Christmas in her heart." Grandmother winked at Meredith.

Meredith nodded. "Oh yes."

I was surprised at the warmth in her tone. She looked genuinely happy to be here.

Grandmother cut cake for everyone. "Don't overeat, okay? This is just a little treat to have with coffee."

"Grandmother, did you prepare a feast again?" I asked sharply, knowing there was more to what she was saying.

"My grandchildren are coming to dinner. Of course I'm preparing a feast. What kind of a grandmother would I be otherwise?"

"One who's ninety years old," I wanted to say, but I knew better. My brothers and I worried that our grandparents overdid it, and we were trying to encourage them to rest and relax and enjoy life. It was going *spectacularly*.

Jake cleared his throat. "Grandmother, I got a call from the cleaning company I hired. You told them that you no longer need their services. Why is that?"

She sighed. "Your grandfather is feeling much better now. Between the two of us, we're doing just fine. It's good exercise for me to do a few chores."

Jake and I exchanged a glance, but Colton just shook his head. Spencer looked at Gabe and mouthed, "Later." As usual, when we needed to convince Grandmother of something, it took a group effort to put our minds together and come up with arguments she couldn't refute. We wanted to take care of them. Why was it so hard for them to let us? They'd looked out for us our entire childhood and adulthood; it was only fair for the roles to reverse now. But that was a conversation to be had another day.

We all ate cake without even sitting down. Grandmother brought out a carafe of coffee too. I glanced at my watch, noting it was five thirty. She always asked us over early for dinner, so that usually meant we still had most of Saturday evening to ourselves.

I had some great plans this evening, and they all involved Meredith.

After we finished the cake, my grandmother brought out fifty or so courses, it seemed like.

"You truly meant a feast," Meredith said as she gazed at everything on the table.

"The only good part about this is that they then have food for about a week, so she doesn't have to cook again," I told her.

Meredith leaned into me, saying in a soft voice for only me to hear, "I like that you worry about them and want to make sure they get help as needed."

"Not easy with Grandmother, but I am persistent," I whispered, the room having quieted as everyone was eating.

Grandmother's cooking was always perfection; every course was delicious, and the presentation, as she called it, was enticing. Usually she prepared everyone's favorites, but after a while, we got tired of the same menu, so she was changing it up a bit more now.

"Grandfather, how are you feeling?" I asked.

"I'm healthy as a horse. I don't know why the doctor keeps insisting I should watch my diet." He'd had a few scares with his heart and needed to be careful from here on out.

"How many times do we have to have this conversation, Abe?" Grandmother asked. Her voice was suddenly sharp. Obviously she was getting tired of his obstinance.

"Grandmother, Grandfather, behave," Cade cut in. "We have guests."

Grandmother looked at Meredith. "You're right. I'm sorry. I'm just trying to keep my husband alive, and it's a full-time job."

Spencer leaned toward Meredith on her other side. "Welcome to the family, Meredith. If someone's not fighting, you know something's off."

"Duly noted," she replied easily.

He looked at me over Meredith's head. I knew he was bursting with questions.

"By the way, Grandmother, Natalie and I want to go see a musical at the theater next week," Jake said nonchalantly. "Want to come with us?"

"Oh, I'd love to!" Grandmother exclaimed.

Thumbs-up to Jake; he did that very elegantly. I knew Grandmother was happy to go, but if she knew we'd had an actual conversation about taking her out more often, she'd brush off our efforts, saying she didn't want to be a burden. It was always a fine line with Jeannie Whitley. The woman was smart.

"Are you sure you want this old bag of bones to tag along?" Grandmother asked Jake.

"Jeannie!" Natalie said, sounding completely affronted. "We love spending time with you. Abe, do you want to join us too?"

"No. The doctor said I should try to avoid events that are very crowded," Grandfather replied.

Grandmother laughed. "*Now* you're bringing up doctor's orders!"

I had to give it to Grandfather. He was smart as always. He'd once confided in me that even though my grandmother was a theater actress, he disliked plays and musicals. But he'd never missed any of her performances, even back when he was running Whitley Industries.

"Never make your wife feel as if what she does or what she likes is insignificant. Even if you don't understand why she loves it, support her. She will appreciate it." I had no clue that those words had even registered in my mind, but they had. It was great advice. Then again, most of the things he said were useful.

After we finished eating, we offered to clean up the table. Grandmother protested, but Jake put his foot down. "We won't hear of it, Grandmother. The least we can do, after you cooked the whole day, is clean up."

"Oh, you boys! You get more stubborn with every year."

"That we do," I said.

"I can't believe she's fighting you about cleaning up," Meredith said as we finished bringing everything to the kitchen and loaded up the dishwasher.

"Yeah, it's an ongoing battle," I said.

"And what was that about Jake and Natalie taking her out?"

"Remember a few weeks ago when I told you I realized she might need a bit more company?"

"Yes," Meredith replied.

"Well, my brothers and I decided to take turns getting her out of the house."

Her eyes widened. "Oh my God, that's so cute! I can just imagine all of you brainstorming this."

"And now, no more talk," I said.

"Why not?"

"I've wanted to kiss you since I got out of the cab."

She smiled shyly, taking a step back and bumping into the kitchen counter. "Oops! Look, I'm trapped here with you."

"Exactly. With nowhere to run." I stepped closer, tilting her head up. "I've missed you."

"I missed you too."

I kissed her the next second without holding back at all. Fuck, how I needed her. It was a need that ran deep, and I hadn't been aware of it until now. For the first time, the past fucked-up week completely vanished from my mind. All I could think about was Meredith: how good she tasted, how delicious she felt against me, soft and trusting.

She moaned against my mouth, and I deepened the kiss. I kept one hand on her upper back, the other on the side of her head, and deepened it even further. I was hungry for her, and the more I got, the more I wanted. I didn't want to stop—not now, not ever.

Her soft lips were inviting. The way she opened up for me, Jesus! My cock stirred in my boxers.

Get a grip on yourself, Cade.

"What do we have here?" Spencer exclaimed.

Holy shit! I'd completely forgotten where we were.

Groaning, I took a step back, glancing at Meredith before turning around. Her lips were completely red and even a bit swollen.

Spencer smirked. "So let me get this straight. Are you two still pretending or not?"

Chapter 18

Cade

"How about it's none of your business?" I asked. I wanted them to know that Meredith was mine, but I didn't like his demanding tone.

"Dude, I need to know. I'm your twin, remember? If I know the details, then we can have a common front with the rest of the guys."

Meredith seemed aware of her swollen lips and was trying to cover them up with a glass of water.

Is she nervous? Why?

"I'm going to the living room," Meredith said. "Jeannie wanted to show me some pictures."

"Sure," I said sort of absently, wondering what the hell Spencer was talking about.

"Dude, what the fuck?" I exclaimed the second Meredith was out of the kitchen.

"Huh?" Spencer asked innocently.

"We're not pretending about anything. I just didn't have time to update you or anyone else. And why does it matter? Couldn't you just go back to the living room when you saw we were having a moment?"

"What the hell's your problem?" He seemed stupefied.

"Didn't you see? You've made Meredith uncomfortable."

Spencer narrowed his eyes. "Okay, let me get this straight. You think me walking in on you is why she felt uncomfortable, or the fact that I had to ask if you're pretending?"

I blinked. "I don't get it." My twin was speaking in circles.

"Man, and I thought you were smart."

Gabe walked into the kitchen just then too. "Hey, is everything okay? Meredith looked a bit out of it there in the living room."

"Yes, we're just discussing who's at fault for that," Spencer said. "Picture this. I walk in, and I find them kissing."

Gabe looked between the two of us, confused. "I thought this wasn't the real thing between you and Meredith. Did I miss a memo?"

"Jesus Christ. There is no privacy in this family. None whatsoever. None." It was getting on my last nerve.

Spencer threw up his hands. "Exactly, right? So that was my question. Meredith excused herself and went to the living room. Now this dickhead thinks it's my fault."

Gabe considered this. "I mean, it is. Why did you have to put the man on the spot?"

"Thank you, Gabe." This was unexpected support. Usually my youngest brother played devil's advocate for whomever was under scrutiny. "Now, before either of you get to question me anymore, I'm going to see what's happening in the living room. I don't want our grandmother suffocating Meredith."

"Too late, dude," Gabe said. "She was getting out family albums. Why do you think I suddenly thought the kitchen might be a better place to be? She's gotten Natalie trapped too."

We all liked to indulge Grandmother, but looking at old photos was an activity we unanimously hated, mostly because she always wanted to start with childhood ones when our family was still complete and apparently happy. That was what hurt the most —that it was all just for appearances. Everything was built on a lie as far as we were concerned. I never could figure out how our father managed to juggle two families, or why he even wanted to. I'd never asked Mom, obviously, and Grandmother only brought up the topic once and then declared she never wanted to speak of it again. The only woman who could probably have an inkling was Nancy, my half brothers' mother, but it wasn't a question I really wanted answered. It simply boggled my mind that he'd gotten away with it for so many years.

I burst out laughing when I entered the living room. Colton and Jake were with Grandfather in a corner of the room, sharing whiskey. They'd chosen the seats farthest away from Grandmother, who was on the couch with Natalie on one side and Meredith on the other. Good God, Gabe was right. She had a stack of twelve albums next to her. If she had her way, she'd hold the ladies hostage the whole evening, showing them all the albums. I needed to save Meredith. She might not know she needed saving, but she did.

I walked straight up to them. Colton and Jake called my name to deter me. "Hey, dude, we can make you a drink," Jake said. That was their attempt to save *me*, but I didn't need any of that. I needed Meredith.

"Grandmother, I'm going to have to whisk Meredith away," I announced.

"Oh, already?" she asked, and I could hear the disappointment in her voice. I loved her dearly, but this was where I drew the line.

"Yes, she and I have plans tonight."

Meredith looked at me in surprise. I winked at her. This wasn't how I planned to tell her, but I had no other choice.

"Oh, of course. I don't want to be a third wheel. Natalie, darling, do you and Jake also have plans?"

It was on the tip of my tongue to say, "Yes," just to get her out of this situation, but Natalie was too nice and cared about my grandmother far too much.

"No. I'd love to look at all of the pictures. I can't wait to see more photos of Jake when he was a kid. He definitely had a growth spurt later on, didn't he?"

"Oh, yes he did," Grandmother said confidently.

Meredith grinned, turning an album around for us all to see. "And Cade wasn't such a looker in middle school, was he?" She showed me the picture. I was scruffy and thin.

I shrugged. "Better late than never."

"I agree," Meredith replied, placing the album back in my grandmother's lap. "Jeannie, it was lovely seeing you. Thank you for welcoming me into your home."

"Of course, my girl. You're always welcome. I'm so happy my meddling worked out so fast. I have my hands full with these boys. Two down, so many more left to go."

Meredith blinked. "What do you mean?"

"Don't ask," I warned her.

"Okay," she said quickly, getting up. My grandmother started getting up, too, but Meredith waved her hand. "No, no, no. Don't get up on my behalf. I'll just tell everyone goodbye before we go."

We headed to my brothers and grandfather before we departed.

"Good to see you, Meredith. And thanks for making my grandson happy—and my wife. Very important," Grandfather said.

Meredith laughed. "You're a good sport, Abe. As usual." She had a way with charming my family. I hadn't expected it, to be honest.

I held her coat as she slipped it on, and then we stepped out of the house. She immediately exclaimed, "Oh my God, I forgot how much I love your grandmother. Why did you pull me away? Those photographs were amazing."

"Because I do have plans for you, and we should get going because the place closes at ten."

"Oh!" She clasped her hands together, shifting her weight from one leg to the other. "I kind of thought it was just a ruse and you wanted us to leave for some reason."

For the first time, it dawned on me that maybe Spencer hadn't been a complete idiot. "Why would you think that?" I asked.

"Well, I thought that, you know, the longer you keep up the deception, the easier it is to be caught in a lie."

I closed the distance between us instantly, cupping the sides of her head and looking at her intently. "If that kiss in the kitchen and the past week weren't proof enough, then maybe this will be. Meredith, this isn't a ruse, or a sham, or whatever you want to call it. You have to know that. What we have is real."

She parted her lips. "Oh, I mean... Well, I..." She was flustered. My woman was flustered. That never happened.

Pulling herself together, she grinned widely at me. "Okay then. Where are we going?"

"It's a surprise. You'll love it."

Chapter 19

Meredith

I couldn't believe that he'd brought me to the SoWa Winter Festival. It was on Washington Street all the way to Southend.

"I can't believe it," I gushed. "I didn't even know they were open yet."

"And you call yourself a Christmas enthusiast," he said. "I guess everyone decided to start Christmas earlier this year." He sounded like a total grump.

I never understood people who complained about Christmas starting early. It was the happiest time of the year. I started my countdown to the holiday in August, and that was after I celebrated Christmas in July. This was one of my favorite festivals in the whole city.

"What do you want to do first?" I asked.

"You're in charge tonight. I've never been, so..."

I turned to him, gasping. "That can't be true. You're a SoWa Winter Festival virgin?"

He frowned. "I don't like the word *virgin*."

I grinned. "You don't, huh? I think I'm going to use it a few more times just to rub it in. Okay, I'll give you a tour. Let's start by buying something to drink. I love mulled wine. Or they have also these Christmas cocktails. I can't make up my mind."

I was so excited. This looked like something out of a fairy tale.

We went to one of the food trucks on the Trail of Light. I chose a Christmas cocktail, and so did Cade. I had no clue what was in it, but it was definitely not just one type of liquor. I knew mixing alcohol was maybe not the best idea. On the other hand, you kind of needed it to brace against the cold. I'd stupidly dressed in sexy garters again instead of putting on wool tights, thinking we were going to stay indoors.

"Okay, let's start with a walk through the Pine Forest," I said. This place was a true winter wonderland. There were ice sculptures at the end of the Trail of Light, past the food trucks. Walking through the Pine Forest always brought me joy. "When I'm here, I feel like I'm a kid all over again. My parents used to bring me here every year."

"My parents weren't big on Christmas things, but my grandmother is. This is good." Cade nodded at his cup.

“You sound unsure. I scared you with that pumpkin drink.”

“Your words, not mine.”

"Oh, alcohol is a must for this stroll. Otherwise, you end up with frozen feet and hands. Ask me how I know." I kept sipping my drink. It definitely had rum and possibly champagne... or vodka... or maybe all three? I had no clue. I was about to ask Cade what was in his when I realized he was looking at me.

"What?" I asked.

"You're beautiful. I like seeing you so excited and happy."

"You're kidding, right? Seeing Christmas stuff makes me the happiest."

"Yep. I've made a mental note about that. I'll make sure to indulge you."

I grinned from ear to ear. My cheeks were a bit sore, but I was too happy.

We went down around the perimeter afterward, soaking up the lights.

"One day, I dream of moving into an actual home of my own," I admitted. "Something with a porch and a tiled roof so I can put up lights everywhere."

Cade threw his head back, laughing. "I like your criteria."

"Hey, it's as good as any," I retaliated. I couldn't stop looking at all the displays. "Oh, there was a bookshop here last year. I think it might have closed, though." It had been replaced by a shop selling jewelry. "I hope they didn't go bankrupt."

I put my hand on my chest. My heart was hurting just thinking about that, knowing it had been here for as long as I could remember. Yes, you could call me a nostalgic when it came to the holidays —it comforted me.

"She used to give me candy as a kid when my mom wasn't looking. I can probably look her up. Maybe she just found a better location."

Cade didn't say anything. When I glanced at him, I realized he was staring at me again.

"Something wrong?" I asked.

"No, but I can't believe you care so much about everything."

I shrugged. "It's just who I am."

"I'm starting to learn that."

I brought my paper cup to my lips, then realized it was empty. "Oh, I finished my cocktail."

"Here, you can have some of mine," he said. "Actually, you can have all of it."

I took his cup, and my eyes bulged. I glanced up at him. "You only took one sip."

He cleared his throat. "It's a little too... Christmassy for my taste."

I burst out laughing. "Obviously—it's a Christmas cocktail. My God, you're a Grinch. I wouldn't have taken you for one."

"I'm not, I just like celebrating Christmas, you know, on the day itself. Not for what feels like half a year."

"Grinch," I repeated, taking a sip. His cocktail was even more delicious than mine.

I figured it might not be the best idea to drink all of it, too, because I might get super tipsy and have a hangover tomorrow. But between feeling cold and feeling tipsy, I'd go with tipsy every time.

The whole place seemed like something out of a painting. There were carolers somewhere, their light music filtering through the air—it was definitely live and not a recording. Decorations were literally everywhere, and I felt like a bobblehead looking left and right and every which way. Some of the shops had chosen simple themes, either red and gold or white and green, some silver and blue. Some were multicolored. I preferred them the most, as I loved color. For me, Christmas wasn't about a color palette or about what was trendy this year—not even about Santa Claus, although sitting on his lap as a kid had been great fun. No, for me it was a celebration for the soul, the heart, and the family.

"Easy!" Cade exclaimed, putting his hands on my arms, stopping me so abruptly that I nearly spilled the rest of his cocktail.

I looked up and realized I had been about to walk headfirst into a booth.

"You didn't see this? You were headed right for it."

"Um, no. I was a bit too lost in my daydreams." I glanced at the cup. "And in this."

Holy shit! I'd nearly finished his drink as well. I looked behind me. We'd already finished strolling Payer Street. *When did that happen?*

Cade chuckled. "You're drunk."

"Yeah, like a skunk," I agreed. "I can't even argue. I don't really feel drunk, but almost knocking into the booth indicates I am."

A female voice broke the air. "Cade, what are you doing here?"

Cade and I turned in the same direction. I blinked, wondering if my eyes were playing tricks on me or if I was looking at the most beautiful woman I'd ever seen.

"Esther," Cade said curtly.

Esther looked like an angel. She had light blonde hair that was completely straight, and she was wearing a beret that matched her scarf. Her coat was elegant, hugging her shape, and only reached her knees. Slim calves peeked out, ending in gorgeous stilettos. How was she wearing them in this weather? I looked like a snowman with my thick winter jacket and my UGG boots.

"Aren't you going to introduce me to your friend?" she purred.

"Meredith, this is Esther," Cade said.

"Nice to meet you," I said, reaching out to shake her hand. I felt Cade put an arm around my back.

"Babe, you're freezing," he murmured.

"Well, I've run out of alcohol," I said.

"Babe?" Esther said, laughing. "That's a joke, right?"

What the fuck? I looked straight at her, wondering if my drunk ears misunderstood her tone or her implied meaning.

"What's your problem?" Cade asked. His voice was belligerent.

Nope, I hadn't misinterpreted. He was pissed.

"You can't be dating her. She looks like a fucking Christmas globe, round and red."

Oh my gosh. How can someone be so hateful?

"Shut your mouth. You don't disrespect her like that," Cade chastised her.

"Hey, I'm right here." I got in her face. "You can't talk to me like that." All through high school—college too—mean girls tried to make me feel like less of a person. As I became an adult, I refused to put up with that. Yes, it hurt when I was called names or talked about, but what I looked like didn't define who I was.

She snorted. "Oh, you're bitchy, too, and drunk. My God, Cade. I'm not even going to tell people we dated, knowing you keep this sort of company. It's going to look bad on me."

"Feel free to never mention my name," Cade said nonchalantly. "I don't ever mention yours."

Esther's eyes turned hard. She tightened her coat around her, looking even slimmer than before. I didn't think that was possible. Next to her, I really looked like I was a freaking basketball rolling down the street.

"He has standards, you know," she said, staring at me. "He might have forgotten them, but not for long. He'll kick you to the curb soon enough."

"Fuck off, Esther," Cade said before I could say it myself.

So I added, "Right now."

She smiled at us, almost viciously. "My pleasure."

"Come on, let's go," he said, keeping an arm around my shoulders as we walked.

I tossed the empty cup in a nearby bin a bit more aggressively than necessary. Esther pissed me off. I let her bring up some of those old feelings, which made me even madder. As a kid, I always felt a little troubled because of my size. But then I learned that size didn't define me. If someone insulted me, it always boiled down to their own insecurities. Esther obviously didn't like the fact that Cade was with me and not her.

"I'll get us an Uber," he said. "Do you want to go to my place?"

"Sure." I couldn't tell if Cade had just brushed off the whole encounter or was hiding his take on the whole thing.

A couple minutes later, we were already inside a car. I was quiet during the drive, completely pissed. Who did she think she was? I hated that it affected me so much. Esther tried to embarrass me in front of Cade. That was plain cruel.

I'd always been confident, especially after graduating. Then again, perhaps my confidence had also stemmed from the fact that there were fewer bullies in adulthood. In high school, no one had a filter; they said whatever they wanted, even if it hurt people. But grownups usually had better manners, except for this bitch.

Don't react like this, Meredith. Someone else's opinion of you doesn't diminish your worth.

But no matter how much I repeated that in my mind, I couldn't help but think about the fact that Cade used to go out with someone who looked like a model.

Oh God. I'm not just jealous. I'm drunk *jealous.*

Cade moved closer to me. “Are you okay, there, drunk girl?”

I nodded, pressing my lips together. I kind of wanted to laugh and cry at the same time.

“Why so silent?”

“I'm afraid I'll make a fool of myself,” I whispered.

Where did that confession come from?

He winked, interlacing his fingers with mine. “Got it. Then let's go home.”

Chapter 20

Cade

Meredith was quiet on the drive home. So quiet, in fact, that I thought she fell asleep when she rested her head on the window. It was only when the car arrived in front of my building and I leaned in to wake her up that I realized she wasn't sleeping at all.

"We're here, babe," I said.

She nodded, straightening up. She was still a bit tipsy.

"Stay put. I'll go around and open the door for you."

The cold bit my cheeks when I got out of the car. I hurried to her door, opening it and then holding out my hand for her. She gripped it tightly and leaned on me as she got up. I was steady on my feet, supporting my woman, and immediately put an arm around her as we walked up to the building.

"Man, it's cold," she said. I unlocked the door as fast as possible, waiting for her to step inside first. "This place looks amazing." She glanced around the second I turned on the light in the mudroom. “Do you have a fireplace?”

“Yeah.”

“I didn’t take you for the type to live in a brownstone.”

“What did you imagine?”

“A penthouse.”

“Not my style.”

I looked at her closely. She seemed completely different than back at the fair. Something was off. "Babe, what's wrong?"

She shrugged.

"Esther bothered you," I concluded.

"Obviously, and I hate that because I'm always so confident, and I don't let people get to me."

"And I love that about you."

"I don't want you seeing me like this."

My woman was feeling vulnerable because of that snotty bitch. Esther and I had gone out a few times but were never a thing. Conversations were dull, and we had nothing in common.

"I don't mind. Babe, I'm honored that you can feel this comfortable around me, that you're showing me this side of you. Really, it’s okay."

"But I don't want to show it to you," she whispered.

"I'm sorry we ran into her."

"Who was she?"

"We dated a year ago. I met her at an event—the Coffee Formation. She was one of the presenters the host hired. It meant nothing." And that was an understatement.

"Sure seemed like it did to her, since she is still bragging about it."

"Forget about it. I never felt a thing for her. I don't even want to compare her to you. You mean so much to me, Meredith. You're fucking gorgeous." I was going to show her that tonight so she had no doubt. "If I could, I'd go back in time and cut that fucking conversation short before it even happened."

But that was impossible, so I was going to do the next best thing. I was going to show Meredith exactly the effect she had on me.

"Now, let's get all these clothes off you," I said, starting with the thick scarf around her neck. Then I lowered the zipper of her jacket. I put both our coats on the chair by the entrance, not bothering to hang them up.

"Let me start with that," she said, pointing to my shirt. "How can you still look this hot in winter? Aren't you cold? What are you made of?" she mumbled. I liked her when she was tipsy. She had no filter, and I liked listening to her inner thoughts. The one downside was that she took forever to unbutton my shirt. I helped her by starting to undo them from the bottom up. I finished all of them by the time she undid the second one.

"Someone's in a hurry," she said with a lazy smile.

"No, babe, I'm going to take all the time in the world with you. I just want to get these clothes out of the way. I want to see you. I want to feel you. Every inch of your gorgeous, sexy body."

She sucked in her breath. "Let the best one win."

"At what?"

"Taking off clothes."

"Babe, no offense, but I think I'm going to win that one."

She giggled. "So am I." She shimmied her hips. "Go on, ravage me."

"I will. First, I want to kiss you."

She tasted like cherries and rum. Everything she drank tonight. I couldn't understand how the simple act of kissing this woman had such a profound impact on me. I didn't want to stop savoring her, not even long enough to take off her clothes. I ran my hands down her sweaterdress as she pushed her hips into me. I groaned. And just like that, I needed skin-on-skin contact more than my next breath.

I grabbed the hem of her dress, knowing this one probably didn't have a zipper. And I was right. It came off easily as I pulled it over her head. Her hair was in complete disarray, making Meredith look wild, and I loved it. Her eyelids were hooded, and she bit her lower lip.

"I'll take care of the rest," I said. She didn't say anything, just leaned against the wall while I slowly peeled off her garters. "Your lingerie is driving me crazy."

"I know," she murmured, her inhibitions gone, left back at the festival, thank God.

I kissed up her thigh, stopping at the hem of her panties. I felt her suck in her breath and tighten the muscles in her belly.

No, I have a better plan. I stood up.

"What are you doing?" she murmured.

"Not here in the foyer. I want you on a horizontal surface, so when I make you come and your knees give out, you have all the support you need, babe."

She exhaled sharply. "Cade!"

I liked seeing her at a loss for words. I led her to the dining room, patting the table. "Sit here. But first lose your panties."

She cleared her throat, pointing up and down at me. "First I'm going to get you naked." She took off my undershirt and then opened my belt buckle with surprising dexterity, considering how much trouble she had with the buttons on my shirt earlier. She pushed my jeans down, along with my boxer shorts. "Oh yeah." She palmed my cock as I stepped out of my jeans, and my eyes rolled into the back of my head when I felt her thumb and then her tongue slide over the crown.

"Meredith," I groaned. I looked down at her. "Fuck me! You're so sexy." I loved seeing her on her knees, taking me in almost to the base of my cock while looking me straight in the eyes.

She pulled back, licking her lips.

"Come on, beautiful. Sit on the table like I told you to."

She hopped onto it, and I parted her thighs wide, but not before I reached around her back and undid her bra. It snapped open, and then she let it fall to her middle. I pushed it off her belly, and it landed on the floor.

“Meredith, I'm clean.”

She licked her lips. “So am I. And on birth control. We don't need a condom.”

"I want to memorize everything about this moment. Seeing you naked, thighs spread wide for me, right here on my dining room table. I want you everywhere in this house—on my desk, my couch, my bar, the bed, the shower."

Goose bumps broke out over her skin. First only on her thighs, then also on her arms. I pulled her to the very edge of the table, kissing her mouth softly.

She cupped my face with both hands. The unexpected tenderness stirred something inside me. She parted her legs even wider as I stepped between them, rubbing the length of my cock up and down against her entrance and her clit. She shivered every time I touched the crown to her clit. I increased the pace, knowing deep in my bones that I could make her come just like that. I wanted it. I wanted her to come once before I buried myself deep inside her and took what I needed. This was just for her.

I felt her entire body brace for orgasm. Her nails grabbed at the table. The muscles in her back tensed. She pushed her pelvis back and forth in a small movement. Clearly she needed more friction. I explored her beautiful, voluptuous body with my hands. I liked this position; I could easily reach down her thighs *and* her torso.

"Oh my God, Cade! Cade, I need you."

I took both her hands, putting them on me. I knew she wanted to dig her fingers into something, and the table wouldn't do. My skin would, though. I liked feeling her unrestrained pleasure rippling through her body.

She exploded beautifully, thrashing around on the table, crying out my name. I wanted to kiss her, but it was impossible.

Fuck, I was nearly losing my mind! I needed to be inside her, but I was determined to let her ride out this wave of bliss. Even though my cock was pulsing like mad, I rubbed it up and down her clit, drawing in a deep breath and expelling it even slower, all the while kissing her neck.

When her breathing fell back to a normal rate, I straightened up, looking at her, and then stepped back so we weren't touching anymore. I knew she needed to catch her breath. Her eyes were unfocused, and she had a mark on her lower lip from where she'd bitten it.

"I love seeing you this wild."

"You make me wild. I didn't even know... what you... could do to me." She wasn't coherent, but I knew what she was getting at. Fuck yes, it filled me with a caveman sort of pride that she hadn't done this with anyone else.

I stepped back farther, holding her hands. "Come on, beautiful. Down from the table."

"Why? Your next plans include the bed?"

"You bet. I'm going to need you to lie down for what I have in mind."

She shivered as she turned around, walking in front of me. I liked seeing her walk, her hips moving from side to side. The sight of her gorgeous ass turned me on just as much as her screams had a few minutes ago.

We walked up the stairs to the next floor. In the bedroom, I only turned on a few of the lights, the ones over the dresser.

"Get on the bed, Meredith. Hold your hands close to the headboard."

The headboard was a wood panel with an intricate pattern. I'd never paid much attention to it before, but now I had a good use for it.

"Why?" Meredith asked.

"You'll see."

As she climbed onto the bed, I went to my dresser, taking out two ties. She exhaled sharply when I returned.

"I want to use one of these to cover your eyes and the other to tie your hands to the headboard. I promise it's going to make everything I do to you so much more delicious."

She pouted. "But that's going to limit what I can do to you."

"Trust me, watching you come is reward enough for now. What do you think?"

"Yes. I want to try everything."

I started by putting the tie around her eyes. I made sure she couldn't see much, though it wasn't important for her eyes to be completely covered, only enough so she couldn't fathom my next move. Then I used the other tie for her wrists.

"They're very loose. Are you comfortable?" I asked.

"Yes." She tugged at them lightly.

The sight of her tied up in my bed like this was insanely sexy. She was sitting with her ass by the headboard, legs spread wide and bent at the knees. I pulled at her ankles, and she understood my message—I wanted her lying down.

I dragged my fingers from her ankles up to her knees, then moved to her inner thighs. Going farther up, I parted her legs even more. I positioned my mouth right over her pussy, blowing cold air over it before pressing the flat of my tongue straight over her opening.

"Cade!" she screamed, pushing her heels down into the mattress. She shoved her pelvis against my mouth, and I knew exactly what she needed.

I pressed my tongue inside her, alternating between that and paying attention to her clit. She was wild. I felt her tug at the ties, writhing around on the bed. Then I kissed back up, because I wanted to see her up close when she came undone for me. I moved my mouth in a slow, torturous kiss over each breast while I slipped my fingers inside her, pressing my palm on her clit at the same time.

"Oh my God. Oh my God." She clamped her thighs together, trapping my hand. I stilled, watching her intently, drinking in the way she gave in to me.

This orgasm was even more intense than the one before. I took off her blindfold when she seemed to have come down from the release, then I undid her hands as well.

"Oh my God. I didn't even know I could come twice."

"You'll come again for me before the night ends, babe. When I'm inside you," I assured her.

I kissed her long and deep, feeling the vibrations of her body against me before straightening up. Resting on my knees, I lifted her ankles off the bed, keeping her thighs to the side, and put two pillows under her ass until her entrance was level with my cock.

"What are you doing?" she murmured.

"You'll like this angle, babe, I promise."

When I couldn't stand it anymore, I slid inside her. She was still pulsing. The skin-on-skin contact sent me into a tailspin. Pleasure was already building in my body, and I buckled forward at the unexpected shot of heat. I straightened up, dropping my head back.

"Fuck!" I exclaimed. "Have I died and gone to heaven?" This couldn't be real. The sensation was impossibly good. Nothing I'd experienced before had ever come close to it.

"Cade... Cade," she chanted. She tugged at the remaining pillow next to her. I instinctively knew she wanted to cover herself with it.

"I want to hear you. I want to see you," I murmured as I moved my hips back and forth.

Her eyes widened. "Oh my God, how is this happening?"

She rolled her own hips back and forth, and I knew what that meant. She was close again. Her nerve endings were so sensitive. She probably hadn't even finished coming yet. I brushed her clit on every thrust, feeling her pussy get tighter and tighter around me.

"Cade, oh my God."

Another shot of pleasure made me buckle, but this time I didn't straighten up. Instead, I put a palm on the mattress, leaning over Meredith. I took her nipple into my mouth, circling it with my tongue.

She came almost violently, squeezing so tight around my cock that my breath was cut short for a few moments. My entire body seemed to be frozen in space. All the sensations were concentrated in the places where our bodies touched. And then I gave her all I had. My climax had never felt this good or this powerful.

Meredith was mine. And I knew without a doubt that I was hers too.

Chapter 21

Cade

I woke up early the next morning, got out of bed without waking Meredith, and headed straight down to the living room. Glancing at the fireplace, I made a split-second decision. I wanted to surprise Meredith this morning. I texted Cal, asking him to bring by breakfast stuff and wood. He replied immediately. I was going to chat with my brother about paying Cal extra. Jake had assured me he was compensated handsomely, but I believed in treating people fairly, especially when they went above and beyond. I'd given Jake shit for having someone chauffer him around, but I was starting to see the benefit.

Forty minutes later, breakfast was on the kitchen island. Meredith was still asleep. That gave me enough time to surprise her.

It had been a while since I lit the fire, but YouTube was very informative. I didn't usually bother with it because it seemed impractical. I mean, I could just turn up the heat if I wanted to get warm. When I first moved into the brownstone, I'd asked about removing it, but it was too much of a hassle, so in the end, I just let it be.

"Oh my God." There was my surprise. The fire was more of a

flicker, but when I turned around, Meredith stood in the doorway, mouth open, eyes sleepy and wide at the same time. Her hair was in complete disarray, full of snarls. She was wearing the robe I gave her last night after we showered. "When did this happen? You had wood to start a fire?"

"No. But I have my ways of getting what I need to keep my woman happy," I said, walking up to her.

She yawned, running a hand through her hair, then stopped midway, dropping it. "Oh God. My hair is a mess. I didn't even check my appearance."

"You look gorgeous." I leaned into her, but she stepped back quickly, covering her mouth with her hand.

"Nope. Morning breath. I didn't mean for you to see me like this. I was just lured here by the smell of burning wood. I'll be right back."

Turning around, she darted out of the living room. I didn't want her worried about her appearance when she was around me. I got hard seeing how she looked right now, after being ravished by me and *only ever* me. I was going to have her over as many times as it took until she was completely comfortable here.

Damn. I couldn't even believe my own train of thought.

I took the food Cal brought out of the containers. I never ate at home in the mornings, so I had nothing in the fridge and had asked him to bring breakfast bowls from a nearby restaurant that prided itself on being the city's best choice for brunch and breakfast. It was so popular that they started having a takeout menu too.

Meredith came down fifteen minutes later. The fire was much stronger than before. She looked stunning, yet I still preferred the natural, early morning version of her.

"See, now I look like a human," she said. Her hair was shiny and falling in a straight line down her back and shoulders. Her face was fresh. "You can kiss me all you want."

"You're gorgeous no matter what, babe. Loved the way you looked before."

"Right. Especially my hair. Looked like a bird's nest."

I looked straight in her eyes, touching her cheek. "Fuck yes, I like it. It meant you woke up in my bed, and I'm the first to see you today."

She licked her lips, blinking slowly. Then her stomach rumbled.

I kissed her forehead before motioning to the kitchen island. "Breakfast is ready."

"Wow, you had all this?"

"No. Cal brought it, along with the wood."

She sighed. "Can we eat in front of the fireplace? It's so gorgeous."

"Anything to make you happy. Sit down, and I'll bring you your breakfast."

Smiling from ear to ear, she sat on the couch, then swung her legs up next to her. "This place is amazing."

"I like it," I said, sitting beside her on the couch and handing her a bowl.

"By the way, Natalie and I exchanged numbers at Jeannie's house. *Aaand* she and I have been talking about taking Jeannie out. Maybe to have a pedicure or something. Do you mind?"

"Fuck no. Of course not." Mind? How was she even real? I couldn't wrap my mind around this.

"Okay." She looked down at the bowl. "Is this from that fancy breakfast place? I saw them on Instagram."

"Yeah."

"You do spoil me. Let's see what all the fuss is about." She put her spoon into the yogurt and granola before placing it in her mouth. "Hmm, okay, I'm totally sold."

I took a spoonful too. "This is really good."

"So, how do you like your house?"

"It's cool. It just feels a bit claustrophobic. The idea of a brownstone sounds good, but it just doesn't really feel like a house. The backyard is a joke."

She rolled her eyes. "Oh please, keep telling me the downsides of living here."

"I probably sound like a snob."

"Nah, just hard to please. But you're forgiven because you also made this happen." She pointed at the fire and at the food. "It's the best morning ever."

This was all it took to make her happy? Hell, I was going to just keep doing it, then.

"I love Sundays," she murmured.

"What do you usually do?"

"It depends. It's the one day of the week where I don't have anything scheduled. I just play it by ear. You?"

"I'm playing tennis with my half brothers. Actually, Spencer might be there today too."

"Even in this weather?"

"They have indoor courts at the club."

"Nice. So, that's the secret to your hot-as-hell body. Tennis."

"Yeah." I made a split-second decision because I didn't want to stand up my brothers, but I also wasn't ready to bid Meredith goodbye in two hours. "Want to come with me to the club today?"

I wanted her to meet the rest of my family so she didn't think I was keeping her a secret from anyone.

"I don't play tennis."

"Trust me, most people don't go there to do anything besides just hang around. You can go to the sauna or steam bath or even try your hand at playing if you want to."

"Okay. I can't wait to meet your half brothers." She took another spoonful of granola. "Oh my God, this is orgasmic."

I grunted. "Meredith."

She cleared her throat. "Oops, sorry. I got lost in this."

"If I hear the word *orgasmic* out of your mouth again—"

"Will you give me one? Because I'm all up for it."

"Hell yes I will."

WE ARRIVED AT THE CLUB TWENTY MINUTES BEFORE I was supposed to meet my half brothers on the court because I wanted to show Meredith around. Turned out they had workout clothes for sale in the club shop, something I hadn't known until today. Meredith needed an outfit.

"You're getting access key, and you can get in everywhere. Want to try on some clothes?"

"Yes," Meredith said. "They look great."

"Put it on my account," I said.

Meredith snapped her gaze to me. "No, Cade, I'm buying it."

"I invited you here. It's on me."

She held my gaze. I wasn't going to relent.

"Why don't you two take your time to decide? You can pay when you check out," the woman behind the reception desk said, clearly uncomfortable.

"Sure, thanks a lot," I said.

"Which brother owns this again?" Meredith asked as we moved past the desk.

"Nick. It was the smallest Whitley business when he took over, and now it's one of the biggest fitness companies in the country."

"Is there anything Whitley Industries isn't doing?"

"Not really." Despite everything my father had done, I could admit he'd been a genius. I'd once asked him why he'd started so many different branches. Back when Grandfather was running it, it only operated in the healthcare, coffee, advertising, and magazine industries. My father told me he got bored quickly, that he loved starting things from scratch. Probably explained why he felt the need to have a second family.

Nate, Leo, Maddox, and Spencer were all on the tennis court when I arrived. Meredith insisted she might need longer to change and that she'd meet me here. She was so funny about everything, worried about me spending money on her, like she was concerned I'd think she was taking advantage of me. *Silly woman.*

The indoor courts were underground. It was smart of my brother to use the space, but they were claustrophobic. I missed playing outdoors.

"What's that I hear?" Leo said lazily. "You brought Meredith?"

"I did," I said. "I wanted her to meet you."

"It's a good thing I came here, then. You won't be able to play for shit," Spencer said.

"Want to bet?" I challenged.

"Hell yeah."

Maddox and Nick exchanged a glance.

"Is that her?" Maddox asked, nodding behind me. I turned around.

Meredith looked stunning in her gray-and-black workout clothes. They showed off her curves beautifully.

Fuck me. I wanted to take her somewhere and be all alone with her, as if I hadn't had her this morning already. But there was never enough when it came to Meredith.

"I heard the word *bet*," she said as she came closer. That was Meredith to a tee. Giving my brothers sass even before I formally introduced her to them. "I hope it's not against my man losing."

Hearing her call me her man filled me with pride.

"Meredith, with all due respect, we kicked his ass last time. Rumor has it, it's because he was too busy mooning about you," Leo said.

Asshat. My brother seemed to have made it a habit of embarrassing me lately. What had gotten into him?

"He hasn't told me any of that."

"No, I suspect he was trying to save his manhood. But Spencer is always here to beat it out of him," Nick offered.

"Weren't you supposed to always have his back, Spencer? You know, as his twin?" Maddox asked.

"Yeah, but that got boring, so now I'm just stirring things up," Spencer said.

Maddox moved over to Meredith, extending his hand with a grin. "I'm Maddox, by the way," he said, shaking hands with her. Nick and Leo did the same.

"It's great to meet you guys." She looked around, taking it all in. "This is a fabulous place, Nick."

"I'm glad you think so," Nick replied. "If you want a membership, just say the word, and I'll make it happen. On the house, of course."

"Wow. Generosity is a family trait, I see."

"No, no. Everyone else is okay, but I take the cake," Nick said proudly.

"You guys have nicknames for each other? Are you the cocky one or something?" Meredith asked.

Maddox burst out laughing. Leo jerked his head back in surprise.

"I was hoping to meet you soon. You were all Gran talked about at Thanksgiving. And Friday too," Nick said.

I frowned as I was inspecting my racket. "You went to dinner this Friday?"

"We go sometimes on Fridays," Maddox mentioned.

I glanced at Spencer through the racket. "Since when?"

"I don't know. A while. You guys didn't know, huh?" Leo said.

"I think it's time we tell our grandmother that we're all grown men. She doesn't have to tiptoe around us," Nick said on a chuckle.

"Yeah, tell that to Jake. Or to Colton," Maddox added.

"Come on, man. That's not fair," Spencer said.

"Yeah. Jake's come around," I replied. Though Colton hadn't yet. "Why doesn't she just make one dinner on Saturday and have us all over?"

"I suspect she thinks if we all hang out too often, things would escalate," Maddox said. "Now come on. Let's start the game."

"Am I playing first or Spencer?" I asked.

"You go first. I'm just going to stick around, maybe keep Meredith company," Spencer said. "And when they kick your ass, I'll take your place."

"Babe, you can go look around the club. You don't have to stay here," I told her.

“I want to. Just for a set or two, maybe. I want to see you play. Or, if Spencer is to be believed, get your ass kicked."

I scoffed. “That won’t happen.”

Famous last words.

I lost the first set spectacularly. I’d never played so badly.

"You’re on a losing streak," Spencer announced as we all took a break and headed to the juice bar upstairs.

"And I thought I might bring you luck," Meredith said, shimmying her hips. "I think I’m better off doing something else if I distract you that much." She batted her eyelashes. "Although you losing on my account is good for my ego."

Maddox laughed. "God, you're funny."

"I'm glad you think so," she said.

“No wonder Gran likes you,” Leo added. “Although two successes in her matchmaking is giving her ideas for all of us.”

“No one else in your family is seeing anyone?” She sounded stunned.

Maddox cleared his throat. “Not seriously.”

Leo turned to Spencer. “Although you were going out with that chick a few months ago.”

Spencer waved his hand. “She’s been gone from my life for a while.”

“Come on, let’s get you your prize for making me lose,” I whispered in her ear, immensely enjoying the way her skin turned to goose bumps.

I put an arm around her waist, leading her up to the bar. We each got one of their blends—carrot and apple. Watching Meredith slurp her juice and enjoy it with her eyes closed, humming in contentment, was testing my control. I led her behind the bar, needing to be alone with her.

"Why don't we go back to your brothers?" she asked once we emptied our glasses.

"Just want a moment alone with you. You look amazing in these clothes."

I kept my hand on her waist, brushing my thumb along her skin. I wanted to devour her.

"Sorry you lost because of me."

"It wasn't you. My mind was still on what Maddox said, that Grandmother is having two family dinners." I didn't know why it was impacting me that much. "It annoys me that even so many years later, it still takes a lot of effort for us to come together as a family."

I understood why Grandmother did it. If we got together too often, there was always a risk that we'd end up in an argument.

Stupidly, I felt betrayed because she'd kept this from us. What the hell? I wasn't five years old.

"Families are tough. When I'm with mine, I basically have to play referee over who gets to talk more," Meredith commented.

"We also have to play referee in my family, but it's to make sure no one's fighting too much."

Our family experiences were completely different, and I was sure it was also shaping our expectations for the future in wildly different ways.

"I think it's great that you all are making an effort."

I shook my head. "Sometimes it gets on my nerves. It shouldn't be an effort."

"You guys have a terrible history. I don't think most people would even contemplate getting to know their half brothers. Tensions are bound to happen from time to time. But just because some things aren't easy doesn't mean they're not worth it."

Meredith was amazing. She didn't shy away from challenges. Most people were the exact opposite. In fact, Esther had even gone as far as insisting that my half brothers probably weren't legally entitled to Whitley Industries, and we should get rid of them. And she and I weren't even that close. I was actually pissed she'd said anything at all. It wasn't her place. But Meredith was different, and I wanted to hear what she had to say. I respected her.

She put her hands on my neck. The heat from her palms seemed to melt the tension there. I could feel the calm seeping deep into my body.

"That's better," she murmured. "You were so tense."

"*You* made it better."

Being around Meredith was addictive. She was incredible in so many ways. She exuded confidence, always had, and I loved that about her.

A beeping sound came from somewhere close.

"It's not my phone," I stated. "I don't keep it on me when I'm at the club."

"Oh, it's a rule? I didn't know. Let me just check who it is." She took it out from her back pocket, frowning at the screen. "Sonya said she wants a meeting tomorrow. That's strange. She never messages on weekends, or even outside of business hours during the week."

"What do you think it's about? There's been no word on the sale. My CFO reached out, but it didn't go anywhere," I mentioned, not sure if Sonya had told Meredith that.

"I asked her, and she was vague about it. Either she'll circle back after the holidays or she's dropped it." She put her phone back in her pocket. "Never mind. I'm going to worry about that tomorrow. Today is all about getting to know your half brothers and seeing you move that gorgeous ass on the court."

She was smiling, but I felt the change in her body. Her shoulders stiffened, and her arms were tense.

I took a page out of her own book. I wanted to help her get rid of the tension, so I pulled her even deeper behind the bar where no one could see us. Then I palmed her ass with both hands.

"Hey, I didn't say that to give you ideas."

"But you did," I growled. "Anyway, what are you going to do about it?"

"I'm just going to enjoy it." She grinned.

"Great plan."

"What do you think is happening back there, brothers?" Nick's voice boomed. It was close enough that I assumed they'd come around the bar's counter.

"Don't want to know. They've been gone for a while," Maddox replied.

"Who's up to betting?" Leo asked.

Meredith pressed her lips together. "Come on, let's just enjoy the day. And you stop focusing on the two dinners thing, okay? There's nothing you can do about it, so let it go. At least for now."

Reluctantly, I stepped back, following Meredith's lead.

Before I met her, I had a tendency to act upon things right away. If there was a problem, I fixed it. Ideally, I'd like to talk to my brothers or even my grandparents about this dinner thing. But Meredith was right. I had to let it go.

She and I had agreed that our relationship was casual, but I couldn't deny that it was changing me. There was a before Meredith time and an after Meredith time for me. And I wasn't sure I'd ever want to go back to *before*.

Chapter 22

Meredith

The next day, I knew something was weird at the office as soon as I got in. My coworkers were in a frenzy.

What's going on? I headed straight to Sonya's office.

"Hey, Sonya, our meeting starts in ten minutes."

"Yes, it does."

"Do I need my laptop to take notes?"

"Oh no, you don't. It's going to be short."

I decided to ask her point-blank, since her answers were curt. "Is everything okay? The whole team seems in an uproar."

"I'm guessing you didn't check on the contest?"

My stomach bottomed out. Cade hadn't mentioned anything either, though he probably hadn't looked at the updates—and I actually forgot to. We'd been together the whole weekend, and he'd been the only thing on my mind.

"No, I didn't. Is there news?"

"Yes. We didn't make it to the next round."

I felt as if someone had pulled a rug out from under me and I'd fallen nose first against her desk.

"Oh, I'm so sorry. I really thought we were going to make it into the finals. We had a very good product. What was the grade?"

I was truly stunned. I hadn't expected this. "Oh, now I want to rush back to my computer to look at it."

"We didn't get the feedback yet. Our score was high, but I assume the others got an even better grade. I'm disappointed, of course, but as you know, I had a purpose when I entered the competition, and I'm close to finalizing it," she continued.

"Okay. So are you moving forward with Cade?"

"No, I honestly didn't like Mr. Whitley's attitude. I would've thought he'd be more open to us, given your relationship with him."

I pressed my lips together to stop from making a sassy remark. That was unfair of Sonya. One thing had nothing to do with the other.

"In the meantime, I've been in talks with the Bean Masters."

"Really? They're interested in buying?"

"Yes. I've spoken with the CEO at length."

"As long as you're happy with the person who takes over your company, that's all that matters."

Sonya cleared her throat. "Alfred Danvers wants me to go to his office with a presentation. I'll think about whether or not I should include you on the team."

I blinked. That was like a slap in the face. I was her VP of marketing. That was my job. "Why shouldn't I be included? I prepped everything with Arthur for Cade."

"The reason I'm not sure you should be on the team is that I made a mistake of telling Alfred about you and Cade. Your relationship."

What. The. Hell? How in God's name would that have come up in a conversation? A business one at that?

"And?"

"Apparently, he's not a fan of Cade, so he didn't take it well that someone from my team was... well, he put it as 'fraternizing with the rival.'"

I stared at her. "What are you not telling me, Sonya?"

"Look, nothing is set in stone yet, obviously. All I'm asking is for you to be polite when you eventually meet him."

"I'm always polite." Sonya's passive-aggressive way of handling our conversation was starting to piss me off. There was obviously more to it, and apparently she didn't think I needed to know.

"He doesn't have spectacular manners, if I'm honest. He likes to push people's buttons. So, if and when you two meet, and he remarks on something you're not okay with, just let it go."

It was on the tip of my tongue to ask, *"Or what?"*

Is it just me, or is Sonya acting extremely belligerent today?

"Let me ask you something else, Sonya. What do you think will happen to me if you end up selling to him?" Though from what she'd already said, I knew my answer.

Sonya pursed her lips together. "I think that depends on how you're going to get on with him." She didn't meet my eyes as she said it.

"I appreciate the heads-up," I said. If she ended up selling to him, I would be in need of a job. I'd assumed that would be the case from the get-go but had held on to the hope that I'd fit into a new team.

What a clusterfuck. I couldn't believe it. I was being punished because I was in a relationship with Cade when it all seemed to be quite different a few weeks ago.

"Do you want me to put together the marketing part of the presentation, even if I'm not allowed to actually present it?" I asked.

"Yes, please. You can use a lot of the stuff you prepped for Cade Whitley. It was a very good presentation."

"Thank you." At least she acknowledged my work.

I was fuming when I returned to my desk. I couldn't believe things had turned around so fast.

I was starting to get a headache. I tapped the screen of my phone to see if I had any missed calls in my absence. I didn't, but I had two messages from Cade.

Cade: Good morning, beautiful. How did your week start?

Cade: I know Mondays are usually shit. If that's the case, tell me and I'll send reinforcements.

Despite everything, I chuckled. It was as if we had an unspoken connection.

I replied to him as I clicked around on my computer to check if any other unforeseen meetings had popped on my calendar—yeah, I was good at multitasking.

Meredith: Send all the reinforcements you can. The week started off weird.

Cade: I just heard from Sonya. She told me she no longer wants to continue negotiations with me and that she's been talking to the Bean Masters.

Meredith: Exactly.

There was no point telling him that Danvers didn't plan to keep me around. It was my shit to deal with.

I'd barely put my phone down when it vibrated again.

Cade: I don't like Alfred Danvers. We don't see eye to eye on many things.

No shit.

Meredith: Did you make it to the next round?

Cade: Yes.

Meredith: CONGRATS. We need to celebrate.

Cade: We have time for that. But let's focus on you. How can I make your day better?

Oh, I had so many ideas. He could whisk me away and do all sorts of delicious stuff to me.

Get it together, Meredith. This is Monday. You still have five days to slog through before you can feast on Cade for forty-eight hours straight.

Meredith: I don't think you can. I just have to suck it up.

He called me the next second. "Meredith." His voice was almost a groan.

"Yeah?"

"I know just what you need," he said.

"Oh, I doubt that." But despite the fact that the morning had such a spectacularly shitty start, I was already feeling better. I twirled around in my chair, looking out the window. I loved the view. How much longer would I have it?

"No, I can't blast right through your door, throw you over my shoulder, and take you away, but I can do the next best thing."

"And what's that?"

"I can whisk you away this evening."

In a fraction of an instant, my budding headache completely vanished, just like that. Cade was magic, I swear to God.

"Really? Where are we going?"

"I don't know yet. I'll figure something out this evening to make sure you forget all about this craptastic day."

"Oh, that's a very good word to describe it." *It's only nine thirty in the morning, but this day is already better.* “But wait. Natalie and I are going out with Jeannie after work.”

“We'll figure something out.”

"Okay. Damn, I have to go. Our mutual friend Arthur, our CFO, is calling me.”

“Talk to you later.”

“Bye.”

I spoke with Arthur on the phone for a couple minutes. I wondered what he thought about the new development, but it wasn't my place to ask. I wasn't nosy. This was Sonya's business, not mine. I simply had to follow the instructions and do my best for the company.

After I hung up, I did something I usually didn't do during my work time. I opened my private folder where I had my personal financial spreadsheets. Even if I was unemployed for a couple months, I still had enough savings to be able to continue helping out my parents with their rent. That should be enough, right?

Stop this, Meredith. It's not like you to procrastinate. You have a job right now. Make the best of it.

At around eleven o'clock, there was a knock at my door, and Diana, one of our assistants, stepped inside. "Meredith, I have something for you. A delivery boy just brought it. I think it's some samples."

"Thanks." I took the box. It had no sender or a recipient. As carefully as possible, I put it on the desk and opened it up.

Oh my goodness. There were three *pastéis de nata* inside, and there could only be one person who sent them. I snapped a picture and sent it to Cade.

Meredith: Is this your doing?

He replied a few seconds later.

Cade: Obviously. Who else knows what your favorite treat is? Wait, don't answer that. I don't want to know.

I chuckled, typing back.

Meredith: My sister and parents know, and that's about it. Why did you pass it off as a sample?

Cade: I didn't want to make a fuss about this being from me.

He was charming and thoughtful and whip smart. All that made him insanely attractive to me.

Meredith: Thanks. I feel better just looking at them.

I immediately shoved one in my mouth, humming.

Cade: Good. That was my goal. I can't wait to see you tonight.

I grinned from ear to ear as I typed back.

Meredith: I can't wait to see you either.

I put the phone down, sighing. I'd never experienced anything like this before.

Usually the only person I shared my bad days with was my sister. Once, with an ex, I'd made the mistake of telling him when I came home from work one evening that it had been a difficult day, and he said he didn't want me to bring down his mood with any of that. Since then, I'd never bothered.

But Cade didn't hesitate to ask me how my morning was, and now he was going out of his way to make sure the day wasn't complete crap. I was going to spoil him rotten this evening and show my appreciation in every way possible.

Chapter 23

Meredith

"Girls, this is... You're ridiculous. You're young. You don't want this old hag cramping your style."

Natalie laughed. "Jeannie, where do you even get that expression from?"

"I'm trying to keep up with slang. I always had to stay on top of things in my working days. I'd usually bring some modern flare to my interpretations. Not classic ones, of course. I wouldn't make Shakespeare say 'cramp your style.' But as I reached my seventies, I didn't want to be out of touch."

Jeannie lit up when she spoke of her acting days. Natalie and I had gone back and forth about what to do with her, then decided getting mani-pedis was an activity everyone enjoyed.

"This place looks amazing," Jeannie went on.

Natalie nodded. "I discovered it recently. I love the nail bar. It's so relaxing. It's almost like a visit to the spa."

They didn't have an actual bar, despite the name, but they served drinks and had decorated everything, so it resembled an oasis in nature. The three of us were sitting in a semicircle, and our respective professionals were explaining the procedure to us. I thought that was pointless because everyone knew how to get their nails done, but Jeannie was having a field day with it, so what did I know?

"I want red nails," Jeannie exclaimed. "I've had a french manicure for so long. I'm sick of it. They should call it the old lady manicure."

"Hey, I like them," Natalie said.

"Girls, mark my words. Go for red while you're young enough. You'll have plenty of time for nudes and french manicures when you're an old bat."

I burst out laughing. "If there's anyone who shouldn't refer to herself as old, it's you, Jeannie." She truly was sharp as a whip. One could only hope to reach that age and be just like her.

"I saw a tea shop next door. I'll go in after we're through and buy Abe some hibiscus tea. He loves it." It was so endearing how she always seemed to be thinking about her husband.

"You spoil him rotten," Natalie said.

"Oh, I do. I think spoiling each other is a prerequisite of a long and happy marriage."

As the manicurists started to work on our nails, I listened to Jeannie intently. I always liked to listen whenever my parents spoke about their marriage, but she and Abe were an entirely different level altogether. They must have had something like six or seven decades together. That was remarkable. Natalie was also leaning in a bit. We made eye contact, and she winked.

"It doesn't even have to be big things. Just small things that show appreciation on a daily basis. It's important to keep it up, especially when you're going through hard times."

Definitely wise words.

"But how can you do that?" I asked. "Typically, when you go through a hard time, you're not in the best of spirits. The last thing on my mind is someone else."

"You're right," Jeannie said, looking at the nail polish she'd chosen. It was the brightest red in the color palette. "And that wasn't always easy." Suddenly her eyes looked sad. "After Ryan, the boys' father and my son, showed his true colors, it was an especially difficult time. Abe was angry, almost constantly. Bitter that our only son had turned out to be... well, not the good person we'd hoped we raised. I have to admit it was a tough time. It's hard showing love when the other person is bad tempered all day long, but that's especially when they need it. When you both need it. They need the reassurance of knowing you're still there for them even when they're not at their best. Abe was there for me too. Sometimes it's easier to show up for the other person than it is for yourself. And that's okay."

Her words went straight to my heart. I was going to remember them for the rest of my life.

"I'm sorry your family went through that," Natalie said.

Jeannie shrugged. It was still a sore point for her after all these years. Then again, how could it not be? "I wish we could've protected the boys better."

"Jeannie," I said gently, "you did your very best."

"I hope so. Colton and Jake took it so hard. They'd wanted to keep their younger brothers shielded, but it was impossible. And then their mother got ill. My poor girl. I know the doctor said she'd had the melanoma for a while, but I firmly think it started after Ryan broke her heart, and no one will be able to convince me otherwise."

"Oh, Jeannie, don't say that," I said. "Illnesses are unfortunate mishaps."

"I think Cade was the angriest out of everyone. He changed from that boy who played harmless pranks to someone who the school viewed as dangerous. I didn't know how to reach him. No one could." And just like that, her expression changed as she said, "But let's not talk about anything sad anymore. I'm making that a rule we follow for the rest of the day."

"I like it," I said.

"So do I," Natalie replied.

"I do have an important question for you two girls," Jeannie whispered conspiratorially. "You can tell me not to butt in."

Oh yeah, like that would ever work.

Jeannie's eyes twinkled. "Are either of you planning on giving me great-grandkids?"

I'd never blushed so fast in my whole life. Natalie looked like she was about to choke on nothing at all. All three manicurists were fighting their laughter, enjoying our discomfort, I supposed.

"Um... I, um... You know Cade and I just started seeing each other," I mumbled.

"Okay. I take it that's my cue. I'm butting in."

Natalie narrowed her eyes at Jeannie. "You're doing that thing again that you did when you told Cade about Meredith."

"What's that?" I asked.

Natalie leaned forward, making eye contact with me. "Apparently, when it comes to matchmaking, she has two strategies: one where she's completely sneaky and one where she's only partially sneaky."

Jeannie shook her head. "No, I was completely up-front. Sometimes it helps to tell people what you plan for them. Even if they reject the idea at first, it's there in their brain, percolating."

"Oh, I see. It's sort of like that movie *Inception*," I said, even though it really wasn't. That movie had boggled my mind, but Leonardo DiCaprio was hot in it, so I'd watched it.

"Okay, got it. I did butt in. I won't ask again." Jeannie looked mighty pleased with herself.

We made chitchat while we got our nails done. Jeannie regaled us with stories from her time as an actress. She'd truly lived an amazing life. She said she hadn't wanted to travel a lot because it would take her away from her family, and that limited her options a bit, but she had no regrets.

Once my nails were dry, I texted Cade with an update.

Meredith: We're done with our nails. Jeannie is happy. I think she had fun.

Cade didn't answer right away, so I put the phone back in my bag and focused on Jeannie as we entered the tea shop. The store was packed, which was surprising for a tea shop and the time of day. On the second floor, they sold very cute cups and plates and other accessories that looked delightful, so I marked this as a place to return to.

"Do you want us to drop you off at home, Jeannie?" Natalie asked after Jeannie bought tea for Abe and we'd stepped back out onto the street.

"Only if you girls have plans later."

Natalie and I exchanged a glance.

"No, not at all. We saved the evening for you. Why? Are you in the mood for something?" I asked.

Jeannie nodded. "Yes, please take me to a fancy bar. I need a cocktail. I haven't even opened a bottle of wine lately because I didn't want to tempt Abe."

Jeannie Whitley was feisty, and I was here for it.

"I know a bar a few streets away," I said. We were near Beacon Street, where I'd been with Everly a few times.

On the way, we admired window displays, oohing and aahing at the holiday decorations. We stopped in front of the one right next to the bar. It was magnificent, with huge red bows and gold details.

"I can't believe I found my soul sisters when it comes to admiring Christmas decorations. Sometimes I think I'm adopted. My own family doesn't get the fuss either," I said.

"Really?" Natalie asked. "Mine loves it. God, I hope they're going to join us for Christmas."

Jeannie glanced up at her. "They said they would."

"Oh, I know. But now they're having second thoughts because a few hotels around are organizing events for tourists between Christmas and New Year's Eve, and they're thinking maybe they should do the same. I miss them."

"Where are your parents?" I asked.

"Greece."

Oh man. I understood where Natalie was coming from. If my family moved across the ocean, I'd probably be sad all the time. I couldn't even imagine it.

"Okay, let's go in before we freeze our ears off," Jeannie said.

I felt my phone vibrate in my pocket and took it out, thinking it had to be Cade. No, it was a message from Sonya.

Sonya: Hey, apparently the gala for all the finalists is in three weeks. Alfred Danvers said he'll be there too. We're invited as well even though we didn't make it into the finals. I think it's going to be a good opportunity for you to meet him.

Damn. I thought nothing could put a damper on the evening, but that definitely did.

"What's wrong, girl? You look pale," Jeannie said.

"Just some news from work."

"Nothing a cocktail won't solve," she said with a wink.

I looked over her head at Natalie, who just shrugged and smiled.

Is Jeannie intending to get drunk tonight?

Turned out she didn't. The woman could hold her liquor. Natalie and I, not so much.

Cade texted me just as we asked for the bill.

Cade: How is the evening going? I'm picking you up. I'm still going forward with my plan to spoil you.

I grinned as I typed back, bringing the phone close to my face so I could see the letters properly. I wasn't drunk, but I was definitely a bit tipsy.

Meredith: We're ready to go. Natalie already texted Jake. This is our address.

It took forever for us to pay. Afterward, I had an idea, inspired by the wisdom Jeannie shared earlier. "If you want, you can go downstairs. I need to buy something first."

On the way in, I noticed they were selling bottles of champagne from a local producer. Usually it was exorbitant to buy bottles of alcohol in the bar, but this one was reasonably priced. Besides, tonight was a special occasion. My man was one step closer to winning the contest and cleaning up his company's reputation.

"Sure, I think Jake will be here any minute," Natalie said as she and Jeannie put on their coats.

After they left, I went to the bar. I had to wait behind a couple who ordered cocktails before my turn came. The neon lights behind the bar seemed ethereal when we first arrived, but now they were hurting my eyes.

"Hi. I'd like to buy one of the bottles you have on display in the fridge by the door."

"Sure thing. Want us to package it as a present?" the bartender asked.

"Not necessary," I said. I was certain we were going to pop it open tonight. It was even chilled, though it would warm up by the time we got to the brownstone.

Five minutes later, I was downstairs in front of the building. Jake and Cade were already here. Natalie and Jeannie were inside Jake's car.

"Wow. You guys got here fast," I said, clutching the bottle of champagne in my arms.

Jake smiled at me, noticing my purchase. "Good thinking. This one just told me he made it to the next round."

"Oh yeah. We're going to celebrate, don't you worry." I winked.

Cade put an arm around my shoulders. "Come on, let's get inside the car. Your teeth are chattering." And they were.

"It's way colder than when we went inside the bar earlier."

"Have a good evening," Jake told us.

Cade opened the door for me, and I slid inside, practically melting into the warm seat. I was still holding the champagne bottle.

Let the fun begin.

Chapter 24

Cade

We arrived at the brownstone twenty minutes later.

"I'm going to put this in the freezer real quick," she said, shimmying her hips through the house. "Oh, you got more wood delivered?"

"I prepared everything to start a fire."

"And I thought this evening couldn't get any better," she said. Her energy was addictive.

She busied herself in the kitchen while I started the fire. I was much faster with the whole process now.

When I was confident it was going strong, I joined her in the kitchen.

I went up behind Meredith, kissing her neck. To my surprise, she'd already taken out champagne glasses.

"How did you know where they were?" I asked.

"Oh, I saw them when I emptied the glasses from the dishwasher. Do you mind?"

"No, I want you to feel comfortable here, Meredith."

It made me happy that she knew where everything was, that she felt at home here.

I turned her around slowly. "I've never been this close to anyone."

"Neither have I," she admitted, her eyes searching mine.

"When I saw today that we made it to the next stage, I didn't think about celebrating with my family. I wanted to celebrate with you."

"Really?"

"You're important to me, Meredith. You're an integral part of me."

I tilted closer, kissing her slowly. She tasted like orange juice. She moaned against my mouth, putting her hands on my chest. Breaking the kiss, I smiled down at her.

"Champagne first," she said, "or I have a feeling you're going to make me forget all about that."

"You're right." I took the bottle from the freezer, popping open the cork and pouring it in glasses. It had chilled surprisingly fast. I was going to take the bottle with us. I had plans for the rest of it. "I'm sorry you didn't make it to the next round." I meant it sincerely. She'd put in a lot of effort.

"Honestly, it doesn't matter. It was only a means to an end for Sonya anyway. But for you, the win itself is important. And I'm so happy for you." She was genuine; I could see that in the way she looked at me. It slayed me.

I felt invincible when I was with her, and I wasn't talking about business. I felt as if I could take anything life threw in my way. It was incredible.

We clinked glasses. "Bottom's up," I said.

But we only took a few sips before I put down the glass, and she did the same. I was too hungry for her to drink champagne. I put a hand on the back of her head, kissing her even deeper than before. With my other hand, I grabbed the champagne bottle, then walked her backward.

"Where are we going?" she muttered.

"In front of the fire. That's where I want you tonight."

I wanted to claim her in a primal away. The rug in front of the fireplace was thick enough to be comfortable. I put the champagne on the floor.

"What are you going to do with that?" she asked.

"You'll see." She was wearing a skirt and a sweater, a change from her usual dresses. Those came off quicker, but this wasn't bad either. I took off her sweater, and then she shimmied out of her skirt and tights.

"I will never tire of looking at you. You're so damn sexy." Her curves were endless, and I wanted to worship them.

"Mmmm," she muttered, coming close to me. "You should wear these shirts more often."

"Why, because they're easier to take off?" I asked.

"That, too, but also because your muscles look so damn delicious in them." She took it off right away, then moved her mouth to my chest and continued in a downward trail, lowering herself to her knees. She undid the belt buckle of my jeans and yanked them down before doing the same with my underwear. I kicked them to one side. Fuck, I was so hungry for her.

"I like this. Already hard for me." She palmed my cock.

"I've been hard for you ever since we stepped through that door," I admitted.

She licked once from the base up to the tip. I dropped my head back, groaning, moving my hips back and forth. Then I straightened up, focusing on her again. She was like a vision on her knees in front of me. The fire lit up half her face and body. She lowered her mouth on my cock, and it was all I could do not to thrust even deeper.

Pace yourself, Cade. Pace yourself. But I was hanging on by a thread. Her mouth felt spectacular around me.

I took a step back, lowering myself to my knees as well. She pouted. I grabbed the bottle of champagne and instructed, "Lie down."

She did as I asked. I dripped champagne on her chest, then

everywhere I found a dimple from where I could drink, before licking it up. Then I spread her legs wide open and poured right over her pussy.

"Oh my God, Cade."

I put my mouth on her clit the next second, catching the champagne and sending her into a tailspin. The liquid was cold; my mouth was hot. Meredith bucked her hips, grasping at the carpet with both hands, kneading it between her fingers. I circled her clit with the tip of my tongue, feeling her entire body vibrate. I'd never tire of making her come, of bringing her so much pleasure that she completely lost herself.

"Oh my God, Cade. Cade." She chanted my name faster and faster. I didn't increase the rhythm of my tongue. I knew she desperately needed to come, but if I dragged it out just a bit longer, her release would be that much stronger. My erection was damn painful, trapped between the floor and my thigh, but right now it didn't matter. She was all that mattered.

Her entire body shook when she gave in to her orgasm. I interlaced my fingers with hers, keeping her hands tight in mine while she wriggled along the floor, and then I kissed up her body, over her belly and her breasts.

Her smile was sated, her eyes unfocused. She licked her lips, lifting her head, and I kissed her. It was more frantic than before. I touched her everywhere I could reach. My cock was now trapped between her belly and mine.

When her eyes focused again, I kissed one corner of her lips before pushing myself back on my knees. I drew my hand down her inner thighs, resting them on her ankles.

"Turn around," I said. She swallowed hard. "On all fours. I want to be inside you while we both watch the fire."

Her eyes glinted as she moved swiftly, turning around and pushing that gorgeous ass up to me. This right here was everything I needed to be happy: Meredith on all fours in front of my fireplace. I gripped my erection, and I didn't tease, not even one bit. I was too hungry for that. I needed her too much. I pushed inside, moving slowly, inch by inch, feeling her warmth, her perfectly pink and snug flesh. Being inside her without a condom was the best thing in the world.

"Oh my God, Cade," she exclaimed when I was inside her to the hilt.

I wasn't gentle or slow. I gripped her hair, threading my fingers through it as I moved my hips back and forth, determined to give her all of me. I didn't want to hold anything back. I thrust and thrust until I felt her grow tighter around me, and then I moved faster still.

"This is... Oh my God." She lowered her head, and I let go of her hair.

She put one hand under her forehead and brought the other to her clit. I felt her fingers at the base of my cock on every thrust. I came at the same time she did. One second she was tightening around me—the next I was shaking uncontrollably, calling her name. My knees turned so weak that I had to put one hand down to support myself. Then I turned us both onto one side. She was shaking too. I held her from behind, arm around her waist.

"Oh God, that was so intense," she murmured as we lay down on the carpet.

"I've got you, babe."

"Yeah you do," she murmured.

I kissed the side of her neck.

"Are you comfortable?" I asked.

"I'm perfectly happy."

Hell yes. I wanted her to feel like she belonged here. I had the burning desire to intertwine our lives. How had that happened? I liked this feeling of her being around the house, hearing her footsteps on the hardwood floors.

For my entire life, my instincts had told me that settling down was not an option. For the first time, I was doing my best to fight that instinct.

Chapter 25

Meredith

The celebratory banquet was in one of the smaller ballrooms of the Taj Boston. The committee really hadn't spared any expense for this competition.

I walked around, drinking in my surroundings. It was a relief not to be in the running anymore. I'd spent the last three weeks focusing on all our Christmas promos. In theory, I shouldn't care about the outcome of tonight, but I was keeping my fingers and toes crossed for Cade to win.

We decided to come here separately and to stay professional the whole evening. I wondered if I could stick to that, considering he was going to wear a tuxedo, but I was going to try my best.

I was a bit uneasy tonight. Same as Sonya. She emphasized how important the meeting with Alfred Danvers was, and I wasn't going to screw this up for either of us. I wanted her to sell the company. She seemed to want to retire, and although I really wanted to keep my job, it didn't appear as though that was possilbe.

We had a small table for Sonya's Blends with four seats, which was surprising considering Sonya and I had been the only ones who'd ever gone to these events. But this time, there was a place for Arthur as well as our VP of sales. Sonya had invited them for Alfred's benefit. Since it was Friday evening, most people were hoping the event would end quickly. I was among them.

"Oh, you're here. That's good," Sonya said, taking me by surprise as I was about to sit at our table.

"Hey, I didn't see you. I looked around for everyone."

"You and I are early, although Alfred is already here. Come on, I want to introduce you to him."

"Of course. Don't be nervous, Sonya."

"Honestly, I can't help it. Being here tonight makes it all the more real. If I don't manage to sell the company, I'm stuck running it for a few more years, and I'm honestly exhausted. I've been working for forty years, and it's time to retire."

I felt a rush of sympathy for her. Being a business owner was always heralded as one of the best things a person could do. But you could leave a job at any time, whereas you couldn't just up and leave your company.

"It's going to work out. I'm sure of it," I encouraged.

"Alfred, I want to introduce you to Meredith," she said when we approached another round table. There was only one person there for now, even though there were places for six. "This is Meredith, my VP of marketing."

"How do you do?" I said as we shook hands.

He smiled. "It's great to meet you. Sonya told me you worked on the presentation she pitched to me."

"I did. "

"I'm going to leave the two of you to get to know each other a bit and get myself a cocktail," Sonya said.

I'd never seen Sonya so nervous. There were servers circulating with trays of champagne, so clearly she just needed an excuse to get away. I was determined not to ruin this for her.

"So, what do you think?" I asked as soon as she was gone. "Think our customers would be a good fit for your portfolio?"

"Yes, it would be a very promising start in niches I haven't bothered with until now."

"I'm sure your customers will appreciate our special products. And vice versa—our customers will embrace the mainstream products in your portfolio as well. I already have a few ideas of how we can marry the two." I wanted to show him that I was dedicated to my job and that I'd already put thought into this.

"Meredith, right?"

"Yes," I said. Something in his eyes chilled me to the bone.

"Look, I appreciate your enthusiasm, but I'll be honest. If this merger goes ahead, I will bring my own VP of marketing, and I would prefer if you're not part of the team going forward."

I steeled myself, rolling back my shoulders. "May I ask why?"

"I'm sure Sonya already spoke to you about this."

"I would like to hear it from you." I didn't want to provoke him. I just wanted him to look me in the eye and tell me to my face that he wanted to let me go just because I was in a relationship he didn't like.

"I don't like Cade Whitley. I've dealt with him in the past, and I'm no fan of his. Frankly, the fact that you're in a relationship with him is worrying."

"I'd never share trade secrets or company information with him."

"I have a very hard time believing that. I wouldn't feel good knowing that someone in my company is so close to the enemy."

"The enemy?" I asked. It was on the tip of my tongue to tell him that was a little dramatic, but I didn't want to lose my job right now, even though I clearly didn't have a future if the acquisition went ahead. I was fighting to keep my composure. "I'm sorry you feel this way." Close-minded was another word for it. "You know, there's no legal framework for firing someone because they're in a relationship with someone working in the same industry. At most, you can ask someone to disclose that information, though even that isn't legal."

He waved his hand. "I don't care about the legalities. I'm just telling you the way I prefer to do things."

"Right. Well, I see Sonya coming back with her drink. Let's not ruin her evening," I said. "She has enough at stake right now and doesn't need to know that you've practically dismissed me."

He narrowed his eyes and nodded. "I respect you for that. I was sure you were going to throw a fit the second she returned."

"Not my style. Not at all."

Sonya took one look at me, and her expression turned stony. I was sure she could tell exactly what had happened.

“Everything all right?” she asked.

I nodded. “Yes. I’m going to get some air.”

What I needed was to step away from Alfred Danvers. But I was here tonight to keep my fingers crossed for Cade. I wanted him to win—I couldn’t wait to see Jeannie and Abe’s joy when he succeeded.

Cade

TONIGHT WAS MY NIGHT. I FELT IT IN MY BONES. I KNEW we were going to win. Not just because we'd put a lot of hard work behind this—everyone else had too—but I trusted our products. I knew our quality, and I knew the committee would see it. Tonight, I was finally going to clean up the company's name.

As soon as I entered the ballroom, I looked around, wanting to catch Meredith’s eyes. I was all on board with her plan. We didn't have to parade our relationship, but I wanted to see her. Ideally, I wanted her up there onstage with me when I received my award.

I tried to find her, but the room was full to the brim. It was impossible to distinguish one guest from the other. There was a table chart next to the entrance, but that was it. I found my table easily enough. Sonya's Blends was right across the room. I instinctively looked over there, but Meredith wasn't at the table. Maybe she hadn't arrived yet. Sonya was chatting with Alfred. He was definitely one of my least favorite people. I didn't like his business practices. I was surprised Sonya wanted to sell to him at all. Then again, it was none of my business.

I went to our table, even though the rest of the team hadn't arrived yet. There were three other seats. I took out my phone, intending to text Meredith, when someone walked up to me. I glanced up from my phone, pocketing it.

"Sonya," I said.

“Cade.”

"To what do I owe the pleasure?"

"Look, I've handled all of this badly. I'm sorry about that."

"No need to apologize. Business is business. You didn't like my approach, and it's your prerogative to look for another buyer. One you're comfortable with."

She flashed me a smile that seemed forced. "Yes. Well, I'll be honest. I would rather you buy me out, but if the price isn’t up your alley, what can I do? Alfred is a bit..."

A waiter came to us with a tray of champagne glasses. I grabbed one and took a sip. She played with the pendant at her neck, which was a huge gold thing. Something I'd only ever seen my grandmother wear.

She continued, "I don't like him very much, but I do like the money he's offering."

I respected that. "Is Meredith here already?"

"Yes. She was actually chatting with Alfred before I went back over to them. I think she went to clear her head. She's upset."

I squared my shoulders, putting down the glass of champagne. "Why?"

Sonya pressed her lips together. "Alfred told me he made it clear that once he takes over, he won't keep her around. He's not happy that she's in a relationship with you."

"What the fuck? That's none of his business." Why hadn't Meredith told me that?

"I don't like how he's handled the whole situation either."

Fuck this. I wasn't going to allow it to happen. Meredith worked hard. She deserved her job. Hell, she deserved far more than that. She wasn't going to lose it just because Alfred didn't like me. That wasn't how business was conducted. I was even more disappointed in Alfred than before.

Sonya started to turn away. "Anyway, I'll leave you alone now. I'm rooting for you, by the way. I do like your products and everything you've done for the company over the past years."

"Do you know where Meredith went?"

"No, I honestly don't know. I'll keep my fingers crossed for you," Sonya said before leaving.

This was utter horseshit. My previous good mood had completely evaporated.

I took my phone from my pocket again, calling Meredith once, twice, three times. She didn't answer.

Where is she?

I had no idea how to find her, but I knew exactly what to do next. I was going to talk to Alfred.

There were still a few minutes until the winner would be announced. I caught up with him at the bar. He ordered a gin and tonic. I took another glass of champagne, since I'd left mine at the table.

"Alfred," I said curtly.

He turned around, raising his eyebrows. "Already drinking champagne?"

I cocked a brow. The waiters were circulating with champagne. Everyone was drinking it.

"You're so sure you'll win?" he continued. "The rest of us are going to give you a good run for your money. You're not the hot shit you think you are."

I couldn't believe Alfred was still holding a grudge because my company had a higher market share than his. Usually I'd give him a cutting reply, but tonight my main priority was Meredith. I didn't want to do anything that could affect her situation even more.

"Listen, I'll cut right to the chase. I heard you've got a problem with Sonya's employee, Meredith?"

He snorted. "Good God, that place is very unprofessional. She already came gossiping to you?"

"I spoke to Sonya, actually."

He shook his head. "She's terribly defensive of that girl."

"That's because Meredith is great at her job, and I don't see why her personal life should get in the way of her continuing to do that job."

"I'm not keen on keeping someone close who's sleeping with the enemy, so to speak."

"The enemy? That's dramatic. There's no reason Meredith should lose her job for something that's personal and doesn't affect her work. Our relationship has nothing to do with her performance."

He snorted. "That's just like you, Whitley. You like to keep it in the industry, huh? First Esther, and now this poor woman."

I stared at him. "How do you know Esther?"

"Word gets around. She was the hottest woman at the Coffee Formation event. I can understand Esther, but Meredith? What did you do? Hook up with the poor woman, hoping to get insight into the competition?"

Unbelievable. His insinuation was way off track. I didn't use people to get my way. Maybe that was how he operated, but not me.

"Meredith is a brilliant woman and a damn good person. I won't allow you any disrespect toward her or me."

He scoffed. "Yeah, yeah. Get off your high horse. You're probably not even serious about her."

I didn't think I could dislike this Alfred guy even more. I'd wasted enough time with him. I had to find Meredith.

Chapter 26

Cade

Unfortunately, I didn't get the chance to find my woman because Harley, the committee head, walked up onstage and spoke into the microphone. "Welcome, everyone. Please take a seat at your respective tables. We're going to announce the winners soon."

I looked at my table and noticed that half my team was already here. Meredith was still not at her table. I called her again as I walked to my seat, but she didn't pick up. Damn it, I wanted to talk to her. She needed to know I would fix this, that I'd never let anything happen to her.

As I sat down, John addressed me. "Sorry we're late, boss. There was a long line at drop-off, and the cab refused to let us get out until we reached the entrance."

Harley walked onstage again.

"Okay, I think everyone's here. We had a few mishaps at the drop-off line. We're sorry for that. We didn't account for everyone arriving at the same time. I'm happy we've all gathered here together. It's been a couple of interesting months. My colleagues and I had a hard time evaluating all your product lines. That's a compliment to all of you for having such quality blends. Even those of you tonight who aren't finalists should be proud of your products."

I personally considered it cruel to invite companies that were already disqualified, but it worked for me. It meant I could share tonight with Meredith. I was getting impatient; I wanted Harley to announce the winner and be done with it.

I couldn't believe it. I'd looked forward to this evening ever since the competition was announced, but now I was ready for it to be over.

I finally caught sight of Meredith as she sat down next to Sonya. She was so far across the room that I couldn't see her properly, but I managed to catch her attention. I held up my phone. She shook her head. I knew she was trying to be professional, and I was tempting her. I was going to catch up with her as soon as possible. But simply seeing her helped my mood. My pulse slowed. I could finally focus on the presenter.

"All right. As you know, we have only one award, but we'll do the honorable mentions first. Now I'll get to it right away. I've kept you all in suspense for long enough." Yes, she fucking had. "For honorable mentions, we have the following..."

She called the names of the other businesses and competitors. I was so fucking happy that Alfred's company hadn't even made that. He was among the finalists, so in theory, he could still win. But I knew in my gut, he wouldn't. His products weren't top-notch. I was honestly surprised he'd made it this far in the competition. I kept my eyes locked on the stage.

We had to win. For my grandparents and for my family's legacy.

"And the winner is... Whitley Industries with The Boston Coffee Expert. A round of applause, please. I would like to welcome Cade Whitley to the stage to say a couple words."

Fuck yes. I looked around at my team, congratulating them.

"Well done, everyone." I stood up. "Well done." They all clapped, smiling.

I didn't register anyone else in the room. Except Meredith. I looked straight at her as I walked up to the stage. The presenter gave me a gold plaque. I didn't have time to read what was on it. I lowered it, grasping it tightly in my left hand. I spoke into the microphone.

"Thank you, everyone. This is a great honor. I'll be honest, I was looking forward to stepping up on this stage ever since the competition started." Several people in the audience laughed, but I heard some groans too. "As some of you might know, The Boston Coffee Expert had a couple of rough years, but since I took over, I made it my life's ambition to restore the quality to what it was during my grandfather's time. I'm dedicating this prize to him and my grandmother."

I wished they were here, but I'd instructed Rupert, my VP of sales, to film this so I could send it to them.

I looked at our table, nodding and holding out the plaque toward my team. "Thanks to everyone on my team. They're all dedicated hard workers and stuck with me every inch of the way. Thank you."

I nodded at the presenter, stepping down from the stage and walking toward my table.

“Congratulations, Cade. I already sent the video to your grandparents,” Rupert said.

“Thank you.” I shook hands with everyone. They'd put a lot of effort into the competition. We'd had a discouraging few months, what with the mishap in Jacksonville. Rupert himself had joined me there. He'd found the subcontractor who ended up saving our asses. I was proud of my team.

My phone rang a few seconds later. My grandmother was calling. I answered right away.

"Cade, we are so proud of you. Even if you didn't win, we would still be proud of everything you've done,” she said.

“And the man you've become,” Grandfather added. “Congratulations, boy.”

Both their voices were uneven. My throat closed up, hearing this high praise from the two people who meant so much to me.

"Thank you both. I did it for you, for us." As I put the plaque on the table, I searched for Meredith across the room. I wanted her here with me to share the celebration. I was damn proud to be celebrating with my grandparents and my team, but something was missing.

Meredith was missing.

Meredith

I was clapping so hard that my palms were itching.

"I knew he'd win," Sonya said.

"I had the feeling too." I nodded in full agreement. I hadn't hoped he would win just because the product deserved it, but also because I knew how much it meant to him. How I wished I could be closer to celebrate with him.

"I was hoping that ass wouldn't win," Alfred said behind us.

Sonya sighed. I was taking my cues from her, and it seemed even she was unhappy having to schmooze with him. Were we supposed to keep this up the whole evening? I was already exhausted from my previous interaction with him. Why did he come over to our table again anyway if all he could do was be negative?

"I'm going to have a word with the committee afterward. It's unacceptable that I didn't even get an honorable mention," Alfred said.

What a sore loser!

"I'm going to get another cocktail," Sonya said, standing up from her chair. "Anyone else want something?"

She couldn't keep ghosting me whenever Alfred approached.

Arthur and our VP of sales went with her, once again leaving me with him.

To my dismay, Alfred sat down in the chair Sonya vacated. I put on my poker face. I only had to keep the charade up for a bit longer.

"Meredith, how do you feel about not even making it to the last stage?"

Is that a trick question? "Disappointed, of course. But the caliber of participants was very high."

"You're a diplomat. Might make a good asset on my team after all."

"Oh?" I asked in surprise. For some reason, I'd warmed to the idea of looking for a new place to work, just because Alfred seemed like an asshole.

"Whitley's a dog. He's not serious about you."

I blinked, sitting up straighter. I felt as if he'd slapped me.

"You spoke with Cade?"

"Yes, he cornered me at the bar, and one thing led to another."

Cade would never tell him our relationship wasn't serious. He just wouldn't.

"Anyway, the guy is an ass. He probably just used you to get information on Sonya."

I was so sick of Alfred. I knew Cade, and this couldn't be further from the truth. His company could buy Sonya's tenfold. He didn't care about the strategies of a minor competitor.

"If you'll excuse me, I need to go to the restroom." I took my bag, hurrying out of the room. I suddenly felt like I couldn't get any air. I couldn't be around Alfred any longer. He was completely toxic.

And he was wrong. Maybe he hadn't made up talking to Cade, but just misunderstood. No, I was sure Alfred misconstrued it all and twisted the conversation to his benefit.

Then again... Cade and I had never spoken about where this

relationship was going. Hell, we weren't even referring to it as a relationship.

I took in a deep breath when I stepped into the dark corridor, needing to calm down a bit. There was too much commotion in the ballroom. I felt like I couldn't even hear my own thoughts.

Cade cares about you, Meredith. He said you're important to him. That you're part of him. That's all you need to know.

Still, caring about someone didn't mean you were ready for a relationship, or that you wanted to commit.

Holy shit. I was all jittery.

Come on, Meredith. This isn't the time to have a meltdown. Put your big girl panties on.

But I couldn't do it. I couldn't give myself a pep talk and walk back inside. I needed to get out of here.

I took my phone out of my purse, forcing myself to take deep breaths. As I shot Sonya a message, I also realized I had about six missed calls from Cade.

Meredith: Not feeling well. Do you mind if I take off?

Sonya: No, you go. I might do the same thing. I can't seem to get rid of Alfred.

Well, good luck selling him the company. Even she couldn't stand him.

My mind was racing. God! Was Cade not ready for a relationship? He'd told me repeatedly that he hadn't had anything like this with anyone before. I took it as a romantic sign, but what if what he actually meant was that he wasn't ready for more?

I wanted to be here for Cade and celebrate with him. And yet I knew the second I was face-to-face with him, I'd question him about the conversation with Alfred. I didn't want to ruin this evening for him. We could talk another time. But I couldn't stay here.

Since everyone was still in the ballroom, there was no line at the coatroom. I got mine right away and tightened it around my middle, then put on my beanie as well before I stepped outside.

The cold whipped my face as I looked for a car. I finally went to the doorman and asked, "Where are all the cabs?" There had been a million of them dropping off guests when I arrived.

"I'll call one for you, miss. They're one block down there." He pointed to the left.

"Thank you." No way in hell was I walking that distance. I'd freeze. I closed my eyes because the wind made them watery.

It already smelled like winter and Christmas—which was in two days. The first snow wasn't too far away. I was always right about that.

I took in another deep breath. Christmas and winter were usually my happy places. They gave me good vibes, and I needed all the good vibes I could get right now.

Chapter 27

Cade

I looked for Meredith everywhere, but as the event ended, I still couldn't find her. I'd kept an eye on Sonya's table, but Meredith had left a while ago and hadn't returned.

"I'll take you all out to dinner next week," I promised my team. I didn't schedule anything for the evening because I didn't want to jinx the odds. They deserved the best for all the effort they put in this, but tonight I wanted to celebrate with my family, and with Meredith.

"Give your grandparents all our best," Rupert said.

"I will."

Instead of heading to the exit, though, I went to Sonya. She put her bag on her shoulder, smiling at me.

"Cade, congratulations. I'm so happy for you. Don't tell Alfred that."

"Don't worry, he and I are done talking. Where is Meredith?"

"She left a while ago. Alfred cornered us again. I have to put up with him because I still want his money, but Meredith doesn't, so I told her she could go if she wanted to."

"She left?" I was shell-shocked. I wanted her next to me, to share this moment with her.

"Yes, a while ago. I thought she might have told you."

I'd checked and didn't have any messages from her.

"Anyway, congratulations again, Cade. I need to go. Alfred wants us to continue chatting."

I wasn't paying attention to Sonya anymore; I was fixated on what had happened to Meredith. She wouldn't have left without notifying me.

"Thank you," I said, stepping away. I took out my phone and called her a couple times, but she didn't answer. I wasn't going to wait around to find out what happened to her.

Outside the building, it was madness trying to get an Uber or a cab. Everyone else was trying to do the same. I walked a couple blocks before I could finally find a car. I gave the driver Meredith's address.

I didn't try calling her again on the way; in my experience, when people didn't answer their phone twice, they were unlikely to do so if you persisted. I practically jumped out of the car when I reached Meredith's building and went to the intercom, pressing it a couple times. There was no answer. *Where is she?*

I was worrying in earnest now. Maybe she was sick?

I took out my phone, intending to call her this time despite my previous conviction that it was of no use. I was surprised to see a message from her.

Meredith: Hey, sorry I left without telling you. Alfred told me about the conversation you had with him, and I didn't want to overshadow your win with any talk about that.

I stared at the phone. *Talk about what? Overshadow what?* I replied immediately.

Cade: Where are you? I'm at your place.

Meredith: I came to my parents' for the evening. Our conversation can happen another day. I don't want to spoil anyone's day.

Cade: You wouldn't spoil anything. What do we need to talk about?

Meredith: Alfred implied that you're not serious about us.

The bubbles on the screen indicated she was still typing, but I replied right away.

Cade: I absolutely didn't. HE implied that.

Meredith: I thought that might be the case... but you and I never defined our relationship, did we?

Meredith: And SEE? Here I go, overshadowing your win.

I cut in before she could jump to any further conclusions.

Cade: I'm coming to your parents' house.

Meredith: Please don't. Just enjoy this, okay? I know for a fact that your grandparents are waiting for you at the house to celebrate. Don't make them wait much longer. We'll talk tomorrow. I mean it.

This woman was amazing. She was probably reeling from the shit Alfred spewed, but she cared about my grandparents more.

I had two choices: I could go up to her parents' home right now, or I could go to my grandparents. But if I'd learned anything about Meredith since reconnecting with her, it was that she didn't say things she didn't mean. If she wanted us to talk tomorrow, it meant she couldn't do it today. It didn't mean she wanted me to go running after her. She was a strong woman. My instincts told me to go to her parents' house, but I wanted to do what was right for her, not for me.

"Welcome, brother," Spencer said half an hour later, opening the door to my grandparents' house.

"What are you doing here?"

"We were all on standby, waiting to see if you'd win, and then Grandmother asked us all to come over."

"Wait, who else is here?"

"Everyone."

We went straight to the living room. He was right. The whole gang was here, including my half brothers. Good. This was a moment of victory for all of us.

My grandmother came to me first. "Oh, our darling boy, congratulations." She hugged me tightly, and I hugged her right back.

Grandfather, stoic as usual, shook my hand.

"I can't believe you organized this," I said.

"I was certain you were going to win," Grandmother said. "Honestly, if you didn't, I was thinking you could use some cheering up anyway. I baked a cake, and we've got plenty of champagne."

"She's even allowing me to drink for the occasion. Go figure," Grandfather said.

"But where's Meredith? I thought she'd come with you," Grandmother asked.

"She couldn't."

She narrowed her eyes. "I'm going to bring the cake."

"Congrats, dude." Maddox shook my hand. "Maybe you'll get back in a winning streak at tennis too."

"No. I was quite enjoying beating you two," Leo added.

"Congrats for winning," Nick said.

Colton came to me next and clapped my shoulder.

"You honor us with your presence," I mocked him. "I didn't think anything could get you out of the lab."

"Some things are worth coming out for," he said.

Jake and Natalie congratulated me next.

Gabe was last. "This is a fantastic evening, brother. I'm very glad for you. Word of warning: Grandmother was all about Meredith tonight. She might circle back to why she's not here."

"I'm not expecting anything less."

It felt good to be here surrounded by my family. Making them proud was everything I'd wanted, but Meredith was still missing. It had been a mistake not to go talk to her tonight. She might not need it, but I did.

"Is anyone helping Grandmother?" I asked no one in particular. Since everyone was in the living room, the answer was no, so I headed to the kitchen. Spencer came with me.

"Grandmother, do you need any help?" I asked once inside. She was putting frosting on the cake.

"No. I know what I'm doing. I didn't want to put the frosting on before. I don't like the taste of it after it's been in the fridge for too long. But since you're here..."

Spencer cleared his throat. I barely bit down the urge to do the same. She was using her *stern* voice.

"Why don't you tell me where Meredith is? She was very excited about tonight. I told her about my plan, and she assured me she was going to be here."

"There's been a misunderstanding," I said.

Grandmother put down the frosting and straightened up, turning to look at me. She put her hand on her hip.

Spencer groaned. "What happened?" he asked.

"A competitor told her I might not be serious about her."

"What the fuck?" he exclaimed. "Sorry, Grandmother."

She didn't even blink. "I taught you better than that, young man."

"As I said, it was a misunderstanding. Honestly, it's ridiculous."

"Not if she believes it," Grandmother said. Her voice chilled me because she didn't sound annoyed anymore; she sounded concerned. "If it's all a misunderstanding, why isn't she here?"

Spencer shook his head. "Yeah, dude. I'm sorry to say you might have won this prize, and you're a smart-as-a-weapon businessman, but you don't act very smart when it comes to Meredith. Remember the last time we had a conversation about this in this kitchen?"

"Spencer," I warned.

"I'm just saying."

Grandmother looked at my brother. "Spencer, darling, I love you, but you're not helping. Do you mind taking the cake out? I want to have a few words alone with Cade."

"Yeah, I'm out of here," Spencer said, immediately grabbing the cake and heading to the living room.

My grandfather came in at that moment. "Jeannie, leave the man alone. He's had a big win."

"So?" Grandmother asked.

I almost laughed; she sounded unimpressed.

"You can do this later," he continued. "Don't spoil his evening."

"Let her talk, Grandfather."

To my astonishment, Grandmother shook her head, pursing her lips. "No, he's right. Let's all go to the living room. This can wait." She didn't sound as if it could wait, but she walked toward the living room faster than I thought she was capable of.

Grandfather cleared his throat. "I couldn't help but overhear your conversation."

I wasn't surprised about that. Neither of us had kept our voices down. "Did everyone hear?"

"No, they were in the living room, too far off. But I was coming to get all of you. Listen, you know I'm not a man of many words. Your grandmother usually does all the talking."

"I know. That's how you are."

"Yes, but sometimes I think that if your father had had another example growing up, he might have turned out differently."

I stared at him. "I really doubt that."

"He never expressed his emotions, and I know he got that from me. So, I only have one bit of advice to give you: make sure you do. Does Meredith know she's important to you?"

"Of course." And yet, as I said the words, I realized Grandfather was right. She didn't. I'd never told her I loved her.

Chapter 28

Meredith

"Honey, are you sure you don't want to stay any longer?" Mom asked as she walked me out of the house.

"No, it's getting late."

"But it's Saturday tomorrow," Everly protested. "And Christmas Eve."

I texted her after I left the event. When she told me she was at my parents', I came straight over, and I spent the evening with the three people who meant the world to me. It was time to go home, though. I hadn't told them I was most likely out of a job—I didn't want to worry them when nothing was certain—but I knew if I stayed longer, I was likely to spill the beans.

My sister dashed to the door as well. I kissed her cheek and then also patted her belly. I was always hoping to feel a kick, but so far, no such luck. Mom took a step back, and my sister whispered in my ear, "There's something you're not telling us."

I smiled, just shaking my head. I knew she'd catch on eventually. Good thing I was leaving.

Traffic was light, so I arrived home in no time. After removing my coat and shoes, I headed to my bedroom, taking off my clothes. I took a long shower, rewinding the day in my mind. After stepping out, I cleansed my face of makeup before applying night cream.

Then I slipped into my bed, grabbing my phone. As I suspected, my sister had messaged me.

Everly: What happened?

I typed back quickly so she wouldn't have a chance to worry. I hadn't told her or my parents anything about Cade either.

Meredith: Nothing! Don't worry. Just tired.

That wasn't a lie. I *was* tired. But even so, instead of going to sleep, I opened the website of my favorite ornaments shop. They had next-day delivery. I'd braced myself for Everly to insist, but she didn't. Knowing her, she was probably already asleep. Poor thing. She'd napped at my parents' too.

Some people were addicted to buying shoes. I was addicted to buying Christmas ornaments. I scoured the internet for a couple hours and was about to open yet another site when a message lit up the screen.

I bunched the covers to my chest when I saw a message from Cade.

Cade: Are you still up, beautiful?

I licked my lips, sitting up straighter in bed. My fingers tingled with excitement.

Meredith: Yes. Splurging my net worth on Christmas ornaments.

I swallowed hard.

Cade: I have a better idea. Meet me at Harvard Square at 10:00 tomorrow and I can indulge your addiction all you want.

My heart felt skittish, like it was jumping around in my chest.

Meredith: Game on.

I texted and deleted another reply before deciding on not sending anything else. We'd talk tomorrow. I was determined to keep things light. I wished I hadn't told him all about the conversation with Alfred because I was certain it had been on his mind this evening. But I couldn't come up with an excuse about why I left. I didn't want to lie.

I wished I could've spent the night with Cade's family at Jeannie's and Abe's, but I thought I did the right thing. I didn't want to be a Debbie Downer, and I was afraid I might've done that based on the way I was feeling earlier this evening. After I spoke with Cade, I'd have to tell Jeannie I was sorry for not showing up. I knew she was excited about celebrating Cade's win and wanted me to be there.

The next morning, I was out the door super early. I was sure he'd sent the wrong time—I knew for a fact that they opened at eleven o'clock because I'd been there for the last couple years almost religiously—but I was too anxious to see him to care.

When I arrived, I let out a sigh. This was where I first saw Cade. If I closed my eyes, I could still see my booth. A shiver went through me as I remembered how my entire body tightened up when I laid eyes on him the first time. God, I'd been so on edge.

I was even more on edge now when I saw him walking toward me just as I was getting out of my Uber. The nearest booth was open. He was smiling widely, hands in his pockets. I quickly glanced around. All the booths were already open, and there was no one here except Cade and me. I'd forgotten my beanie, so my ears were freezing. The air didn't smell like mulled wine yet like it usually did.

"I feel like something's happening, but I don't know what," I explained, looking around again. "How is this even open?"

The nearest sales associate cleared her throat. "This gentleman here made a very convincing case for us all to open earlier—something about impressing his girlfriend. I was skeptical, but when he told me how much he cares about her, I fell hook, line, and sinker."

"And me," the elderly woman in the booth next to us added. She sold hand-knitted scarves and beanies. I knew that because I bought one scarf from her every year.

I looked back at Cade. "How did you manage that?"

"I told her this is one of your favorite Christmas markets, and it's also the place where we first met. I thought it was appropriate to bring you here to tell you everything I have on my mind."

I swallowed hard, clutching my purse to my chest. "When did you do this?"

"Last evening. I thought, 'What would make Meredith happiest?' A Christmas shopping spree without anyone crowding you. But first, Meredith, we need to set something straight."

"Oh, here it goes," someone murmured.

"I think everyone's listening," I whispered.

"Yeah, I haven't thought this through," Cade said, looking stern. "The one benefit of crowds is that the sound gets lost. Come on, let's step away."

We went farther away from the booths, under a huge tree.

"Meredith, last evening was a complete blur. I wanted you by my side the whole time. I didn't tell Alfred anything he implied to you. You have to believe me."

"I do. Deep down, I didn't believe it, but..."

He took my hands in his, tilting toward me until our foreheads were almost touching. "I love you, woman. I realize I haven't told you that before, but I plan to tell you every single day of my life. How can you doubt that?" He put his hands on my face. Immediately, I realized he was trying to warm up my ears with his thumbs. He remembered they always froze!

"And I love you, Cade. But we never spoke about what this is between us, or if we're ready to commit."

"I know I told you I've never done commitment in my life, but it's what I want with you. You are all I want for the rest of my life. I don't even remember who I was before you." He tilted even closer, and now our foreheads were touching in earnest.

I melted against him. I needed his heat, and all his beautiful words.

"You're cold," he said.

"Just a bit."

In a flash, he unbuttoned his jacket and opened it so I could make even more contact directly with his body.

"Aren't you cold?" I asked.

"No. Don't doubt us again, Meredith."

"I'm sorry I did, but I was already on edge because of everything with Alfred, and when he said that, I just... I don't know. I'm sorry I left. I know it was an important evening for you, and you wanted us to celebrate it together."

He touched my jaw with his thumb, before touching my ear again. "You really are freezing."

"Just a bit," I admitted.

"We have the rest of our lives to celebrate together, babe. I love you so much."

“I was so happy for you, so proud. I wanted to jump on that stage and then jump you." I chuckle. "Actually, no, I had a more elaborate plan in mind. I wanted to lure you somewhere quiet and jump you."

He grinned. "You can do that right now. I'm all yours to lure and jump and do whatever else you have in mind."

"I love you so much," I murmured.

"And I love you, too. I know this started out with a bang, and I can't promise that things will always be smooth sailing, but you and I, we’re a team, no matter what. Alfred was way off track."

"You don't need to explain. I understand. So, what do you want to do now?"

He wiggled his eyebrows. "Your choice."

"Well, since you so romantically arranged for them to open earlier for me, why don't we make a round?"

"That's not what I thought you were about to say."

I laughed softly. "But you've gone to all this trouble. Besides, this is hands down your most romantic gesture ever."

"I'm always happy to make you happy, Meredith,” he said as he took my hand, leading me back to the booths. "All right, you've got twenty minutes until the rest of the customers arrive. Go wild."

When I told him this was the most romantic thing someone had done for me, I wasn't joking. I knew some dreamed about going to Bergdorf Goodman or another department store after closing time to have the place to themselves. All I wanted was the Christmas market. I already knew most of the booths, of course, but there were some new ones as well.

I bought garlands for my mom because I knew how much she wanted them, as well as treats for my sister. But I was antsy. Even though I loved being here, I wanted to look at everything at my own pace. I also wanted to be around Cade. I was yearning for it.

Once I bought my obligatory scarf and beanie, I turned to him and said, "I'm ready to go now."

He smiled lazily. "You only saw about half the booths."

"I know, but it's... Oh, I still have fifteen minutes. I did all of my shopping in five. Will you look at that?" I bounced up and down on my toes. "I guess I'm anxious to be alone with you."

"I thought you'd never say that. That's all I want."

"Okay, then let's go."

"Are you sure? Because I'm willing to wait."

"I thought you just said you were hoping I'd say I wanted us to leave?"

"Just trying to do the right thing."

"I love it when you try." I could torment him for a while longer, but the truth was, I longed for us to be alone.

He kissed my forehead. "Come on. Let's go."

"Fine."

"Don't those two look cute?" the sales associate from the scarf booth said, making me giggle.

We went outside the market, and I glanced up and down the street. "Should we Uber, or did you come with your car?"

"No, I Ubered here," he said and instantly pulled his phone out, tapping the screen.

A few minutes later, we were in the car, speeding toward my home. It was the closest of the two. He interlaced our fingers together, squeezing mine lightly.

I felt so blessed to have him in my life. And I was going to do all I could to keep him there... forever.

Chapter 29

Meredith

As soon as we got out of the car, we practically ran inside the building. I felt his breath at the back of my neck as I unlocked my door.

I was shaking slightly. The second we were inside, we got rid of our jackets, and then Cade kissed me. I loved feeling his mouth on me. I lit up everywhere his lips touched. He trailed his mouth from the corner of my lips, down my jawline and my neck, and continued down my body, stopping at the hem of my dress. I smiled when I felt him grin against my skin.

Oh sweet Lord. I'd forgotten to get rid of the tights. I might love the cozy months, but I had to admit, getting naked for sexy time always felt like a job. He lifted my dress, cinching it around my waist, and then pulled it over my head.

I was wearing a simple cotton bra, but judging by the hungry look on his face when he straightened up, staring down at my breasts, he didn't care one bit. I felt so desirable right now, and I loved it. I loved him. I yanked my tights down.

"Leave your underwear on," he commanded in that hot voice that turned me on completely. "I'll take care of those."

"Yes, sir," I murmured, stepping out of my tights.

I took off his shirt quickly, touching his chest with my fingertips and trailing my mouth down in a straight line until my jaw brushed his belt buckle. I pulled back a bit, taking it off and then making quick work of his underwear and jeans. His cock was already semihard. I looked up at him, straight into his eyes, then opened my mouth and took him in all the way, putting my hand on the base. I felt him go hard in my mouth, and it was such a turn-on. I was desperate for him.

"Meredith." His voice was a deep, delicious groan.

I stared at him as I moved my head up and down.

"Let's move onto the bed," he said. "That way I can touch you all you want and need. I'm hungry for you, babe."

He took my hand in his, helping me to my feet. My entire body was on edge as I led him to the bedroom. I walked in front of him, swaying my hips, feeling completely confident. I was naked in front of the man I loved.

But it had always been this way between us. I never felt insecure around Cade, because he always wanted me and proved it over and over again. I was a confident woman, but there had been times in the past when I didn't feel comfortable naked. With Cade, it was different from the start. It was like he worshipped my body.

God, I loved him.

When we reached the bedroom, I stopped next to the bed. I felt Cade right behind me. He lowered my panties, kissing a trail down my right ass cheek before coming back up.

"Lie down on one side," he said in my ear.

Biting the inside of my cheek, I put one knee on the bed before lowering myself onto my right side. He mirrored my position, only upside down.

My mouth was level with his erection. I licked my lips, gasping when his fingers brushed my clit. I instantly realized I was in trouble. How could I focus on his pleasure when I was coming unraveled? I palmed his cock, licking the tip, squeezing my eyes shut when he put his mouth on my clit. This feeling was surreal.

I felt so impossibly turned on. He alternated movements, applying pressure with his fingers on my clit and licking it again. I jerked my hips forward, knowing I wouldn't last long. Then he parted my legs even wider, sliding two fingers inside me at the same time as he circled my clit with his tongue.

I was done for. I pulled my hand back as my entire body jerked. My legs and my thighs cramped, and I opened my legs wide, falling onto my back on the bed.

"Fuck, you're so beautiful, Meredith. So damn beautiful." He turned around on the bed until his mouth was level with my chest, then kissed down my sternum and under my left breast, teasing me as he circled around the nipple. My pussy pulsed as if he were still touching me there.

When he clamped his mouth around my nipple and pressed two fingers against my clit, I nearly came again.

My hips lifted off the bed. "Oh my God."

"I love seeing you like this, knowing I'm the only one who can bring you to this state. You're the only one for me," he whispered while I was lost in all the sensations he ignited inside me.

I slowly regained my sense of space and time as I came down from the high of the orgasm. His gaze was on me. I felt it reach me somewhere deep inside.

He was mine, and I was his.

Cade looked down, positioning his cock at my entrance. I cursed when I felt the tip. *Oh heavens!* If just the tip was causing this reaction in me, how was I going to take him all in? I couldn't understand how he always brought me to this state of hypersensitivity where every touch felt like it was too much and simultaneously exactly what I needed.

He pushed in. I closed my eyes, internalizing the pleasure. My hearing was sharper, and I felt his intake of breath and the vibration of his body against mine. I knew a groan was building deep within him. When he was buried inside me to the hilt, he rewarded me with that groan. It was guttural, loud, and filled me with pride.

I parted my legs even wider, pulling my knees up higher. I didn't have any leverage like this, but I could take him in even deeper. I couldn't get enough of his mouth exploring mine, of feeling every delicious inch of him inside me, thrusting hard.

A vibration started deep in my body, and my muscles tightened.

"Cade, I can't any more."

"Come for me, babe. I want to hear it. I want to feel you."

His words brought me even closer to the edge. I felt him push himself off me for a few seconds, and I was about to protest because I liked the skin-on-skin contact.

But then I felt his fingers on my clit, and I was lost to the world. My vision faded, and I arched my back off the bed. I wasn't in control of my body or my reactions. I cried out his name, thrashing around, shimmying my hips on the bed.

I felt his orgasm rise before it gripped him. His entire body clenched before his release. I blinked my eyes open, watching him. It was such a sexy sight. His muscles and veins were prominent as he contorted from the effort. I only caught a glimpse of him before he lowered his mouth to my neck and buried it there while he thrust harder and harder, then stilled inside me completely.

That was all I wanted. For us to be as one. I needed it.

Cade turned onto one side, kissing my forehead and playing with my hair. I smiled up at him, completely blissful. I couldn't believe how much I'd given myself to this man. I didn't even think I had it in me. For the longest time, love was something that seemed out of reach for me. Something that happened to my parents and sister but couldn't happen to me.

"Your smile is gorgeous," he said.

"I like when you talk sweet to me."

"It's true," he replied. "I mean every word I say." He kissed down to my ear, tugging at my earlobe with his teeth. "I'm so fucking happy today is Saturday."

"Why?"

"Because I can spend all day doing this: worshipping you, showing you how much you mean to me."

If anyone told me that I'd be spending this Christmas Eve being spoiled by this man, I wouldn't have believed it.

I kissed his shoulder, drawing my hands down his impressive biceps. "I want to soap you up," I announced. "Let's go to the shower."

Grinning, he rolled off the bed, holding my hand and helping me up. Thank God he did, because my thighs were still feeling a bit mushy, like they couldn't sustain my weight. *Oh, the power of the orgasms this man gives me.*

My phone beeped somewhere in the apartment. I glanced around before remembering I left my bag at the entrance.

"Let me check really quick that it's not an emergency," I said.

Cade pinned me with his gaze. Clearly he wasn't on board with my plan, so I dashed out of the bedroom.

I found the phone easily enough in my bag. I only glanced at the message Sonya sent me for a few seconds before I burst out laughing.

"Something happen?" Cade asked.

I hurried back to him. He was already in front of the bathroom door.

"Sonya said she's not selling to Alfred after all, that she can't sell to someone she can't stand."

"That's good news. What's she going to do?"

"I don't think she knows yet," I replied. "And I thought this day couldn't get better."

He growled, stepping closer to me, taking the phone out of my hand, and throwing it on the bed. "*I* am going to make this day better."

"You're jealous of Sonya now?"

"Yeah. Today I want you all for me."

"I'm all yours, Cade, to do whatever you want with me."

A smile played on his lips. "Exactly what I wanted to hear."

Chapter 30

Meredith

Three months later

"Fifteenth time is the charm?" I asked Cade.

He wrapped his hand around my chin, placing a quick kiss on my lips.

"I have a good feeling." There was a twinkle in his eyes.

We'd taken house hunting very seriously over the past few months. We'd seen fourteen, but we found something about each one that we didn't like. I wasn't getting my hopes up for this one. Leo was showing us the homes personally; he hadn't even sent us pictures of this one.

He'd gone above and beyond in helping us find the home of our dreams when he could've just sent one of his employees with us. He was the CEO of a real estate giant, so he certainly didn't have time to waste with us, but he did it nonetheless. Cade spoke to him a few hours ago and decided we should go see it.

We'd been mostly living at Cade's place and had been talking about the future, family, and life together. Getting a home was a priority, though, as we both wanted something with a yard.

I sighed, completely content with my life. I was working as VP of marketing and interim CEO. Sonya still hadn't found a buyer, so she was stuck running her company. Whenever she went on a trip, I replaced her as CEO. Through the grapevine, I heard that Alfred's company was in serious financial troubles. Served him right.

Cade kissed my hand as we rounded the corner of the street. I'd never been here before. It was a family type of neighborhood. The homes were elegant and huge. I noticed one that caught my attention right away. It was newly built, or at least newly renovated.

"Oh, look at that. This one's beautiful."

Cade smiled at me, kissing my hand again. "That's where we're going, babe."

"That's on the market?" I practically yelled, sounding hoarse.

He parked right in front of it, and I jumped out the next second. Leo was looking very pleased.

"I can't believe it. What is this place even doing on the market? When did it come up?" I asked.

"This morning." Leo looked at Cade. "I figured this was exactly what you're looking for, so I told my team to keep it offline until I could show it to you."

"Give us the keys. We'll take a look by ourselves," Cade said.

"Sure, here you go." Leo handed them to Cade.

"Wait. How come it's on the market? It looks new. Please tell me someone didn't get a divorce while they were renovating it. I don't like bad vibes."

I knew it was silly, but a long time ago, I'd promised myself that I'd never buy a home where the owners were forced to sell.

"No, nothing like that. They put a lot of work into this home, but when they finished it, the husband got a very good offer to work in Dublin for a few years. They decided it made no sense to pay the mortgage on this place if they had another home in Dublin too."

"Their loss, our gain," Cade said. "Come on. Let's check it out."

"There's a porch," I told him as he took my hand, leading me up to the house.

"I know. The second he sent me pictures, I knew exactly how it would look decorated for Christmas and Halloween."

"Wait a second. He sent you pictures? Why didn't you show them to me?" I asked.

"I wanted you to see it outright."

"Oh, wait. Is this a wraparound porch?"

His face lit up with a smile. "Yeah, it is."

I walked from one end of the porch to the other, taken aback. "Oh my God. This is absolutely beautiful. I can see us throwing family parties here."

Cade chuckled. "Want to see the inside too? Or we can buy it just based off the porch if that's what you want."

Grinning, I went back to the door. "Let's go inside."

The second he opened the door, I knew why he'd said he had a good feeling. The place had such beautiful character. It was a dark gray day in Boston, and still the house seemed full of light. It had enormous french windows, which I adored.

The living, dining, and kitchen area were one huge space. I could already see it full of both of our families.

"I think everyone would fit in here," I said.

"I'm sure they would."

"Let's check upstairs," I said. The house had four bedrooms and en suite bathrooms. "Wow. I mean, I'm not even sure if we'll need all the bedrooms."

He wiggled his eyebrows. "We can make good use of all of them. Didn't you say you wanted three kids?"

I blushed but grinned.

As we came back down to the first floor, I glanced into the backyard. There were old fir trees on the property. A sense of peace washed over me as I took them in.

"Want to take a walk?" Cade asked.

"Sure. I can't believe there are even two fir trees," I said, clapping my hands and looking around.

"I bet you can do a lot with them at Christmas."

I smiled sheepishly. "I was just thinking about that. How did you know?"

"Because you're mine, Meredith. Mine to love and make happy. Look at that smile. I'm so proud to be your man."

Tears threatened to spill, but I forced them back, even though they were happy tears.

"Cade, I love you so much."

"I love you, too, babe." He squeezed my hand as we walked under the fir trees. "So, what are you thinking?"

"I think this is our place."

"I think so too. It's the one." His voice was soft. "You're the one, Meredith."

As if in a haze, I realized what was going on at the same time that he lowered himself in front of me on one knee. He reached into his pocket and took out a ring box. I hadn't even noticed the bulge in his coat.

"You're the one, Meredith," he repeated. His voice was stronger now but still soft and full of emotions, and I... well, I was completely overwhelmed. My pulse raced, my stomach cartwheeled, and my knees weakened. And those tears? They threatened to spill over again. "I want to make a home with you. I want us to be together every day and every night. Will you do me the honor of growing old next to me? I promise to love you every single day while we build a life together."

"Yes, yes. I want to be your wife, Cade." I swallowed past the lump of emotion in my throat. The ring looked a bit like a flower. It had a round diamond in the center and several triangular ones around it, like small leaves. It fit me perfectly.

I put my hands on Cade's shoulders and then bent at the waist, pressing my lips to his. The kiss was soft at the beginning, but then he deepened it, tugging me downward. Then I was on my knees, too, and we were kissing like two teenagers.

I couldn't believe it. I was with the man I loved, and we were about to buy the house of our dreams.

When we paused to breathe, I laughed against his lips. He chuckled. Before I knew it, we were both laughing without any restraint. My knees were wet. I bet his were too. The ground was still damp from the early morning dew.

“Leo is probably still waiting outside," Cade said eventually.

"Probably. Is this why you didn't want him to show us the house?"

"Yeah. Didn't want anything between us."

I was so full of happiness. *God, is this my life?* I could hardly believe it.

We both rose to our feet, looking a bit silly with our wet knees, but I couldn't care less. We walked around the house, not wanting to take any dirt inside.

Leo heard us and looked up from his phone. His eyes were fixed on our knees. "Do I even want to know what happened?"

I held up my hand, pointing to my ring finger.

"Holy shit. I didn't see that coming at all. I take it you liked the house?"

"Yeah, we're making an offer," Cade said.

"Congratulations are in order, then. For the house and the ring."

"Don't sound so stunned," I said.

Leo shrugged. "No offense meant. Just didn't think you were going to be the one to settle down after Jake. Tell me the truth—was it the house that convinced you to say yes?"

"Yeah, dude. That was it," Cade deadpanned.

“I should advertise that. 'Whitley Real Estate will help you find your dream house. Maybe to get a ring too.'”

"Such a romantic," I replied.

"Not my strong suit."

"Hmm... that's what Cade said as well. Do we know who your grandmother has her eye on next?" I had to ask. I still couldn't believe Jeannie and my mom thought Cade and I, after all these years, would be perfect together.

Leo looked perplexed. "Not me, I hope."

Cade glanced at me, then threw his head back, laughing. "See, that's why I love you. You know just how to shut him up."

"I take this as a cue that you two want to be alone," Leo said, sounding as if he wanted to put as much distance between himself and us as possible. Like falling in love was catching or something.

"You're a smart man," I replied. I liked Leo, but I wanted to be alone with my man right now.

Cade put an arm around my shoulders, kissing the side of my temple after Leo got into his car.

"How are we celebrating this?" I asked.

His eyes flashed. "Let's go to my place, and I'll show you."

I smiled, pulling back a bit, rising on my tiptoes, and bringing my lips close to his. "You don't have to tell me twice. Let's go."

Epilogue

Cade

"Meredith, you need a break." I walked up behind my fiancée in our new kitchen, putting an arm around her waist. She wanted to prepare everything herself for our housewarming party. I'd tried to warn her that with so many people, it was going to be a massive undertaking, and we should at least cater part of it, but she insisted. We spent all morning prepping 'finger food.'

I kissed the side of her neck. She was tense, so I stepped back, putting both hands on her shoulders, massaging them.

"Oh yeah. You can do that any time you want," she murmured.

I groaned, imagining what other sounds I could get out of her. That desire only intensified when she bit her lip.

"You think they'll like it here?" she asked.

I bunched her dress, putting my hand on her leg. I loved feeling her skin. It was soft and so damn kissable. *She* was kissable. "Of course they will. Why are you so nervous?"

"I don't know. I just want everyone to be happy in our home."

I kissed the back of her hand. "I know they will be."

"Thank you," she murmured, "for finding this gorgeous place and indulging me."

"Meredith, indulging you is my honor." I lived for the moments when her face lit up. I made myself a promise to give her at least one reason to be happy every day. "I love you, Meredith."

She sighed, putting her hands on my neck. "How can you make me melt every time you say that?"

My chest was bursting with pride. That was exactly the effect I wanted to have on her.

As I kissed her forehead, the doorbell rang.

I groaned. “How can they be here so early?”

“I bet it’s my family,” she replied.

"Ready?"

She nodded excitedly. "Yeah."

Meredith was right. Her mom and dad had arrived along with Everly, Derek, and their daughter, Kate. Everly had the baby the day after Christmas, which made the holiday even more special for everyone.

“I love this house so much,” Meredith’s mom said.

“You two did a great job with it,” her father added.

Everly kissed my cheek. “And you keep doing a great job of making my sister happy. I’m a big fan of yours, just so you know.”

“Very big,” Derek clarified. “Stop raising the bar, man. It’s hard to keep up.”

“Awww, but you’re lovely for trying,” Everly told him.

He looked stunned. “Trying? Not succeeding?”

Everly kissed his cheek.

Meredith immediately took the baby from her sister's arms. My wife-to-be was a natural, and I could already picture our children filling up our house in the future.

"Oh, you’re so cute. When did you get so big? Isn’t she gorgeous?" she asked me as her family went into our living room. "Cade, what's that look in your eyes?"

Instinct. It was pure instinct. Seeing her with the baby wiped out every rational thought.

"Imagining you as a mother."

Her eyes widened. "Okay. I didn't expect that."

"Neither did I," I admitted, and kissed her forehead.

She smiled sheepishly as we went to the living room. I was in charge of drinks and brought out a few plates with finger foods too.

Meredith didn't seem to want to part with the baby. She sat down with her in her favorite corner of the L-couch. She'd decorated our house in painstaking detail and had made it into our home. We both loved it here—though I'd be happy anywhere as long as Meredith was by my side. She was the most important thing. Everything else was just a backdrop, nothing more.

Before Meredith, all I cared about was restoring the reputation of The Boston Coffee Expert. I'd always considered that my legacy. But now I knew better. This was my true legacy, the life I was building with Meredith.

My family arrived shortly afterward. Meredith gave the baby back to Everly as she rose to greet everyone. Grandmother and Grandfather came with Jake and Natalie.

"Your home is beautiful," Grandmother said as she touched my cheek. "You did good finding this place."

We had a few things updated to our liking, so we didn't want any visitors until it was completed. Honestly, that was more Meredith's thing than mine; whatever my fiancée wanted was good with me.

Meredith immediately took my grandmother's arm and said, "Oh yes he did. I owe you a huge thank-you, Jeannie."

"What for, darling?"

"For raising him to be such a gentleman."

"That wasn't all me."

"By the way, I've looked at the theater program. They're playing *Romeo and Juliet* next month. I could practically hear Cade's eyes roll into the back of his head when I asked him to go with me. Would you like to accompany me instead, Jeannie?"

Something tugged deep in my chest. That conversation with

Meredith had actually gone in a completely different way. She asked me if Grandmother would like *Romeo and Juliet*. I told her she liked everything. I couldn't believe how much she cared for my grandmother's well-being.

It was easier to entertain Grandfather. All my brothers and I had to do was show up at his house and talk business with him. We usually kept out the challenging parts, but he was a smart man and could read between the lines.

Gabe and Colton arrived next.

"Colton!" I was stunned. "Thanks for coming, man. I wasn't counting on you showing up."

Gabe pointed a thumb at himself. "I get all the credit for this, okay? I dragged him from the office."

"He did," Colton admitted. "I lost track of time. But I'd always planned on coming."

"Yeah, brother, you always lose track these days. What would you do without me and Spencer?" Gabe asked. "Now that Jake and Cade are busy with their women, it's down to me and Spencer to nag you."

"Where is Spencer, by the way?" I asked. "I thought he was coming with you guys."

Gabe shrugged. "I don't know. He said something about an emergency and also not to worry."

"What the hell?" I took my phone from my back pocket, checking the text messages. I had one from Spencer: **I'll come a bit later.** Fair enough. That didn't seem like he was in trouble. Although, he did have a calm way of handling things.

Back in the living room, our families had already spread out, relaxing and talking like they'd known each other forever. Meredith and her mom were at the kitchen island. Everly and her husband were sitting at one end of the dining table along with my grandparents. I couldn't help but laugh. I knew my grandmother would start her campaign for a great-grandkid again after spending time around a baby.

Natalie and Jake sat on the couch next to Gabe. They were talking in low voices, and I instantly knew something was off, so I headed over to them.

"Spill it," I said as I sat down.

“We don't know anything for certain,” Gabe qualified.

"Come on, don't bullshit around. What's happening? Is it about Spencer?"

He nodded.

“I damn well knew it."

“Remember Naomi?” Gabe asked, and I blinked.

“The woman he dated a million years ago?”

“No, not a million. It was, I'd guess, about a year ago? Probably less. Actually, way less,” Gabe corrected. “Anyway, he's meeting her right now.”

“That doesn't sound like a problem to me.” Spencer was meeting with his ex. Big deal. I couldn't understand why Gabe was up in arms.

"Come on, lighten up. You're going to worry the rest of the family," I said.

"No, he won't. Our grandparents aren't paying any attention," Colton said, joining us. He didn't even ask what we were talking about, so clearly he was in the know. “They're far too entranced by Meredith's niece. That's not boding well for the couples in our family. She's going to start nagging about great-grandkids again.”

“I agree,” I said.

Gabe waved his hand. “I think she's more into matchmaking than actually having great-grandkids.”

"Yeah, she does seem to enjoy it a lot," Colton said.

I grinned. “Worried?” He definitely sounded like he was. I liked teasing my oldest brother. I was happy Gabe managed to get him here.

“I don't even have time to breathe, let alone for Grandmother to make any other plans for me, which leaves Gabe and Spencer as well as our half brothers as possible candidates.”

"No, I'm not worried at all," Colton said. "I just don't need her interference."

Jake snorted. "Good luck with that."

I started to laugh. "I told her the exact same thing, and it had zero effect."

Grandmother had made up her mind when it came to matchmaking Meredith and me. But I wasn't complaining, not in the slightest. Some people met through fate, others because Jeannie Whitley decided it was time.

Twenty minutes later, the doorbell rang. I opened the door, and Spencer and Maddox stepped in. I immediately knew something was wrong with my twin.

"What happened, dude?" I looked at Maddox, who just shook his head.

"You have something to drink?" Spencer asked.

"Yeah, what do you want?"

"Whatever's strongest," he said.

An alarm rang in my mind. My usually relaxed brother needed a strong drink? That was a bad omen.

I went to the kitchen to make him one.

"I can't believe your brothers couldn't come," Grandmother told Maddox. She was still on the couch, cuddling Meredith's niece.

"They're traveling," Maddox said. He kissed Meredith's cheek, handing her a bouquet of flowers. "You have a very beautiful home, Meredith."

"Thank you," she said.

I gave Spencer the drink. He took a sip immediately. I wanted to know what was going on, then realized there was a real possibility that he might not want to talk about whatever was wrong with the family all around us.

But Spencer surprised me. "I need to share something with all of you." He spoke loudly enough that everyone turned to look at him as his voice resounded throughout the open floor plan. "I'm sorry, Meredith. I don't mean to hijack your housewarming party, but this isn't something I can keep to myself."

"We're here for you, brother, whatever it is," I said instantly.

Colton frowned, putting his drink on the coffee table in front of the couch. So did Jake. Natalie grabbed his hand.

"Today, I met with my ex-girlfriend, Naomi. You all might remember her?"

"Yes, we do," Grandmother said, not indicating if that was a good or bad thing.

"I hadn't seen her in months. Today, she told me she's had my child."

Everyone gasped.

Colton rose to his feet, coming up to Spencer. "What the hell? She never told you?"

Spencer shook his head. "No, I found out today. She only told me because she realized she can't do it. She doesn't want to raise a kid."

"Oh my goodness," Grandmother exclaimed.

Was that a glint I saw in her eyes?

Colton and Gabe started talking at the same time. Jake and Natalie were whispering in low voices, still seated on the couch. Meredith covered her mouth with her hand. Her parents looked stricken.

Grandfather joined us at the kitchen island. "Grandson, we're all here for you, of course."

"What are you going to do?" Colton asked.

"Raise my child, of course." There was no hesitation in his voice.

Grandmother smiled wildly as she teared up. "Is it a boy or a girl?"

"Boy," Spencer said.

"Congratulations. Oh, I've always wanted a great-grandchild. I didn't imagine you'd be the first to give me one, but congratulations. Spencer, it's a blessing, even though it might seem overwhelming at the moment."

Meredith came up to me. I laced an arm around her shoulders, kissing her temple.

“This is a lot,” she whispered.

“I agree.”

“How do you think we can help?”

That’s my woman. Always there for my family.

“He’ll tell us.”

"I'll get my shit together in a couple hours. Right now, I'm still shell-shocked,” Spencer said.

I didn't blame him. Who the hell left their kid?

This was insane. But none of that mattered. All that did was that our brother needed us. And we were all going to be there for him when the time came.

Dear Reader,
This is the end of the book. For a full list of Layla Hagen’s books, please visit laylahagen.com